Listening to van Gogh

A Coming of *Retirement* Age Novel

Live like to it fullest!

By:

James Stevens

James Stevens

Published by Outsource Communications, Inc.

Copyright 2010

ISBN: 978-0-557-17932-9

Cover art: Café Terrace at Night, Place du Forum, Arles, France

By Vincent van Gogh

Dedicated to the loving memory of Lila Rothermel Strasico

1920-2006

Wife of Mariano, mother of Marie and Anne

Loved by all who knew her

"The good of living is in the sweetness of memory"

-Terry Kay

Chapter One

The sleek motorcoach glided quietly south through the rolling hills of the wine country of Burgundy, the passengers' spirits high in anticipation of their arrival at the heart of their trip, the river cruiser, M/S Arles. Their first two days in France had included a city tour of Paris, and an enjoyable side trip to Monet's home and gardens in Giverny, in Normandy. Their most recent stop in Beaune, the heart of the wine district, with its museum and wine caves, had been interesting, but it was the concept of traveling through Provence on a small, elegant, river cruiser that was the main attraction of the tour. Most of the forty passengers were experienced travelers, having watched the landscapes of many different countries through the huge windows of the comfortable vehicles, but the experience of traveling on a private riverboat had its own special appeal.

Gerard, their tour guide and Program Director, watched carefully for the destination signs for Chalon- sur- Saone. He was a young man, in his thirties, slim and nicely dressed in the casual, somewhat careless way that European men do so well. He wore a gray herringbone sport coat over an open collared black shirt, black pants supported by an expensive looking black leather belt with a silver buckle and belt tip. A pair of thin-soled black and gray athletic shoes added the right touch of reckless style. His left wrist sported a large-faced watch he consulted frequently. His dark hair was arranged in a fashionable "chopped" cut. He reached for the microphone in its cradle as the bus slowed for the sharp turn to the river.

"Bonjour. Ladies and gentlemen," he announced, "we are now at the river Saone, and the Arles is just around the next turn. If you read your handout, you know it was built especially for groups like ours for river traveling. There are two decks with cabins, and a third sundeck for watching the countryside glide by. There is a crew of 14, and they all speak English, some better than others. Ladies and gentlemen, your home for the next seven days...the M/S Arles."

Gerard gestured through the windshield at the gleaming white superstructure of the Arles, on the river below them. Wooden deck chairs with royal blue cushions with white trim were in place along the length of the sun deck, waiting for the eager travelers. The Arles' hull was a deep navy blue, with a dark red stripe running its entire length just above the portholes that marked the cabins on the lower deck. The upper deck cabins featured long windows and small balconies just large enough for a small table and two chairs. The entire top structure was a sparkling, almost blinding white.

The happy group exited the bus, gathering at the top of the steps to the dockside, as their luggage was quickly and efficiently removed from the luggage bins underneath the bus. Their bags would be delivered directly to their cabins by the crew. Personal cameras appeared as the group waited for Gerard to direct them onto the vessel.

"Beautiful," was the first audible reaction, followed by several laughs of agreement. The crowd spread along the dock, taking in every angle of the beautiful river cruiser, camera flashes everywhere.

"It's so perfect," a small, trim woman wearing a turquoise top over pale white Capri pants said as she focused on the bow. "It's even nicer than the pictures in the catalog. It's just beautiful, isn't it? Are you happy to be here, Russell?" she asked, touching the arm of the man standing at her side.

"I'm happy to be here," the sandy haired man replied with a smile "For a while there I wasn't sure I'd be anywhere."

She reached for his hand and squeezed it softly. "But it's over now and you're doing just fine. We're going to be living on this beautiful boat for the next seven days, and we don't have to worry about a thing, just relax and enjoy the scenery on the river. Aren't you excited?"

"You're right, Elizabeth," Russell replied. "I am excited, and this is going to be a great experience. Thank you for making it happen despite my grumbling."

"You would do the same for me. And you have. Put all that behind you. This is a new start," she said.

"Attention, please," Gerard announced. He held his clipboard cradled in his arm. "It will be a few minutes while your suitcases are delivered to your cabin. Does everyone know their cabin number? If not, check with me. After you have had time to unpack and refresh yourself, I will take you on a tour of Chalon, a charming and ancient town. This is the only time you need to unpack for the rest of the river trip." He paused, waiting for the smiles of appreciation. He was rewarded with several head nods. "This evening we will meet the international crew, and celebrate a welcoming dinner on board. Watch your step on the gangplank as you board. Use the side rails if you need them." He scanned the group, nodding at the most elderly-appearing. "At the front desk just inside, state your name and cabin number, and you will be given your keys. Take your time unpacking, and please move around and explore your new home. There is a full bar in the lounge area, here at the stern, or back end of the boat, if you would like a drink. There is also free coffee in the lounge. We are ready." Gerard waved back to the Purser's signal.

The group moved patiently through the check-in process, their travel experience in place. Gerard saw that the two elderly women, Agnes and Shirley, who might need assistance, were boarded first. The gangway was narrow, wide enough for one person at a time, and about twelve feet in length with chain side rails at waist level.

Three couples, obviously traveling as a group, were enjoying a laugh, sorting through carry-on bags as they organized a welcoming buffet in one of their cabins. They were all berthed on the main deck, next to the travelers who couldn't manage the stairs to the lower deck, or who preferred the premium location. There was no elevator between decks.

"Bonjour, our name is Hunter, Russell and Elizabeth, assigned to cabin five," Russell greeted the white suited crew member. An attractive young women handed him two brass keys attached to a mahogany tag, and directed him to the stairs to the lower deck.

"Your cabin is the last one on the left. Welcome to the Arles."

The Hunters descended to the lower deck, Russell stopping at the highly shellacked wooden door, fumbling with the brass key. He finally got the right combination of turning the key and pulling on the brass handle and entered the room. The cabin, as expected, was small, about the size of a small hotel room, but very well planned. Two painted wooden chairs with embroidered fabric, separated by a small table and a writing desk, faced a wall mounted television, next to two separate bunks, with slide out storage drawers underneath. A rectangular window a few feet above water level allowed greenish tinged sunlight into the cabin. On the wall opposite, a folding wooden door opened to a full length closet for hanging clothing. A shower stall was in a separate room, next to the room containing the toilet and sink.

"What do you think?" Russell asked.

"I like it," Elizabeth said. "A lot. These wooden chairs are a nice touch, with a very nice desk for writing postcards, and the drawers under the bunks are a great idea. They pull out so they're easy to get to. We can get all of our folded clothing in them. There's plenty of space. "

"I must admit you were right," Russell said as he slowly moved his clothing from his suitcase to the storage areas. "This is a beautiful way to travel and relax. I'm looking forward to sitting on the sun deck, watching the river go by."

"We've earned it, don't you think?" Elizabeth asked. "You need to relax and continue the healing process. After all those years of work, it's time to play," She continued her meticulous unpacking, refolding the packing tissue for later reuse.

"We've always taken vacations," Russell countered.

"Yes, usually to a battlefield, or some other historic site. Or the beach, which I always enjoy.. And, we're going to do more of that, but I want to explore some new places."

"Okay with me," Russell said. "I've had my wake up call. I know I said this before, but thank you for helping me through my difficulties," Russell said, hanging up his shirts.

"That's what married people do. Most men have problems as they get older. We help each other."

"I'd prefer not to get into a big discussion of my problem on this trip. I still remember the people we saw in Florida, reviewing their pill regimen at the dinner table before the 'early bird' special." He finished hanging his garments and closed the empty suitcase.

"I don't think this is that kind of a group," Elizabeth said. "They're here traveling because they still have a curiosity, a spirit of exploring. I don't think they're quite into the nursing home mindset yet."

"I hope not. I'm just not comfortable with medical discussions."

"Most men aren't, are they?" Elizabeth asked, eyebrows raised. "Women talk about everything."

"We are different," Russell said. "Are you ready to go see more of our private yacht, or do you need more time?"

"You know, I think I'd prefer a quick shower. Do you mind? Maybe you could do some exploring and I'll meet you on the sundeck? I won't be long."

"Fine with me," Russell replied. "I believe Gerard said there was a bar nearby. I'll just put these documents in the room safe. It has an electronic lock, , so write down the code we need to enter to open it. How about your birthday? Month, day, last two numbers of the year, skip the 19 bit for the century." He slid the passports and other papers into the safe and closed it firmly.

"Time to explore French beer. I'll see you later," Russell said as he moved to the door, wooden key in hand. He pulled the door closed with a soft click and walked to the stairs, climbing to the main deck where the dining room, bar and cocktail lounge were, stopping at the check in desk, now no longer crowded. He found the gently curving metal staircase to the sundeck, with its open top, and proceeded slowly upward into the bright sun. Russell passed the rows of deck chairs and tables, arranged in perfect order, nothing out of place. This must be what you call 'ship shape' he thought as he walked to the bow of the boat.

Leaning against the white railing, he looked down at the dark green water, then across the river to a small piece of land projecting into the stream. There was no traffic.

It seemed like it had been just a very short time ago, less than a year, that he and Elizabeth had selected this particular trip to celebrate her coming retirement. It had been her choice, and Russell smiled at the memory of her excitement as they had sent off the check. He liked traveling, but also enjoyed being in his home with his books and music and maps. He was not one to seek change, preferring a more stable life. He sometimes envied Elizabeth her eagerness to plunge in to new experiences, trusting that all would be fine.

And then he got the totally unexpected shock of the results of his pre — retirement physical. He turned at a sound behind him, his thoughts drifting away.

A stout man wearing a red cap and red and white striped rugby style shirt with loose fitting khakis greeted him.

"I thought I recognized you. I'm Mel, Mel Weinstein from Palm Harbor, that's in Florida. I believe we met at the Eiffel Tower?" He extended his hand.

"Now that sounds like a line from a Cole Porter song," Russell said, returning the firm grip. "Russ Hunter, from Atlanta. I think we did meet on the Paris bus tour, at the Eiffel Tower stop."

"Right, my wife asked you to take our picture. She's freshening up," Mel tilted his head. "Are you a Cole Porter fan?"

"I guess I am," Russell replied. "I'm more of the rock and roll generation, but I still enjoy great songs and singers like Sinatra, Tony Bennett, Nat King Cole..."

Mel nodded, "I know what you mean. We're the in-between kids, too young for the 'greatest generation,' but too old to be 'baby boomers.'" They leaned against the railing as more passengers emerged on the deck.

"We looked for you on the bus after we stopped at Invalides, but didn't see you." Mel said. "I don't remember you being on the trip to Versailles that afternoon."

"That's because we opted out," Russell explained. "We had seen Versailles on a previous trip and Elizabeth was still a bit jet lagged, so we decided to go to the top of Montmarte, to Sacre Coeur, instead. We had gone there before and had enjoyed the view and the people. It feels like the Paris of Gene Kelly in An American in Paris. We took the Metro and then climbed the steps."

"I'm not too big on climbing steps," Mel said. "I had a slight problem with the ticker, you know?"

"Are you alright? Do you need to sit down?"

"I'm okay now. I exercise every day, take my pills. I just have to be careful I don't overdo anything. The doc said I'd be fine on this trip, just not to push too hard. It's a pain, you know?" Mel huffed."Getting old isn't fun."

"I do know," Russell said. He decided to change the subject. "I think I see Bloody Mary's being offered. Can I get you one?"

"Please, I'll get the next round. I'll watch for the ladies." Mel said,

Gradually the other travelers appeared and began their first exploration of the vessel, pausing first at the entry desk before visiting the bar and dining room where most of the onboard social activity would take place. The sun deck slowly filled as the travelers climbed the metal stairs to the upper deck, hands sliding along the white hand rail. Wooden lounge chairs with thick cushions were spread around the deck, while wooden dining chairs were positioned at a series of wooden cocktail tables under a central canopy that could be unfurled for shade as needed. The Wheel House, where the ship was steered, was forward, with rear windows that allowed a view of the captain and first officer as they guided the river cruiser. A white jacketed waiter circulated through the growing crowd offering Bloody Mary's with protruding stalks of fresh celery, or glasses of wine. The sun was warm, not hot, and a gentle breeze carried away the traffic sounds from the roadway next to the quay. A pleasant smell of fresh river water filled the evening air. The passengers were pleased with their wise decision to select river travel, made many months previously.

Gerard, the Program Director, moved quietly through the crowd, observing their mood, noting the groupings, the conversation clusters, looking for any signs of someone not enjoying themselves. Some people fit in immediately, effortlessly starting a conversation, introducing themselves, while others hesitated, finding it difficult to speak to a stranger, not socially comfortable. It was his job, he believed, to help those shy souls fit in and enjoy their holiday. He noticed two women standing near the rail watching the gathering, obvious candidates for his assistance with his type of social skills. He struggled to recall their names, then glanced at his notebook.

"Bonjour, ladies, Moira, and Katy? Welcome to the Arles. Have you found everything to your satisfaction?"

"Our cabin's okay. Being half underwater bothers Katy, but she'll get used to it, won't you dear?" Moira spoke up. She was wearing a white shirt with long collar points, tucked into baggy beige slacks, topsiders on her feet. A large purse was looped around her arm. Her light gray hair was trimmed short, her face showing no sign of make up, except for a slight tinge of pale lipstick. Her chin jutted forward as she spoke to Gerard.

Katy stood quietly, a half smile for Gerard. She too wore a white shirt, with a pale yellow blouse and a gold chain and cross. Her dark slacks and sandals were practical, and she wore no makeup, not even lipstick. She seemed to be younger than Moira by a few years. She twirled her glass, the celery stalk waving.

"I believe," Gerard said, "you will find that you will spend very little time in the cabin. Most people are only there for sleeping. During the day most of them gather here on the sundeck, or else we will be touring the towns where we stop. The weather has been excellent, and the forecast is for more of the same."

"Let's hope so. We came a long way for a cruise and some sunshine," Moira added.

"It will be nice to sit in the sun," Katy commented.

"But not too much," Moira immediately warned. "You know how you burn so easily. Worse than me, even. The Irish curse."

"Yes, you should use sunscreen when you are outdoors," Gerard said. He turned at an explosion of laughter coming from a small group surrounding two women. They were all clutching Bloody Mary's or wine glasses and laughing at what had been said.

"There is a happy group. Have you met any of your fellow passengers in that group? How about another Bloody Mary? The waiter is taking orders." Gerard steered the reluctant women to the party people. The smiling crowd parted as Gerard introduced Moira and Katy, leaving it to the others to introduce themselves.

"Hi. My name's Larry, from Iowa, and we were just enjoying Sonia's story of her visit to a wine cave in Beaune," he explained, his Bloody Mary pointed at two smiling women. "This is Sonia," he gestured, "and her friend Sally, from Delaware, is it?"

"Right. Rehobeth Beach." Sally, the blond woman, answered, nodding. Her hair was a bright blond, almost golden, not quite in keeping with the rest of her appearance. Her short pants and espadrilles complemented a bright blouse that said "vacation." Bracelets dangled from her thin wrists.

"Anyway, we had no idea how cold it was in there," Sally said. "We were just looking for a place to get a drink 'cause Sonia was upset by the old hospital we had toured, that place they call a Hotel, you know?"

"Yes, Hotel Dieu, that was a depressing place. Not too many patients walked out of there," Larry said.

"Right, so we asked some guy at the wine store where could we get a drink and he thought we wanted wine, like we wanted to buy cases of it. So, he sent us down this alley to what they call a 'wine cave,'" Sally went on. "The people were real nice to us, a man and a woman."

"Especially the man." Sonia turned to Moira and Katy. "You see I was wearing this thin blouse, no jacket, and, like I was just telling them, when the cold hit my chest..."

"I was trying to remember my high school French for 'eyes up' when the woman gave the guy a look," Sally laughed.

Moira smiled, Katy hesitated, looking uncomfortable.

"Then we understood why the man and woman were both wearing these heavy sweaters," Sonia explained. "Once the man got himself under control, they offered us this drink, a Kir Royal?"

She was taller than her friend, dressed in Capri pants and a bright blouse, a pale green scarf around her neck, a gold watch on her slim wrist. Her trim figure spoke of regular workouts. "It was delicious. Sweet and fizzy, just what I wanted. I liked it so much I asked what it was and the guy explained it was a drink made with a wine like Champagne, and a sweet liqueur called Cassis. I wrote it down. Cassis is wonderful, both the red and the white."

"You tasted both?" Larry asked, his voice rising, a grin on his face.

"Oh, yeah."

"Then," Sally interjected, "they started with the wines. Just a little cup for each wine. They used a pipette, like we used in the hospital where I worked, for drawing a sample from the barrels. We were the only ones there, and we didn't know you were supposed to take just a taste and spit it out. We just kept drinking these little cups of wine, being polite."

"Thank God the other people showed up," Sonia said. "First they explained how you're supposed to spit and not drink everything, and then they told us the wine we were tasting was very expensive, if we wanted to buy it. We got out of there as fast as we could. When we hit the sunlight, I felt like I was hit by a truck. I got back on the bus and slept all the way till we got here. The first thing I did in our cabin was take a shower. I'm sticking with Perrier for a while." She shook her glass, the ice rattling.

Elizabeth and Ruth arrived on the sundeck, searching for their husbands in the milling crowd. They had met in the passageway, and immediately recognized each other from the previous day. They found their spouses sitting quietly, sipping their drinks.

"Hi, we found you," Elizabeth smiled. "You remember Ruth, don't you?" she asked.

"Of course. We met at the Eiffel Tower. Isn't that a great line for a song? Mel and I think so," Russell said, rising to his feet. Mel followed.

"We were just eavesdropping on our fellow travelers' stories," Mel said. "Would you like one of these?" He shook his glass, the green stalk of celery waving.

"Yes, I would. Ruth?"

"Of course. We're in France on vacation."

Mel flagged the waiter and reached for two of the tall glasses.

"To the start of a new adventure, a new country, new friends, new experiences," Ruth raised her glass in a toast they all joined.

"Russell was telling me you have been to Paris before," Mel said as they formed a seated circle.

"Yes, we have," Elizabeth responded. "A few years ago, Russ had to go to Scotland on business, and his company agreed to some vacation time in the UK, so I packed a bag and flew to London where we met. We spent most of a week there, then Russell surprised me with a quick trip to Paris. Just 3 days, but we saw a lot."

"What a nice surprise," Ruth said.

"Well, when we first met," Russell explained, "we were both in college, and I was so broke I was selling my books from one semester to buy new ones for the next course. That's how we met, when I sold her a Spanish book, half price." He took a long sip, pushing the celery aside.

"But the new books you were buying were full price, right?" Mel asked.

"Right. Not exactly a money making scheme. I was just trying to survive. Anyway, I promised her that someday I would take her to Paris and we would stand at the top of the Eiffel Tower, which we did," Russell said. "We arrived in the afternoon, and it was one of the clearest days in the history of Paris. You could almost see Dover from the top of the Tower, it was so nice."

"That's a lovely story," Ruth smiled. "Have you done any other traveling?" She raised her glass.

"Yes, we went to Belgium when I had to go on business. Then we decided to visit Italy, and we started exploring on our own. This is our first river cruise. How about you?" Elizabeth asked.

"It's our first river cruise. We did some ocean cruising, but didn't really enjoy it. Then we started exploring Europe, and fell in love with Italy and Spain. We decided to try this after Mel had a slight setback and we got tired of lifting suitcases every day." Ruth said.

"A wise decision," Russell said. "Elizabeth, you were right in insisting on doing this. I feel totally relaxed and we haven't even left the dock yet. Life can be good."

Their conversation was interrupted by an announcement from Gerard of a brief walking tour of Chalon, leaving in one hour. With a glance at his watch, Gerard left the sundeck, moving quickly to the office of the Ship's Purser, Giovanni Strazzeri, a veteran sailor and business friend of Gerard's.

He knocked politely on the office door, which automatically locked when closed. The Ship's Purser was the officer responsible for all accounting onboard, and his duties included supervising his staff, overseeing the crew payroll, visa and work permits, and managing currency exchange. On the Arles, the Purser also served as the front desk manager, a position similar to that of land based hotels. He was the man called on for any passenger questions or complaints.

"Bonjour, Giovanni," Gerard announced. "All have arrived, all are in the correct cabins, and a lively gathering is taking place on the sundeck, yes? Once again, you have risen to the occasion."

"Bonjour, and thank you, Gerard. Yes, the first river cruise of the season is about to get underway. The weather outlook is excellent, and we will be off to a wonderful start. The check-in went well, no major problems, no major health issues. A few elderly who may have trouble getting to the sun deck, but overall, a happy experienced group, yes?"

"Good. We do not want any problems." He glanced at his watch. "Anything else I should know? Any special passengers?"

"We have the usual mix of mostly married couples, quite a few women traveling together, probably widows, and one man by himself. That is slightly unusual."

"Yes, I noted that. His name is Mr. Durgan," Gerard explained. "I met him in Paris, of course, and he was on the tour of Giverny, but kept to himself. A widower, I believe. He should be popular with the single women. I didn't see him at the gathering on the sundeck," Gerard said, head cocked to the side.

"I'm certain he will make an appearance."

"So, you have copies of all my documents, guest lists, yes? I assume the itinerary remains the same? No problems with low water in the river or malfunctioning locks?"

"No. The water level is high, the locks are all working well for our descent," Giovanni said.

"Well, I have a walking tour of Chalon to conduct soon, and then we have the welcoming event with the introduction of the crew. Will you be doing that, or the Captain?" Gerard asked.

"I do all of the social events," Giovanni replied, shuffling his papers into a neat stack. "I am the permanent Master of Ceremonies, as the English say. We have an excellent crew, almost all experienced on Arles, with a few new waitresses, from England. Our chef is Paul, and I think he is the best. Terry, from Leeds, manages the dining room service and is completely reliable. He is in his fourth year with us."

"It seems you are fully prepared for the new season. My travelers are ready for a new adventure and whatever tomorrow may bring. C'est la vie!"Gerard said as he returned to his cabin and his laptop to check for new messages.

Chapter Two

Returning to his cabin, Gerard did a quick scan of his email, and a glance at his daily itinerary. Everything was on schedule, moving nicely. He did not like to get off, or worse, behind schedule, on his tours. He was a seasoned PD or Program Director now, a proven veteran of the tourist trade for both land tours and river tours, which he preferred. A few more years, two at most, and he would be ready to move to the high end, semi-private tours for the very wealthy clients, the celebrities seeking quiet villas and evening tours of famous places. Or, perhaps he would become a regional director for the agency, with a staff of his own PDs, young people with degrees in Fine Arts and excellent people skills. That was what the business was all about, wasn't it? Understanding people and their needs?

He liked the Americans, with their eagerness and their generosity. They were almost totally ignorant of the history of other countries, but most were willing to learn, given time. He, Gerard, knew how to introduce them to his beloved France, with its long history as the leader of culture for Europe. When they returned to their home states, Iowa, Georgia, New York, they would carry with them a special feeling for France that would never fade.

The initial meeting in Paris had gone well, all passengers arriving safely at the hotel in Montparnasse, all their luggage intact. Most struggled through the evening welcoming meeting, fighting sleepiness from the long flights and the six hour time change from the East Coast. He greeted them, made his announcements, handed out needed forms, and had them introduce themselves before offering them a wine and cheese reception. It had gone well, with a few minor annoyances, as expected. The elderly woman called Agnes seemed to follow every pronouncement of his with a "can't hear you," complaint, in spite of his correct use of a microphone. She seemed to delight in making the comment, forcing him to repeat himself.

The city tour the next morning went well, with the now refreshed passengers eagerly following his sightseeing directions as the bus toured Montparnasse and the Latin Quarter, the Luxembourg Gardens, and a slow drive along the Boulevard St. Germaine and its famous cafes. After a brief stop at the Eiffel Tower, the tour continued to the Place de la Concorde, the site where the guillotines were deployed to behead the aristocracy during the French Revolution. The Americans were understandably surprised, and shocked, to learn that they were standing on the very ground where hundreds of men and women were put to death by the common people of Paris. He had done his best to explain how the Age of Enlightenment, with its recognizing of the rights of individuals, had led to the revolt by the masses. He, Gerard, told his group that to understand France and the French people, you must first understand what happened at the Place de la Concorde centuries ago. Governments and politicians are never to be trusted. Gerard, smiling at the memory of his performance, glanced at his wrist, and sat upright. Time to start the assembly for the afternoon tour. He picked up his clipboard and jacket and walked quickly to the gangplank.

Gerard gathered the passengers in a loose formation on the dock as they gathered for the short walk through the ancient town of Chalon-sur-Saone.

"Welcome," Gerard said in his deepest voice, "to Chalon-sur- Saone, one of France's oldest settlements. It has been an important inland port since the Canal du Centre was built to connect this river, the Saône to the Loire in western France," Gerard explained. "It also is the birthplace of photography. The inventor Joseph Niepce invented what he called 'heliography' or 'sun writing' when he produced the first permanent photograph. During World War Two, Chalon marked the northern boundary of Vichy France, the French State created after the fall of France to the Germans in1940. We will hear more about that at an onboard lecture in Lyon. The town square is a pedestrian only area with many shops and cafes. We will stop at a chocolate shop where you can make purchases if you choose. Please follow me and pay attention to our route if you wish to return to the Arles early."

"We're off," Elizabeth said. "Are you feeling okay?"

"Yes, I am. For a while, after my bad news, I kind of lost interest in doing anything. I didn't even want to get out of my chair. I guess I was lost in my own world. I'm sorry hon. I'm getting better."

'Good. The boat is a delight, and I like Mel and Ruth. It's nice to discover new friends," Elizabeth said. "And there they are."

The group strolled up the slight hill to the cement bridge spanning the Saone River, turned left to cross the dockside motorway, and entered the small and ancient town, passing the bronze statue of Monsieur Niepce. A pleasant rumble of conversation marked their passing.

"Look at this," Russell called. He was standing at the corner of the small square reading a plaque attached to the building wall. "If my French is correct, this says that across the street here, on that bridge, during World War II, the Germans murdered some young Frenchmen. It lists their names and the date of the massacre. They will never forget, will they?" Russell said.

"And they shouldn't," Mel added. "It could happen again."

"Come along," Gerard said, "I will take you to one of my favorite stores in all of France. To the chocolate shop."

The village square was not crowded in the late afternoon, just a few locals sipping coffee at the sidewalk tables. The tourists wandered in and out of the many small shops, glancing at postcards for sale, wine-based souvenirs, corkscrews made from grapevine roots, and the usual clever T shirts. Gerard gathered as many of his group as he could and escorted them into a patisserie, the French combination of a gourmet delicatessen and elegant bakery. The aroma of the cooked food and the fresh baked pastries was pleasantly overwhelming. Added to the usual mix was the powerful scent of chocolate, as a large display featured chocolate for celebrating Easter. Chocolate eggs of all sizes formed a small mountain in a center display.

"I need to buy my Easter treats," Gerard announced. "You can select your personal favorite pieces, or buy pre-packaged chocolates. I have no will power when it comes to chocolate, especially in this shop."

"If he says he's a 'chocoholic,' I'm going to hit him with a big chocolate bunny," Mel muttered, receiving a glaring look from his wife, Ruth.

"Just kidding" he smiled.

A line formed quickly in front of the display cases, Moira leading, Katy close behind, the others following. Gerard was pleased with the response. He selected boxes of different chocolates, creamy milk chocolate from Switzerland, dark chocolate made locally, truffles filled with raspberry or peanut butter or other rich cream fillings. Free samples of broken chocolate were offered to the visitors who responded with small purchases.

"I may never leave here," Sally announced. "Call home and tell them to sell my car, Sonia. This is so wonderful."

"Sally, remember your pledge about your new image."

"I do, but this is the first time I've ever been in a store like this, with the smell and the arrangements. I just want a small taste."

"Okay, but don't complain to me tomorrow."

Gerard waited patiently in the square for the group to complete their buys in the chocolate shop, glancing at his watch.

"Attention, please. Attention. I will be leading those of you who wish to return to the Arles now. If you wish to stay longer, please do. Just walk to the corner there, turn right, and you will see our beautiful new home. The reception starts at 6:00, so you have time to refresh yourselves, have a cocktail, browse some more, whatever you like. See you then."

"Are you going back now?" Ruth asked Elizabeth.

"We have plenty of time. I think we'll walk a little. I want to see some of the shops along these side streets," Elizabeth said. "Okay?" she smiled at Russell.

"Whatever you'd like, Madame."

"See you later. I have to get into my tux for the dinner," Mel said.

Ruth sighed, staring at him with a practiced look.

The Hunters strolled the side street, Elizabeth enjoying the bright floral displays that lined the sidewalks, delighting in the colors and the variety. Shop owners and clerks stood in the open doorways, smiling at the visitors, encouraging them to walk inside. Elizabeth walked into a small shop.

"These flowers are so beautiful, so perfect. Look at these colors, deep purple, crimson, brilliant yellow."

"Have you given any thought to expanding your gardening efforts when you are retired?" Russell said. "I noticed you've been checking out more gardening books lately," They stopped at a small sidewalk table.

"Yes, I have. I've been thinking of doing more with flowers, adding to that area near the back fence that gets limited sun. I might be able to do some containers there. I'm also looking into possibly adding a small fountain and a retaining wall to build up a soil bed."

"I think you're ready to retire. Would you like a lemonade?"They sat down, facing the square.

"Yes, that would be nice. You know, I really am ready now." Elizabeth said. "You always said I'd know when the time was right, and I do. I want to have fresh flowers in our home, and I want to indulge my own yearnings for a change, instead of listening to others tell me what they think they need. I want us to be happy and focus on us. When you went through your scare, it really got me thinking. For all these years, we've been healthy. We're careful about our diet, we exercise, never doubting we'd always be healthy with plenty of time to do what we want."

"That's true. I guess we have been a bit smug," Russell agreed. "At least I have. Remember when Lenny died? He was fine one day, and then gone in minutes from an abdominal aneurysm he didn't even know he had."

Russell paused as the waiter arrived with their icy glasses of fresh lemonade.

"We talked about how after we retired we were going to have lunch once a week somewhere where we could watch pretty girls walk by, some place like this. God, I miss him."

"The point is you're cured, apparently, I'm fine, and we need to set a plan for us for whatever time we have left. It used to be that retirement was the last phase of life, but I think that's changed. You can start a new retired life, with new rules if you choose to. This cruise is a good start." She sipped her drink, a napkin wrapped around the sweating glass.

"It's a great start, hon. I loved seeing Paris, and visiting that museum, the one with the Monet paintings, the water lilies." He took a long drink of lemonade.

"L'Orangerie," Elizabeth said. "It was an early version of a greenhouse, used to grow oranges in tubs during the winter for the palace, remember? When it was converted to a museum for art, it became the Musee de l'Orangerie."

"Right. I loved that experience. Standing in those two rooms, surrounded by Monet's panels of water lilies, all that deep blue and violet, like being submerged in a pond. When we saw the actual pond at Monet's home the next day in Giverny, I was completely overwhelmed. I will never see paintings the same way again. What an incredible creation to come from a man's mind." Russell traced small circles on the tabletop. "Then you explained how you listen to paintings, and that really surprised me."

"It's just a matter of concentration," Elizabeth said, "a willingness to get involved in a total experience with all of your senses. It's putting yourself in the moment the artist felt when the painting was being created."

"Do you think I could learn to do that?" Russell asked.

"Of course, if you want to. Think of all you have done in your life. Look at the successes we've had. Look around you now," Elizabeth spread her arms to the square. "Nobody gave us this life. We earned it , and it's not over just because you're retired. In just a few days, we'll be walking where van Gogh walked, and lived and painted. You'll be able to listen to what van Gogh listened to at the exact spot where his paintings came to life."

Russell muttered a small "You're right."

"Don't we need to be getting back to the boat?" she asked.

"I think so. Time to meet our crew and let the great adventure begin."

Chapter Three

The travelers dutifully assembled in the bar/dining room to meet the crew who would guide the Arles on its journey. Waitresses offered wine and sparkling water, and small bowls of potato chips and salted nuts were scattered about the seating area. Gerard assumed center stage, burnishing his wireless microphone, silently counting the arrivals and checking them off his mental list. When he was confident all had arrived, except for the mysterious Durgan, he welcomed them and introduced Giovanni to present the crew.

Giovanni enjoyed his role as the Ship's Purser for the Arles. His mixed heritage, Italian father, French mother, ensured his fluency in both languages, and he had quickly learned English on the big cruise ships where he had spent most of his life.

"Welcome, everyone, to the Arles," Giovanni said. "We trust you are all settled into your cabins for our journey through Provence, and that you have had a chance to look about our boat. Now it is time to meet the crew that will be working to see that your journey is a pleasant one. First is our captain, Monsieur Pelletier."

The Captain stepped forward with a small wave, his dress white uniform perfectly pressed. He was tall and slender, with touches of gray at his temples. His face was tanned and his eyeglasses were rimless. He bowed slightly to the applause.

"Next is the Assistant Captain, the man who steers Arles, Monsieur Broussard, and our ship's First Mate, Monsieur Deveraux." The men stepped forward to light applause when introduced.

"In our dining room," Giovanni continued, "Terry is our man in charge of all meal service, serving the excellent food prepared by our Chef, Paul DuBlanc. Terry understands English rather well, being from the city of Leeds, in England."

Terry, tall and reed thin, added a wave of recognition and a smile.

"Behind these men are the waitresses and the housekeepers who clean your cabin every day. And, before I forget, behind the bar is Sophia, joining us from Slovakia. If there is anything we can do to make your trip better, please inform me. All of our meals are served without a seating chart, and I encourage you to try sitting with new people at each meal. And now, if you will be seated in our dining area, we will begin our evening meal service. Menu cards for the meal are on the tables. Thank you and again, welcome to Arles. After dinner, you may want to return to Chalon for a walk or a visit to a club. Any time you leave the boat, please leave your key at the desk. That is how we keep track of who is not on the boat. Enjoy your meal."

The group slowly selected their dinner places in the softly lit room, pausing to greet the newly introduced crew as they milled about. The Iowa group commandeered a table for eight, ignoring the request to meet new people. A young couple, perhaps the youngest couple on board, judging by their appearance, approached the two remaining places at the Iowa table, shyly asking if they might join the group.

"Please join us," Larry called. "We know so much about each other, it'll be nice to hear from someone else. Sit down and we'll all introduce ourselves. I'm Larry and this is my wife, Debbie."

"Thank you. I'm Kevin, my wife, Pamela." The introductions continued throughout the room as the tables filled.

The Weinsteins and Hunters glanced at the two empty tables for four sitting side by side. "Why don't we be good travelers and sit with new people? You two take that table, and we'll get this one and see who joins us, okay?" Ruth suggested.

"She's the one with the brains," Mel said, pulling out a chair for his wife.

Russell and Elizabeth sat at the adjoining table opposite each other, waiting for their new companions.

"Hi, are these seats available? Everything looks so nice. I'm Sally and this is Sonia. We're from Delaware, traveling together." She nodded her head, confirming what she had just said.

"Please, join us. I'm Elizabeth Hunter, my husband, Russell."

Russell stood and introduced himself to first Sally, then Sonia. He recalled hearing their story of the wine caves of Beaune and their introduction to Kir Royales. The sound level rose in the dining area as greetings were exchanged and the meal service began. The waitresses moved quickly and efficiently, bringing new courses and removing the previously used dishes. Terry, the supervisor, moved quietly through the room offering wine selections, watching his staff at work, pointing out needed corrections. He stopped at the small table.

"Good evening, ladies and gentlemen. My name is Terry. Would you prefer the red or the white wine with your meal?"

Terry poured the wine selections as requested, pointed out the card with the evening dinner menu, and wished all a "bon appétit." He turned to the

Weinstein's table where Moira and Katy had arrived and began his greeting routine again.

"Isn't this lovely?" Sonia asked.

The tables were set in the European style, with white tablecloths and napkins. Fine china and silverware sparkled, and wine and water glasses reflected the subdued lighting. The dining room of the Arles had been transformed into a room rivaling that of a four star restaurant. A small sound of appreciation was heard around the room as the different courses were served by the skilled staff.

"For you, our very special soup made only with French mustard," Terry said as he placed the bowls before each diner.

"Mustard soup?" Sally questioned.

"Yes, it is a popular course in French kitchens," Terry added, as the diners began eating.

"It's delicious," Sonia said.

"I agree," Elizabeth said. "So different and so full of flavor. Do you like it?"

"I love it. I probably would never have ordered it, but I will now that I've tried it," Russell said.

"That's one of the joys of traveling, don't you think? Discovering new tastes, new flavors, new ideas?" Elizabeth said.

Russell smiled, aware of the ploy by his wife. She knew just how to push him when he needed it.

The travelers chatted between courses, explaining where they were from in the US, how they had come to select the river cruise they were finally on, and their initial impressions of their experiences. Gerard moved around the room, trying to be inconspicuous, noting the service, the response to the foods served, and sometimes some revealing conversational bits. He noted that the passenger Durgan arrived late and shyly found a place with a table of five women. Gerard would add all of this information to his daily log.

Finally, the last of the coffee was served and some of the travelers moved to the adjacent bar for an after dinner drink. Many of them decided to visit the sundeck for a few quiet moments before an early turn in, with a handful opting for a brief walk in Chalon. They would be underway in the morning at 6:00 a.m., sharp. Then the river cruise would officially begin.

Chapter Four

The travel alarm chirped its wakeup tone as the LED screen displayed the time of 5:45 a.m. Russell Hunter, instantly awake, reached for the clock and quickly pressed the off button, trying not to waken the sleeping Elizabeth. He sat up, pausing for a few seconds to avoid any dizziness when he stood. He visited the bathroom, quickly washed his hands and face, and slipped into jeans and a T shirt. He jammed his bare feet into his walking shoes and reached for his red windbreaker in the small closet.

"Have a good time," Elizabeth mumbled as he opened the door to leave.

"Go back to sleep. I'll bring you some coffee when I get back."

Russell had always been a morning person, instantly awake and recharged when the sun rose. It was his most creative time of the day, and he loved the early morning silence when the rest of the world was asleep. Afternoon was the time for mundane things like balancing checkbooks, returning email, running errands. He was up early on this morning because he had never been on a boat like the Arles, and wanted to watch the casting off and getting underway process. He stopped at the front desk at the large coffee pot and poured fresh brewed coffee into a cardboard cup. The coffee was the strong French variety that he had first tasted in Paris and had come to enjoy. Giovanni was not yet at the desk at this early hour as Russell climbed the stairway to the sundeck, smiling to himself with anticipation.

Russell was a recent retiree, a former marketing executive turned college professor. He was a tall man, just over six feet, with graying hair, and the long lean body of a distance runner, which he had been. He had discovered marathon running in his late forties, and had run this first Boston Marathon to celebrate his 50th birthday, 15 years before. The leanness of his frame had disappeared with the treatment necessary to eliminate the cancer in his prostate, discovered during his pre-retirement exam. An injection to stop his testosterone production and shrink his prostate had caused a four month period of no exercise, and a resultant weight gain. He was shaken by the diagnosis, and depressed by the treatment and the mood swings, even though he had been declared cured at his last examination. Normally an optimistic and outgoing personality, he had retreated inwardly, with no enthusiasm for the future, in spite of Elizabeth's prodding. He had lost his sense of adventure.

Elizabeth Hunter, his wife of more than forty years, was looking forward to her coming retirement from her practice as a clinical psychologist. An attractive and informed woman, she was the guiding partner in a long and happy marriage. She and Russell together shared many things, but held onto and respected each others' differences. She was pleased when Russell had agreed to honor his commitment to the cruise, in spite of his condition. Her hope was to see Russell regain his confidence and delight in learning that was so much a part of him. She was not looking for a retirement with a partner no longer willing to participate in a fulfilling life.

The ship's diesel engines were rumbling quietly, no popping exhaust sounds, just a steady vibration against the hull. The Captain and the Assistant Captain were forward in the wheel house looking at the glow of a computer screen, and the ship's bosun' scurried from the bow to the stern supervising the casting off of the mooring lines. The sky was still dark, with just a hint of light, as the vessel side-slipped away from the dock and began moving down-river stern first, engines idling.

"I thought I was the only early bird," a voice called.

Russell turned to see a younger man behind him, camera in hand.

"Good morning. I didn't see you there. So, you like to watch ships get underway too? Name's Russell." He reached out his hand in greeting.

"I'm Kevin. I saw you at dinner last night. Actually, this is my first time on a boat like this. I thought it might be interesting to watch, and it has been. Why are we going backward? I mean, the back of the boat is pointed down the river, isn't it?" Kevin asked.

"Yes, it is. I think the plan is to go across the river to that point of land where another channel joins the river, back into there, and turn the boat bow first downstream. The channel here is probably not that deep, or maybe it's a traffic hazard to turn around in mid-river. We can ask the Captain when we get straightened out. It's exciting, isn't it?" Russell felt a tingle of excitement as the boat slid along.

"Sure is."

The boat crossed the main channel as Russell had anticipated, eased stern first into the quiet tributary, then reversed with a shudder as the engines were engaged and the bow faced downstream. The Arles was officially underway. During the next seven days they would travel down the Saone to Lyon where they would enter the more well known Rhone River, and continue through Provence to Arles, where van Gogh painted most of his masterpieces. There would be day tours of local attractions in various towns along the river. After Arles they would leave the boat and take a motorcoach to Aix-en-Provence, home of the artist Cezanne . They would also stop to visit the Rhone

American Cemetery where Americans killed in the invasion of southern France were buried, and the tour would come to an end in Nice on the Riviera.

Russell and Kevin stood in silence, the wind flowing over the bow.

"Well, that was worth getting up for," Kevin said as they selected deck chairs at the bow. The morning air was cool, not cold, as daylight filled the sky. Bird cries were heard as the sun moved higher with the dawn. There was no traffic on the placid river, not even a barge.

"Good morning," a male voice called. A short, stocky man stood facing the men, a steaming cup of coffee in his hand. He wore a navy windbreaker and khaki shorts with boat shoes, no socks. He was unshaven.

"Hi," Russell responded. "Morning to you. Come join us. I'm Russell and this young man is Kevin."

The man held out his hand, introducing himself.

"Name's Durgan. It feels good to be on a ship again, even a small one. I did four years with the Navy a long time ago, and I always loved being on the water."

"There is something very soothing about that, isn't there?" Russell asked.

"Yeah, there sure is," Durgan said, taking a sip of the hot brew, a thoughtful look on his face.

"Where are you from? My wife and I are from Atlanta, and Kevin here is from, where?"

"Connecticut. Just outside of Hartford," Kevin responded.

"I'm originally from Leominster, near Boston, small town. This is my first European trip, other than the Med cruise I did with the Navy. Long time ago," Durgan said.

"What did you do in the navy?" Russell asked.

"I was an aerographer. That's a weatherman to civilians. I made Second Class," Durgan replied.

"Did you have much time at sea?" Kevin asked, sipping his coffee.

"Actually, yes. I was on the Mt. McKinley when it was the Fleet Flagship for the Admiral. I liked it."

The men sat quietly, finishing their coffee as the sky lightened.

"So far, this is a great trip," Kevin said breaking the silence.

"It is. Is your wife enjoying it?" Russell asked, draining the last of his coffee.

"Very much. She's almost over worrying about our kids back home with her parents. I figure by the time we get to Arles, she'll be relaxed."

"Moms never are off duty," Russell said. "The worrying part never goes away, even when your kids are parents themselves. Believe it or not, that's the hardest part, letting go when they're adults. But you're not there yet." He stood, walked to a trash container and dropped in his empty cup. "If you don't mind my asking, Kevin, What prompted you to take this cruise? Most of us are retired, but you're not, are you?"

"No, I'm still working and so is Pam. I'm an engineer, aeronautical, and Pam teaches. Our kids start college over the next three years, so we'll be working a while before retirement." He dropped his cup in the trash. "What happened was a friend of mine at work, a designer, booked this cruise, paid deposits, all of that, then had something come up. I had some time coming to me because I don't take much vacation time, Pam had some time, her parents agreed to watch the grandkids. We decided to take advantage of a really good deal before our kids start college and we won't be able to do this."

"Hell of a deal," Durgan said, rising to his feet, stretching his back muscles.

"It makes perfect sense to me," Russell said. "My wife has been after me to travel more, see new places, have new experiences. I finally gave in, now that I'm retired. I don't usually like changes in my life very much."

"How about you, Durgan? Are you retired, traveling with your wife?" Kevin asked.

Durgan shifted in his chair and cleared his throat.

"Well, I am retired, but I'm traveling alone. My wife made this reservation almost a year ago. But she passed away a few months ago. We knew it was coming, and she made me promise to take this trip she had set up." Durgan swiped his hand across his almost bald head, brushing back wisps of hair.

"I'm so sorry," Kevin said. "I didn't mean to …you know."

"No, no… Men don't usually travel alone or with another guy. Women travel together all the time, I mean look how many widows are on this cruise, but men are usually on their own when they lose a spouse. It's just our way," Durgan answered. "I've been keeping quiet about being single, dodging people, so not too many people know. I'm just not ready to get into a big discussion yet, especially with women."

"We'll keep it to ourselves," Russell said.

Kevin nodded agreement.

"Thanks. I just want to take things slowly."

The boat slowed, an audible shift in the engines signaling a slow down as the cruiser approached a lock that would enable the Arles to be lowered to the new river level. There would be many locks to traverse on the journey south. The men moved forward, standing behind the Assistant Captain as he managed the boat's movements from a control box on the port side of the vessel. The man supervising the gates waved to the boat as it entered the lock. Kevin moved back and forth, his camera documenting every action as the lock gates were closed, the water level lowered and the descent of the boat initiated. The gray concrete sides of the lock appeared as the level dropped, the green water leaving muddy traces on the lock walls, the strong smell of river water filling the air. A painted gauge on the gray wall indicated the level of descent by meters.

"Move back or you'll get a shower," the Assistant Captain called cheerfully. The men looked upward at the water dripping off the lock, then hurried under the deployed awning as a small stream of water fell to the deck as the boat moved forward, out of the lock. The men above them on the lock gate waved them on.

"Success!" Kevin called. "Another first. I experienced my first lock. And I am out of coffee. Time to go below and refresh. It's also full daylight, the sun's really up there. When did that happen?"

"I think when we first entered the lock," Durgan replied. "That was really interesting. Thanks for the conversation, Russell. Are you always up early?"

"Usually. Elizabeth is used to it. We have found our rhythm."

"That's an interesting comment," Kevin said as they walked to the stairwell. "I mean, seeing a marriage as having different rhythms. I've never thought of it that way, but it makes sense. I didn't mention it, but my friend who booked this trip – he and his wife just broke up. They're getting divorced, with one very confused little girl. I guess they never found their rhythm, huh?"

"Some never do." Russell turned at the sound of voices coming from the stairwell. The familiar low voice of Elizabeth drifted upward.

"He's up here somewhere. Russ loves being up early, watching the sunrise."

'Watching the sunrise? It doesn't come up without him watching?" Mel asked, playfully. They climbed to the sundeck, coffee in hand.

"Good morning, people," Russell greeted the new arrivals. "I'd like to introduce my new friend, Durgan, from Massachusetts, a fellow retiree and early riser. Sorry, I didn't catch your first name."

"Just Durgan is fine. Good morning." He shook hands with Mel and Elizabeth.

"My wife, Elizabeth, and our new friend, Mel Weinstein from Florida. Where's Ruth?"

"Right behind us, fixing her coffee. It takes a while, don't ask. Nice to meet you Durgan. How was the sunrise? Did you get us cast off or whatever that's called?"

Durgan nodded and smiled. He looked to the stairwell.

Ruth's smile flashed as she reached the sundeck. She held a cardboard cup of coffee in her hand. "Good morning, bonjour, whatever, its morning and we're cruising on a river in France," Ruth announced. "And you are Durgan? Nice to meet you."

"Nice to meet you. Excuse me, I have to go change and shave before breakfast," Durgan explained.

"You know," Ruth said, "you'd think that a nation that built the Eiffel Tower and invented croissants could figure out insulated cups. These things are hot." She shook her hand as she transferred the steaming cardboard cup to her other hand. She blew on her fingers.

"That's why you have to wrap napkins around them like Elizabeth does." Mel said. He handed Ruth a wad of napkins he had tucked in his jacket pocket.

"Thank you, Mel. You take such good care of me."

"That's true. Taking care of others, that's what I do best."

"And you do it so well. I can't believe we're actually away. We booked this cruise almost a year ago, and it's finally happening."

"Time seems to speed up, the older I get," Mel observed. "One day I'm driving all over New Jersey, chasing business, the next week I'm on a boat in France. What happened?"

"We got older. And that's why we need to keep busy doing things like this." Ruth added, waving her cup at the river.

"I'm ready for some breakfast. Are they set up yet?"

"I believe they are. They open at seven, and it's just after seven," Elizabeth said, glancing at her watch. "Could we wait a few minutes while I take a look around?"

"Sure," Russell said. "Breakfast is served until nine, and the whole morning is just for cruising. I'm going to grab another coffee while you guys check things out. We have another perfect day. I'll be back in a minute."

"Don't forget to wrap a napkin around the cup so you don't burn your hand," Mel called to Russell, who nodded and waved.

"Isn't this great?" Elizabeth said to Ruth. "When I looked out of our porthole and saw we were moving, I yelled out loud, 'We're off!'"

"I did the same thing. Mel was laughing at me, but what do I care? It is exciting."

The stairwell was filling with people climbing to the sun deck, eager to see the view of the placid river as the Arles hissed through what was left of a light mist, a small wake rippling the surface. A few early fishermen were on the river bank, preparing to launch their small boats. Waves were exchanged, a universal trait among boaters requiring no language skills. A feeling of total peacefulness filled the air as the travelers sat in their chairs, free of any obligation other than to relax and leave their cares behind.

"Breakfast is being served," Gerard announced from the top of the stairwell. "If you are ready, the dining room is open. Sit anywhere. A buffet table is available, and you can also order a hot breakfast as well. Just tell the waitress or Terry what you would like."

"I guess I'll go down and find Russell. He's been up a while and is probably hungry," Elizabeth said. "Are you ready?"

"Yeah, I think I could eat a little something," Mel replied, pushing back from the small table. He and Ruth rose and followed Elizabeth down to the dining room where Russell waited in the open doorway, chatting with Terry as the diners slowly filed in.

"Good morning," Terry said. "Table for four?"

"Yes, let's do that. We split up last night, but let's have breakfast together over there by the window." Mel said.

"I have been talking with Terry and he says the chef makes great omelets with anything you want. There's a hot buffet line against that wall, and over there at the long tables you have fresh juice, fruit and cereals," Russell said. "Coffee is on the table, in silver pitchers, and hot tea is available in many flavors. A very nice way to start the day."

"I'm for the buffet and those croissants I see," Melvin stated.

"I'm right behind you," Ruth added. "I'll order tea later I guess."

"I'm having tea. I'll order for you if you know what kind you want," Elizabeth volunteered.

"English Breakfast?"

"Done. Russell, what about you? Buffet or..."

"I am going to listen to Terry and have an omelet with shallots and mushrooms. Then I shall have a croissant in keeping with my new policy of showing respect for other cultures. In fact, I may have two croissants. They are fresh baked right here."

"No cold cereal and black coffee? You are becoming daring," Elizabeth laughed.

Terry appeared, with perfect timing.

"Can I get you anything special?"

"Yes," Mel said. "I would like some tea and so would Ruth. English Breakfast, please. I'll be having cereal from the buffet, I think."

"Very good. And you sir?"

"You talked me into an omelet, with shallots and mushrooms please. This coffee's terrific."

"Thank you. It keeps us all going strong." Terry walked into the kitchen.

The dining room filled up as the passengers were seated and figured out the ordering procedure, most opting for the buffet lines and self-service. The conversation level rose as more introductions were made and stories were shared. Gerard stood near the entrance, smiling at the new arrivals, glancing at his watch, delighting in the pleased expressions he saw on their faces. The smiling waitresses moved silently, replenishing coffee and clearing plates.

"Where's your friend Durgan? Have you met his wife?" Elizabeth asked Russell as the Weinsteins returned with their food.

"Uh, about Durgan," Russell said, "he has asked me to not mention that he is traveling alone, not married. He recently lost his wife. She made him promise to take this trip, and he is honoring her wish, but he wants to keep a low profile. Especially around the single women, okay?"

"What did she die from?" Ruth asked. "Do you know?"

"He didn't say. Just that they knew it was coming. Probably some form of cancer, I would guess. He doesn't seem to feel comfortable talking about it."

The Weinsteins settled in, napkins on their laps.

"I couldn't help hearing the end of your conversation," Mel said. "That's got to be tough for him. Men don't do well when they lose a spouse. I'm on the Grief Committee for our neighborhood community center. It's much harder for men, usually. Women lose a spouse and they're still running the home as usual. Men don't know what to do. They don't know how to shop, how to cook, do laundry. That's why so many end up giving up on life."

"Isn't that Durgan?" Elizabeth asked, looking at the doorway. Durgan was freshly shaved, dressed in pressed khakis and a short sleeved polo shirt. "He seems to have found some new friends."

"That's Sally. And Sonia. We had dinner with them last night. Both very nice, both widows. Sally was pretty aggressive about finding a new man, but Sonia was not interested," Russell said. "Sally must have been a busy detective."

"Anyway, they are both very nice, very interested in art, especially Sonia, and they both have no fear of foreign food. We all really enjoyed the mustard soup, even Russell. I wonder if the recipes for the dishes served are available."

"I'll ask Terry. I spent some time talking to him and he is a great host. He'll know," Ruth said. "Our dinner companions were a little strange. Moira and Katy. Two former school teachers. I don't think either one was ever married. Or maybe they just don't talk about it. Katy barely spoke at all. Very shy. Moira talked enough for both."

"I think she's dominated by Moira with her rough, gravelly voice," Mel noted. "I bet she was a heavy smoker. I don't think Katy is very open to new things. She wouldn't touch the mustard soup and she did eat the lamb, but Moira pushed her on that. I'd rather not share a table with them again."

Russell reached for his second croissant. "Our ladies ate everything, including that dessert, Floating Islands? That was too sweet for me," Russell commented as he speared a small piece of shallot. "These are good. Anyway, both of the ladies are pretty lively and interested in art and the local history. Apparently they have been friends since grade school. There seem to be quite a few women traveling together."

"I traveled with other men once. It was called the Army and I didn't like it." Mel nodded emphatically, getting a laugh as he expected.

"Finish your croissant. I want to change and put on some sun screen before going up on deck for the morning," Ruth directed.

"Are you finished?" Russell asked.

"Yes. I think I'll change too. The forecast is for warm weather."

"See you up above. I'll save a deck chair for you."

"The correct phrase is 'see you topside,' if anyone cares." Mel offered.

Terry surveyed the dining room as it emptied of satisfied guests, noting what items would need replenishing, what items were most popular, how the new people performed and what he could do to improve matters for lunch at noon. The new waitress from England, Brenda, had some problems, mostly about traffic flow, but he would talk to her quietly and she would get better each day. As he was directing the clean-up, a loud male voice called to him.

"Nice job, that. Everything done nicely and on time."

Terry turned at the sound, ears picking up the English accent. A bit of Yorkshire, he told himself.

"Name's Barry. From London by way of Yorkshire. I understand you're from Leeds," the red-faced man spoke. He was medium height, about 5 feet, 6 inches, with an ample midsection. Terry remembered seeing him in the back of the room, sitting with a striking younger woman with heavy makeup, and an older man and woman. Their clothes suggested England, especially their stout shoes.

"Terry's the name. Welcome to Arles. We usually only have Americans in our tour groups. Nice to meet a fellow Englishman."

"Yeah, well, we got on at the last minute. Me and my mate Tommy and the ladies. Very nice boat, this. Any chance of getting a full English breakfast along the way?"

"Doubtful, if you mean the fried breakfast with the sausage, bacon, fried bread, et cetera. People are very health conscious these days." Terry glanced at Barry's shirt pocket. "The whole boat is non-smoking, you may have noticed. Even the sundeck. If you really have to smoke, go to the stern as far back as you can, or wait until you get ashore."

"Bloody hell."

"Yes, well, rules are rules. It really is a beautiful cruise, you know. Lots of art and ancient architecture."

"As if I need that. Just so the pub is open."

"That we can do. Nice meeting you." Terry walked to the kitchen to supervise the cleanup. With a short turnaround time between meals, the crew had to step lively. Terry glanced at his watch and poured a cup of coffee for himself. If Barry doesn't like art or architecture, and he didn't realize this was a non-smoking boat, he wondered, then why is he aboard? He would talk to Giovanni about the English arrivals later.

Chapter Five

Russell woke early, just before the alarm was set to go off. He lay quietly in his bunk, slowly stretching, his arms above his head, his back arched. The early morning light filtered through the cabin window, the engines of the boat in a soothing rumble. Elizabeth was soundly asleep in her bunk, her dark hair framing her face. Reaching for the alarm, Russell turned it off. He sat up and swung his legs over the side of the bunk. It had been another good night's sleep, no interruptions, no problems.

He began his usual morning routine, visited the bathroom, got dressed and silently slipped out the door, headed first for the coffee pot, then the sundeck. He paused at the bulletin board to check the posting of the day's activities. The morning would be a slow, pleasant cruise on the Saone, lunch on board, and a stop at the town of Trevoux. There passengers could opt for a visit to a winery with a sampling of wine, cheeses and sausage. The Hunters had decided to skip the tour, choosing to explore the village on their own. Elizabeth had developed an interest in photography, and was rapidly becoming skilled at selecting and composing interesting shots. In the evening, they would attend the Captain's Welcome Dinner.

Russell stood at the bow, enjoying the breeze, the soft sound of the water parting, and the total solitude of the moment. He had looked forward to retirement, anticipating days of visiting book stores, studying his collection of books and maps, watching favorite films and documentaries. He was beginning to plan a trip to follow the original route of the Lewis and Clark expedition that opened the American West when he learned of his unfortunate condition. He was filled with feelings of anger and denial. What had he done? How could this be happening now? Elizabeth was his rock, offering advice, helping him decide between the many treatment options, never giving in to negatives. She had always believed in him. He owed it to her to put the recent past behind him. He was trying.

After breakfast, the passengers gathered in clusters on the sun deck, moving deck chairs in or out of the warm sun. A steady breeze off the river supplied a cooling effect that sometimes led to early sunburn cases. The engines provided a quiet rumble that was soothing as it masked out conversations, and more than one reader dozed off with a book in their lap.

"This is wonderful," the man said. "Morning. How are you?"

Russell was back standing at the starboard rail, watching the wave spread out from the bow, trying not to think of anything.

"Morning to you. Frank, isn't it? Nice to see you again. How are your ladies?" Russell quickly scanned the deck area. He had remembered meeting Frank and his wife, her sister, and a woman friend at Giverny on the bus trip.

"Believe it or not," Frank said, "they're all in one place, each in their own chair, content until the next change in course when they'll have too much sun and need to move again. They're getting better at getting ready on time. I'm not really complaining, but it's almost like traveling with kids again."

"It's something they'll remember forever. I remember doing things with Elizabeth's parents when they were alive. At the time I didn't think her father appreciated anything. We had to drag him to places her mother enjoyed. Then a few years later we overheard him telling one of his neighbors in assisted living about all the great times he had had with his daughter and son-in-law. You never know."

Frank leaned into the railing, facing Russell.

"Well, my wife Angela and I love traveling and that's a big part of our retirement," Frank explained. "Her sister, Ann Marie, is enjoying herself, and she never traveled much. Her husband passed last year after a short fight with lung cancer. He was diagnosed, then boom he was gone. Nothing they could do. The only problem, a small one, is Peggy, Angie's friend from back home. I think she's depressed, even after three years. She's never gotten over losing her husband. He was all set to retire. They had plans to buy a boat, go fishing, you know. Two weeks before he hit the magic number he dropped dead in their driveway, a heart attack. Getting old is a bitch."

"Has she tried joining groups of other women, like the Red Hat ladies, or card clubs…"

"Angela has made suggestions, but Peggy just shuts everything out. Nothing seems to please her. Nothing."

"Not even Giverny?"

"That was a good trip," Frank agreed. "You know, when we signed up for it, I never gave it any thought. I didn't realize it was where Monet lived and all that."

The tour group had boarded the motorcoach in Paris early on the morning of their second day for the ride along the Seine into the southern part of Normandy, away from the landing beaches on D Day. Giverny was a small country village on a railroad track whose beauty had caught the eye of George Monet as he was traveling. He returned to buy a large home with extensive grounds he developed into gardens. He dammed the small stream on his property to create the ponds he made famous when he painted his canvases of water lilies.

It was in Giverny that Impressionism came to life, even though it took years to be accepted by the art critics. Monet established a school for followers of the new method, and a small museum displayed their talents to visitors. Russell had talked with Frank and his ladies at a coffee bar at the museum and had shared their thoughts about painting in general, and Impressionism in particular, while Elizabeth visited the paintings a second time.

The men leaned against the railing, recalling Monet's works and gazing at the riverbank and the plowed fields beyond. A herd of cows, all of them white, raised their heads, watching the boat pass. A deep mooing sound echoed across the water. Several passengers mooed back, led by Gerard, starting a cow dialogue.

"Think those cows do that every time a boat passes?" Frank asked.

"What else is there for a cow to do?" Russell replied.

Gerard had arrived on deck, casually dressed in boat shoes, cotton slacks, a collarless shirt, and yet another sport coat, a pale yellow this time. He looked refreshed and went at least a minute without glancing at his wrist. There was no clipboard in sight. Peace at last.

Giovanni, in his sparkling white uniform, moved to the front of the deck and called for attention. The cruising travelers put down their books and magazines, and the Iowans halted their card game as the Purser and two crew members conducted the mandatory safety lecture and life jacket drill. Passengers were shown where to get a life jacket, and how to put it on correctly, which led to a long series of laughs. The passengers managed to attach the many straps in combinations the manufacturers never thought of. Giovanni took it in stride, having conducted the drill many times each year. He patiently explained that the likelihood of having to abandon the boat was small, but it was best to be prepared.

Gerard struggled to keep from screaming at the confused travelers who defied all attempts to explain the simplicity of the life jackets. He was horrified, thinking that they all would drown if there was an emergency and they had to go in the water. He moved from one to the other, rearranging straps.

"Looks like Basil's back," Russell said, nodding toward the frantic Gerard. He and Elizabeth had concluded that when Gerard was stressed, he resembled Basil Fawlty of the British television show, "Fawlty Towers."

"You're right," Elizabeth said. "He's got that strange light in his eyes again."

The Iowans were back at the card game, life jackets in place. Gerard was speechless at their impertinence.

"Looks like Sonia won't drown. Now Giovanni is checking her again. I think that's the third time." Sonia's head was back, a loud laugh breaking over the deck as she and Giovanni shared a special moment.

Sally stood next to her, her life jacket straps being adjusted by her new found friend, Durgan.

"Don't look now, but Durgan seems to be coming out of his shell," Elizabeth commented.

"Good. He needs that," Russell noted.

The drill ended, the life jackets were removed and stowed by the crew in their special boxes on the deck, and the lazy cruising resumed. Waitresses appeared with Bloody Marys, the green stalks of fresh celery protruding from the salted rims of the plastic glasses.

"You know, I bet you could make money just offering all day river cruising. No stops, no rough seas, no walking tours, just cruising and eating and drinking, just doing nothing. I'd go for it," Mel said, a chunk of celery disappearing in a big bite.

"I agree, Mel. Just doing nothing may be the ultimate vacation. No phones, no email, no TV. Just leave me alone."

"It's a fact. When men first retire, for the first six months all they want is to be left alone and to take a nap anytime they want to. And watch the History channel. Or, as Ruth calls it, the Hitler Channel. That's all that's on anymore. 'Hitler's Generals, Hitler's Weapons.' When they showed 'Hitler's Pets,' she pulled the plug, so to speak."

The men shared a laugh of recognition."Hey, if we don't watch him, he may come back."Russell explained.

"What happens after the first six months?" Elizabeth asked.

"Their wives get tired of it and haul them off to France and other great spots," Ruth said.

"And we appreciate it, don't we, Mel?"

"You are a wise man, my friend." They touched glasses.

The slow cruise continued in the brilliant sunshine as the Arles sailed through the Beaujolais region on the journey to Lyon and the junction with the Rhone River. At Trevoux, the M/S Arles docked next to a small public park with a canopy of shade trees. Gerard assembled and led the passengers who had chosen to visit the winery and a 14th century chapel into the town of "golden stone." Their visit also included a "degustation" of local wine, cheese and sausages.

The on board luncheon was excellent, with sandwiches in the French style, and a few of the guests talked of an afternoon nap. The remaining travelers slowly ambled into the very small river town, or retreated to the air-conditioned comfort of the lounge for more reading and some card and board games. Mel and Ruth decided on the nap option, with a walk later, in the cooler part of the day. Mel was cautious about his stamina.

The Hunters decided to see what Trevoux was all about and aimed for the octagonal tower of the ancient castle, a convenient street map tucked into the back pocket of Russell's jeans. They passed the park, pausing to watch groups of men, young and old, some of them bare-chested in the warm sun, playing a game with small metal balls.

"That isn't Bocce is it?" Elizabeth asked? "I don't see any court."

"No, it's not Bocce. This is the French version where they don't have a court. They can play anywhere there's dirt. The other difference is the thrower has to keep both feet on the ground and stay in the circle drawn in the dirt. Then it's like Bocce where players try to get their ball closest to the target ball, the small one. I think the scoring is the same too," Russell explained. "It's called Petanque, I think."

"Now, where did you learn that?"

"I'm not sure. I did some reading about France and its customs when you were planning our trip."

"You should try it. You were good at Bocce on our Italy trip."

"Oh, I just got lucky with a few rolls. These guys look like they know what they're doing. What a nice way to pass a Sunday."

"Let's check out Trevoux. I want to get some pictures."

They left the park, entering the town, so small it could be called a village. It was Sunday, and the French regarded Sunday as a complete day of rest. The main street was deserted, all the stores closed.

The Hunters walked slowly, looking in the shop windows. Elizabeth stopped and took her camera out of her small bag. The window held a small display of old mortars and pestles, like those used in pharmacies. Moving to avoid glare of the plate glass, Elizabeth took a series of photos.

"How many pictures can you take with that camera?" Russell asked.

"Oh, 3 or 400, I think. It depends on the size of the chip and this one is big."

" 400 photos in one camera? You're kidding." Russell said.

"No I'm not. One chip holds everything. I can even look at what I've just taken and erase it if I don't like it. I can take pictures all day, review them, and select the best, deleting the rest," Elizabeth explained. "It's an incredible breakthrough. And simple. Why don't you try some shots?" She handed him the camera.

"Where do I look?"

"You can just hold up the camera and look at the image in the small screen, or you can hold it to your eye and look through here," She pointed to the aperture. When you press this button, the lens will focus automatically, and you can take the shot."

Russell pointed the camera at a monument of a knight on a horse and pressed the shutter down slowly. A flash went off.

"Did it work?" Russell asked.

"Look at the back of the camera and press the review button. There."

The knight appeared, mounted on the rearing horse.

"Wow. Perfect."

"And, when we get home, I connect this to our computer, and all our photos can be saved there."

"What if we want pictures, prints?"

"I'm just getting into that, but we can load them on a disc and take them to a store for processing, or print them ourselves with the right printer. Or we can send them to our friends with email."

"I say again, wow. This is really something. No more lugging bags of stuff on a trip. Just this little thing."

"You could create your own travel journal, complete with photos. Think about it," Elizabeth said.

"Okay. I got it. You know, other people I talked to about these things started telling me about pixels. Do I need to know that?" Russell asked.

"Not really. Not at this point."

"Good. Let's take more. I'll watch you."

Back on Arles, Sonia strolled the quiet deck in a summer dress, casual espadrilles on her feet. Sally was below in the cabin, watching an old movie musical, the sound turned low. Durgan had begged off a walk with her, claiming the need to write some postcards.

It felt good to be alone for a change. Sonia appreciated her old friend's concerns about her, but she really didn't need help as much as Sally thought she did. She was on her own, but she wasn't lonely, and didn't feel the need to have a man in her life full time, in spite of what her children thought. There was a sense of freedom in not being bound to someone else. Sally disagreed, of course and was determined to find a new mate, if not for herself, then certainly for her friend.

"Bonjour, Madame," Giovanni called as Sonia descended the stairway. "Everything satisfactory?"

"Everything is very satisfactory," Sonia smiled broadly. "Do you actually get paid to do this? Cruise up and down the river, eat wonderful meals, watch the cows in the fields?"

"Yes, Madame, I do. I would do it for free, but I don't want to insult my employer by rejecting a salary. I am happy you are enjoying the cruise," Giovanni stacked his papers and folded his hands.

"I am. It's so restful, so quiet on the river. The breeze feels so nice I could sit here forever."

"You can, you know. We can arrange anything. Are you going ashore today? Later perhaps?"

"Definitely later. My friend Sally, you met her, is resting, but when it cools off I want to go exploring." The breeze picked up as a cloud scurried by.

"Unfortunately, most of the small stores are closed because of Sunday. There isn't a lot to do in Trevoux except for the Chateau. Perhaps a drink at a cafe, some picture taking." Giovanni shrugged, palms upward. "But tonight it is the captain's dinner and you will enjoy that. Here is the bill of fare." He handed her the embossed menu.

Sonia read the card. "Sounds delicious. I love fish. I can't wait to see how you prepare it. Our meal last night was wonderful. The best part is I don't have to plan it or buy the food or cook it. Just sit back and be waited on." She returned the card.

Giovanni smiled as their eyes met in a long silence. "Would you like something from the kitchen now? Terry is in the back."

"No, I'm fine. I do have a question though."

"And what is that?"

"What is that game they're playing in the park over there? It sounds like those shiny balls they're throwing are metal," Sonia looked to the shady park.

The clacking could be heard clearly, and men's voices raised in shouting something in French she couldn't understand. Giovanni moved to the railing, next to Sonia.

"The game they play is called Petanque, and it means 'feet on the ground.' Players must stand in a small circle drawn in the dirt when they throw. They throw out a small ball, then try to get close to it with the other larger balls, like bocce. The closest balls win points. 11 points wins the game."

"I'd like to try it sometime. Will we get a chance?"Sonia smiled.

"You could play there now if you wish. I'm certain someone would be happy to show you how to play." He gestured to the park.

"Would you come with me?" she asked, smiling as she moved closer to him..

"I would enjoy that, but I have my duties here." There was a long pause. "Unfortunately."

"Excuse me, Purser?"" a voice spoke. It was Tommy, the smaller British gentleman.

The Purser turned at the calling of his name and hastened behind the desk. "Yes?" he asked.

"Sorry to bother you mate, but I need to get some Euros."He held a stack of British pounds.

"Certainly, sir," Giovanni opened his cash box. Back to business.

Sonia waved a small goodbye, smiling with enough heat to let Giovanni know she knew. She always knew when it came to men. As she made her way to her cabin, a glimpse of bright yellow in the forward lounge area caught her eye. Sally had a jacket that color. She moved forward slowly until she could see the back of a familiar head, a yellow jacket and the smiling face of Durgan, the widower. He was sitting across from Sally, holding a small black bound book. "Go Sally," She said softly.

In Trevoux, Elizabeth and Russell had climbed the steep hill to the ruins of the Chateau. The view of the Saone below them was beautiful, the M/S Arles alongside the dock. They could see the players in the park.

Elizabeth was taking pictures of huge clumps of wisteria, draped gracefully over the walls and trellises. She approached from different angles, paying attention to the position of the sun. Russell was once again fascinated by the intensity of his life-long partner. They started down the winding road, stopping for photos along the way, Elizabeth reviewing her shots with Russell, explaining what she was doing, and why.

Gerard, meanwhile, had returned with the group that had visited the local winery. He led them aboard, saw that they got their keys from the desk, checked his count once again, and decided to visit the bar and the new bartender, Sophia.

"Giovanni, I am off to the bar and an apertif. Since we are almost in Provence, I believe a Pastis is in order. I will be there if needed. The new bartender is named Sophia, yes?" he asked.

"Sophia is correct. She has excellent English and passable French. This is her first cruise with Arles, but she has been on other boats. She is quite interesting, as you will learn. Your tour was successful, I assume?"

"You mean our little degustation just back? Yes, successful, with just a small annoyance. I will talk with you later. Merci."

Sophia was arranging glasses and bar supplies she would need for the late afternoon and evening activities. The bar was small with just four stools, but most people preferred to get a drink and then sit in the comfortable lounge or go up on deck. She watched to see that only plastic containers were taken outside. She enjoyed working on the small river cruisers, even though the bar and the number of passengers were significantly smaller. She did less well with tips, but didn't work nearly as hard. She could get to know her customers, and that's where the tips came from. What she liked most was meeting all the different people and learning about the United States and all of its different places and customs. They all spoke the same language, but there were differences as distinct as French from Italian. Getting to the United States was her goal, eventually. At just twenty four, with her athletic body, naturally blond hair, and clear blue eyes, she imagined herself in California, teaching skiing at a resort in the winter months and bartending at a beach resort the rest of the year.

"Bonjour, Sophia. Are you open for a weary Program Director?"

"Bonjour, Gerard. I am always available for a Program Director. Did I say that right?" She laughed loudly. "How may I serve you?" She wiped the bar with her cloth.

"I would love an aromatic, delicious glass of Pastis." Gerard sat with folded hands.

"I believe I have a few bottles on hand. Is Pastis 51 suitable?"

"Perfect. I prefer it to the Ricard."

Sophia slid the glass of the murky anise flavored liquid to Gerard, along with a small pitcher of plain water. She added a bowl of olives, the traditional accompaniment to Pastis.

Gerard mixed in the water, about four parts to one of the liquor, stirred the beverage until it assumed a greenish yellow color, then enjoyed a large sip.

"Ah," he sighed, the anise aroma flooding his head. "Perfect. My congratulations."

"Thank you, Gerard. I am from Slovakia where we drink Slivovitz, the plum brandy, and we have rules for that like you do for Pastis. I suppose every nation has a national drink. Americans like Martinis, very dry. I learned all about that on one of my longer trips on the bigger boats. Have you been on the longer cruises?" She wiped a spot on the bar.

"Yes," Gerard said, "I have been with the line for four years and I have taken the Rivers of Russia cruise, the Great Waterways of Europe, from Amsterdam to Vienna, and countless motorcoach trips. I prefer the smaller boats, and Arles is my favorite."

"I like the smaller boats because you can get to know the people. They are usually very nice. Especially the Americans."

"This is very nice," Gerard said, rolling his now empty glass in his hand. "I will allow one more before I begin preparing for the Captain's Welcome Dinner this evening. Do you like Pastis?"

"Yes, but only one. They are very strong for me."

"You know, van Gogh, who lived in Arles, loved to drink absinthe, which was banned later. It tasted like Pastis, a licorice flavor, but it contained wormwood, which some thought caused madness. Van Gogh did go completely mad, you see, shooting himself in the chest. Pastis was the successor to absinthe, without the dangerous wormwood. At least, that is what I was taught. It is the drink most consumed in Provence."

"Now I have learned something new." Sonia smiled.

"I must go. It was nice to meet you. I will see you later, I am sure."

"My pleasure," Sophia touched hands with Gerard in a European version of a handshake. Their smiles lingered.

Chapter Six

The Captain's Welcome Dinner began on time, with Gerard, as usual, glancing between his watch, the fast filling lounge and bar area, and the passageway to the cabins. Terry paused in his directing of the serving staff to assure Gerard that everything was on schedule. They stood next to the bar while Sophia awaited her first order. At the bar, passengers signed for their drinks, rather than paying in cash, a practice that made life easier for her. In just one busy evening, she would remember all the cabin numbers for each guest after the first drink request. She preferred not to have to handle money when the bar was crowded.

"Relax, Gerard," Terry advised, leaning against the small bar. "My staff has everything under control. We do this every week, don't we? For an entire season that's many months long. Only the passengers change. You'll give yourself a stroke, mate."

"Yes, I might, but these passengers tonight are my passengers and I am responsible for their welfare and happiness. You know how one bad report can end a career, Terry. One unhappy person can cause an investigation." Gerard sipped from his water glass.

"But, Gerard, you cannot please everybody all the time, no matter what you do. There's always something you can't control. This morning I had a request for beans on toast for breakfast and the man was quite upset when I pointed out that this is a French boat and we are on a river in France, not in the East End of London. My own countryman, no less."

"Who else eats beans on toast but the English? What are English doing on this cruise? We normally have Americans only," Gerard said.

"I was told the original people who made the booking had to change their plans at the last minute and transferred the cabins to these other folks," Terry said. "Maybe it's an experiment to attract English travelers. You know we prefer to have all cabins filled. Have you talked to them? The men are Barry, the one with the beard, and Tom, the smaller gent. I haven't picked up the women's names yet."

"I can help you there," Gerard volunteered. "The women are Gladys and Martha. Gladys is the younger blonde, the flashy one. They were on my afternoon tour, without the men. They seem quite nice and enjoyed the wine tasting. Gladys got a bit tipsy, but someone always does. They kept to themselves most of the time," Gerard concluded, moving to the entryway to greet the arriving guests, turning on his smile. The men were wearing suits or sport coats, and the women were in cocktail attire, complete with high heels and costume jewelry. They looked very smart, anticipating an elegant evening.

"Terry," Sophia said, "the Englishmen were in here earlier this afternoon, wanting me to open the bar for them. I believe you were watching the supplies being loaded. I explained that the bar was not open and they were not pleased. They may have gone to Giovanni."

"Really? In future, if that happens again, please come find me wherever I may be. The bar is my responsibility, not Giovanni's."

"I'm sorry, I did not know what to do and they were not being nice."

"That's all right, love," Terry reassured her. "I'm not upset with you. Just keep me aware of any problems you have, and I'll deal with it. Between you and me, keep your eye on those two gents. Try not to take any cash from them. Have them sign for their drinks. Something is a bit off with them."

Giovanni called the guests together and explained that following the reception and dinner, the Arles would be getting underway for a night cruise to the city of Lyon, where the Saone River joins the Rhone. The boat would be in Lyon for two days to allow for sightseeing.

After the announcements, the waitresses circulated among the guests with complimentary glasses of wine, while Sophia poured drinks for those who preferred something other than wine.

The passengers moved to the tables for the formal dinner, most returning to what they now considered "their" usual dining seats, with their usual companions. It happened on every cruise. Travelers sought out familiar faces.

Terry's servers moved with speed and efficiency, delivering the courses, refilling wine glasses, anticipating needs, and quietly assuring the diners of an excellent experience. The chef's selections were superb, and even the skeptical diners were won over by the Provencal seasonings.

A large table had filled up with the Hunters, Weinsteins, Sonia, Sally, and Durgan, resplendent in a navy blazer with silver buttons over pale gray slacks. They chattered on, comfortable with each other, reviewing their afternoon adventures. None of them had chosen the optional tour.

"Anybody go on the tour today?" Mel asked the table, over the buzz of conversation.

"We did," came the voice form the adjoining table. It was the voice of Angela, Frank's wife. They four traveler's were seated together as usual. "I swore I wasn't going to eat again until tomorrow after the wine tasting this afternoon. The sausages and the cheeses were so good I couldn't stop eating them. Even you liked them, didn't you, Peg?" Angela said as Frank and the ladies slowly sampled each new taste.

"I try new things," Peg whined. "It's just that I don't like anything that's too burny, you know, when your mouth feels like it's on fire," Peg answered. "I was raised on plain food."

"I like new things. If I want plain food I can stay home and eat macaroni and cheese with my grandkids," Angela laughed.

"Really, it was a good time. Gerard was really funny, talking about cheese. He gets so serious."

As the dessert was being served, Captain Pelletier rose to thank the guests for choosing the Arles, and to excuse himself so that he could get the boat underway for Lyon. He suggested that there would be many photo opportunities available as Lyon had many lighted buildings and monuments to see on the night approach.

The English travelers, Barry and Tommy, were first at the bar, complaining to Sophia about the lack of beer selections.

"You only have 1664, that French swill? Where's a gent to get a decent pint?" Barry demanded.

"We have Heineken in cans," Sophia explained, her eyes searching for Terry. "I'm sorry but we don't have the room for a larger selection of beers."

Terry appeared behind the complaining Barry, nodding to Sophia.

"Good evening, gentlemen. May I help you?"

Barry launched into a lecture on the importance of having a "proper beer" on board. Terry nodded in agreement, then offered each of them a large whiskey and an apology. The offer was accepted, as Terry knew it would be. He was right in his initial judgment. These two would need watching.

The Hunters and Weinsteins decided a stroll on the sundeck was a good idea, with a quick stop for a change to more casual clothing and a needed jacket for the night air. The group dispersed according to their plans, the Iowans retreating to their cabins for after dinner drinks, some couples lingering in the bar, and most intending to watch the departure from the top deck. The English couples sat in the bar lounge, the men now drinking a mixture of brandy and Port, the women sipping Gin and Tonics, no ice, thank you very much.

Gerard survived the dinner, confirming that all passengers had attended, and observing that the food was appreciated by all, especially the soup course. There was still little participation in the cheese course, served before dessert, Gerard's favorite. When he urged people to try the cheeses they did, and enjoyed them, but it was the idea of cheese as a course, instead of a snack, that Americans could not seem to accept. They put cheese on hamburgers. What could you do with such people, he wondered?

Chapter Seven

The Arles moved quietly down the Saone, green and red running lights showing her passage, interior lights dimmed, deck lights as low as possible, the passengers wrapped in jackets and sweaters against the night chill. A glow of light colored the sky to their south, down river.

Below deck, the remains of the Captain's Welcome Dinner were being cleared away as the dining room was reset for the morning meal. Gerard and Giovanni joined Terry who suggested that they have a business talk outside on the stern of the boat. He led them through the kitchen, or galley, to the small outside deck, the smoking area. Terry closed the door behind them.

"Right. Thanks for coming by," he said. "I've noticed some unusual behavior by some passengers and I wanted to let you know about it, and ask that we all keep our eyes on this lot. You know we had two couples join us in Chalon, English couples, my people. The men are Barry, with a beard, and Tom, or Tommy, a little fellow who doesn't say much. The women are Gladys, the flashy looker, and Martha.

"They were on my tour today, but without the men. Gladys got a bit into the wine. Martha managed to control her."

"Is that unusual, Gerard, for women to go on a tour without their husbands?" Giovanni asked.

"It depends on the tour. If we are going to a fabric store or a pottery shop, something very female oriented, the men will choose not to go. And women do not like battlefield tours. But, a wine tasting with sausages and cheese? Yes, that is unusual."

"What do you suspect, Terry?"Giovanni asked.

"I don't really know, but they aren't acting like the usual tourists. The men have no interest in any of the activities, just preferring to spend their time drinking in the bar, complaining about the choice of beers, for example. They don't seem to have any sense of curiosity, or concern about the cruise itself. Do you know what I mean?"

"I believe I do. I visited them to ask about their meal and received a very vague response," Giovanni said. "Sophia had a run in with them, as you know Terry. They wanted the bar open early."

"Right," Terry said. That's what caught my attention. There has been some talk among the other cruise boats of someone passing some queer, you know, funny money, mainly dollars and pounds, for Euros. So, I told Sophia to limit accepting cash at the bar and to have everyone sign their bill to their cabin."

"It might just be me," Terry said, "but something isn't proper with this lot, and I'm going to be watching. Let's keep each other informed, right?"

"Agreed."

"I, Gerard, will observe in the manner of Poirot, one of my heroes," Gerard grinned, waving his finger. "And now I need to get on deck with my little brood."

The Arles had entered the Rhone at Lyon and the passengers were at the rails enjoying the brilliant light show the city offered visitors. Buildings, monuments, bridges and structures of all kinds were illuminated with splashes of color. Heads swiveled as one spectacular display after another was revealed. Cameras flashed in a steady beat in a vain attempt to capture the sight of more than 200 illuminated locations.

Kevin stood in the forward area of the bow, just behind the wheel house, his professional level camera capturing images of the lighting art as they passed by.

"Look, Kevin," Pamela urged, "It's the Eiffel Tower, all lit up!"

Kevin turned to look at the hillside where a structure resembling the Eiffel Tower loomed over the city. It was awash in colored light. He raised his camera and fired off a burst of shots.

"That's the tower shown on the Net. It's actually a radio tower that the citizens created with an Eiffel Tower look to tease Paris. It's next to an ancient church, and it has upset some of the more religious folks. It certainly gets your eye." Kevin said.

Gerard joined the small group of eager photographers. "There has always been a great rivalry between Paris and Lyon, with the Parisians flaunting their supposed sophistication and culture," he explained. "Lyon is 2000 years old, and is rich in history. You will hear more tomorrow in an on-board lecture. We French consider Lyon to be the gastronomical capital of our country, ahead of Paris. The restaurants are superb. In December, Lyon stages the Festival of Lights, an international event with lights of all kinds lighting up as much of the city as possible. It is magnificent and worth a special trip."

The Arles engines were reversed, sending a slight shudder through the boat as it eased into the landing where it would remain for a two-day visit. From the landing the government buildings that lined the wide street facing the river announced that Lyon was a major city with important business to conduct. Bridges spanned the Rhone on either side of the boat as it nestled between the hills at the confluence of the two rivers.

"Time to pack it in," Russell announced as the passengers began retiring. He rose and moved to the staircase, waiting for those ahead of him to descend.

"That was something, wasn't it?" Larry asked. "Nothing like that in Iowa."

"Or in Atlanta," Russell replied. "Where's your group?"

"Oh, we split up sometimes," Larry said.

"Not nearly enough. Hi. I'm Debbie, Larry's wife."

"Nice to meet you a last. It takes a while to meet everyone. I'm Russell and Elizabeth is my wife."

"We've met. I love your necklace. It's perfect with your dress."

"Thank you," Elizabeth said. The group moved forward, starting down the stairwell.

"You have to bear with us a bit," Larry said. "Sometimes we get a little too much of togetherness with our group. Debbie minds it more than me."

They moved carefully in the darkness, watching the metal steps.

"I'm sorry, honey," Debbie said, "but we have known each other since grade school. We play cards together, we go to the same church, we root for the same teams, and we even go on vacations together. We know everything about each other and I get tired of it. I like meeting other people and learning about their lives."

"That's understandable," Elizabeth said. "Russell and I have moved around a lot in our lives, but we're from small towns where people do have lifelong friendships that I guess can get stifling, although that might be a bad word choice."

"It's a perfect word choice. Stifling. That's exactly what it is," Debbie insisted.

"You're just upset because Bob spent so much time looking at the pharmacy exhibit today," Larry explained.

"Well, how much time can you spend talking about all the different sizes of mortars and pestles?' Debbie asked. "I get the point. Put the stuff in and grind away. Boring."

"Things will be better in the morning. We all need some sleep. Nice meeting you, Russell and Elizabeth." They reached the bottom of the stairs on the main deck.

"See you. Good night."

Elizabeth sat in the armchair, slowly removing her shoes, while Russell hung his pants and sport coat in the closet.

"So, what do you think so far?"Elizabeth asked.

"Well, I am pleasantly pleased so far with the boat, especially the food. I like Pastis, and the wine selections have been great. I've tried to write down the names of the wines served at dinner. And the town today was a bit disappointing, but that's because it's Sunday," Russell said, closing the closet door and reaching for his sleeping pants. "I enjoyed learning about the world of digital photography. I'd like to learn more."

Elizabeth leaned back in her chair, stretching her arms, arching her back. "Any time you wish, just pick it up and use it. When we get back, maybe we should look into the courses they offer at Emory for seniors on photography."

She arranged her clothes for the next day while Russell prepared for bed. She was beginning to notice a return to the old Russell, a shift in mood from the cloud of depression that had begun since the loss of his best friend so unexpectedly, followed by his shocking medical news. He had always been so healthy, not even a cold or a headache. If anyone defied aging, he did. He finished in the bathroom.

"Next?" he waved to the small room.

"You know, today in town I had a flashback," Elizabeth said. "Seeing the quiet streets and the shops all closed, it reminded me of Sundays when we were growing up with everything closed, even the movies. I think they called it 'blue laws' or something. Sunday was always the most boring day of the week. All we did was go to church, eat and sit on our front porch."

"I know," Russell said."I remember when our town voted to have Sunday movies. My dad supported that idea. I can remember him saying that kids needed something to do. I was surprised because he rarely said anything political."

"The world has changed a lot since then, hasn't it? No more sitting on the front porch for us, right?"

"Right. Not for Mel and Ruth either. They love to go. Especially Ruth."

"She was telling me about life in Florida, you know, with the retirement villages?"

"Like what we saw in New Smyrna and the 'early birds special' crowd? God, that was depressing. I don't want to live like that if we can avoid it," Russell said.

"Ruth said they moved to Florida because they had family there, and suggested that it was better to move into a new development, rather than an established one."
"Why?"

"The older communities don't welcome newcomers that easily. In a new development, it's like a small family. Something to think about."

"I think I'm going to hit the rack. Sunrise comes early. See you in the morning."

Elizabeth closed the bathroom door. "Sleep well."

Chapter Eight

Russell woke at first light, slipped into his usual jeans and a pullover, and left a note for Elizabeth that he would be on deck or out for a walk, his usual pattern in the morning. He loved the quiet, when the world belonged to him alone. It was his thinking time, and he needed it more and more. He, a man who had never thought about his age, now woke every morning aware of his new time of life, of his diminishing abilities, of the fact that some day he would be gone and the world would move on without him. What would be his legacy? What dreams had he not fulfilled?

He poured his first cup of coffee and climbed the narrow staircase. The air was warm, hinting of a hot day ahead. A small bank of mist, or fog, was layered over the dark green water. The lights of the two bridges burned brightly as dawn light appeared. There was no traffic on the river, just the quiet lap of water against the hull. On the roadway, yellow street cleaners hissed by, spraying and sweeping the wide street. On the narrow quay next to the boat, early morning joggers, walkers, and cyclists appeared. Women, usually in pairs, were the majority. Not a smoker in sight. Who would have believed the world would embrace the concept of fitness as it had? When he watched the black and white classic movies from the forties and fifties that he loved, the main activity was smoking, followed by drinking large amounts of cocktails, Russell recalled. His thoughts were interrupted by a familiar voice.

"Hi. Up early again. I hope I didn't startle you," Kevin smiled, a cup of coffee clutched in his hand. "Where's Durgan?" He scanned the deck.

"Hi, Kevin. I was just thinking of old movies, and women joggers, and how life changes. I haven't seen Durgan yet. Sleep well?"

"Not bad. The bunks are small, but not bad. Pamela falls asleep in a minute, but I'm more of a night owl. She's dead asleep now, so I tiptoed out."

"Good for you."

"You know, I was thinking about what you said about people finding their rhythms in a marriage. Like now, this morning. She's asleep and I'm up and it's okay, right?"

"I think so," Russell answered, sipping the steaming coffee. "We have different needs, so we adjust. It's funny, but one of the concerns people have when they retire is how they will be able to get along with their spouse all day, every day. When you're young and get married, or move in together, it's an adventure, it's fun, and you have plenty to do that keeps you busy."

Russell finished his coffee. "Then you retire and it's mixing two separate worlds again. You have to work out a whole new schedule and division of labor. It isn't easy. But marriage isn't easy , even after 40 or more years. Respect and compromise go a long way. You have to create your own world."

"Yeah," Kevin agreed., looking over the river. "We argue about that sometimes. I tend to spend a lot of my time in cyberspace, the world of technology. It fascinates me," He shifted to face inward. "Are you are into the tech world? I'm lost without my BlackBerry. Pamela isn't. I mean she understands how to use technology, but she doesn't really get into it. She never turns on the computer at home and just surfs, like I do. I can spend hours checking out sites," Kevin proclaimed, coffee cup waving about.

"Which brings us back to rhythms. As long as you respect each others, you can adjust. What does she do while you're lost in cyberspace?"

A barge appeared, pushed by a black and white tug, heading upriver.

"Oh, I don't know. Stuff with the kids, I guess. Or household things."

"You know, Kevin, you might want to find out a bit more about how she sees things when you're lost in space. To answer your technology question, I am aware of it, but my knowledge is limited. I can turn a computer on and I do searches and email, but that's it. I like holding a book when I read," Russell said. "Elizabeth, on the other hand, booked our trip and made all kinds of arrangements on our computer. She spends a lot of time on it and is after me to do more."

Traffic on the streets had picked up, the commuters on their cell phones, waiting for the lights to turn. There were less joggers and walkers.

"Well, I never thought I was deliberately ignoring Pamela, but you may be right, she might think that. Secondly, to me computers are all about being connected. The Internet and the technology open up the world of information in a way we never imagined. Almost anything you are interested in can be accessed now with a few clicks. Sure, there's a learning curve, but look what it gets you. What did you teach?"

"Mainly History and some Political Science at a small community college near Atlanta," Russell said.

"Did you spend time in libraries and museums looking at historical records or artifacts?" Kevin asked."Visit historic sites?"

"Of course. That's where the pieces of the past are. Research is the heart of history."

"Well, how would you like to be able to visit all of the world's great libraries, the museums of Paris, Monet's gardens like we just did a few days ago?

You can do all that and never leave your home if you don't want to, or can't. Technology, properly used, puts you into the center of everything."

"That's an interesting view point," Russell said, leaning on the railing. "I've noticed that as you get older, you become less and less visible. The marketing experts say the elderly aren't 'part of the demographic' whatever that means. The entertainment industry writes us off. We don't like the TV we see, the moronic programs, the idiotic 'reality' shows, but they're not made for us. Our opinion no longer counts. We are forced out of the mainstream of life, disconnected. So, can using technology change that?" Russell asked.

"Technology is all about connectivity," Kevin said. With a computer and a DSL line, or WiFi, no one has to be disconnected. Age is irrelevant, nobody knows or cares how old you are in cyberspace. You can live anywhere and still be just a few clicks away from a world of information. You can explore almost any interest, any subject, all from your home. There is no reason to feel left out."

Russell nodded slowly, deep in thought.

"I think I'm out of coffee. Ready for a new cup?" Russell asked.

"Sure. I could use the exercise too." They went below to the coffee pot, refilling their cups.

"Elizabeth keeps telling me that the best way to handle change is to change, and change first. It bears looking into. I guess you can teach an old dog new tricks. Thank you, Kevin for your help."

"Thank you for yours. I don't want to lose touch with Pamela and our kids."

The men returned to the sundeck, sipping coffee, waving at the now steady passage of barges, listening to the sound of gulls overhead. The bridge lights extinguished as the sun rose higher. Traffic on the bridges was backed up, and the crew on Arles could be heard preparing for breakfast and a day in Lyon.

"I guess I need to get cleaned up and wake Pamela. Thanks again for sharing your thoughts with me, Russell. Can I ask, how long have you been married?"

"Well, we passed the forty year mark, and after that it's kind of a lock. If you can survive raising children, you deserve to spend the rest of your lives together, spending every last damn cent you have left. After kids is when you get back to remembering why you chose each other in the first place."

" I have a lot to think about."

"Thinking is what your brain does when you turn off the iPOD." Russell grinned, showing Kevin he meant no offense with his remark.

"Okay. Next time, we'll cover the basic advantages of digital photography, right?" Kevin asked.

"The dreaded pixel talk?"

"Exactly."

Chapter Nine

Below deck the breakfast serving had started, the passengers settling comfortably into their routines, making their food choices. They were relaxed, pleased with their trip, discussing the previous evenings' activities, planning the new day. Cameras were being passed around, the pictures of the light show of Lyon being reviewed through the miracle of digital photography.

Gerard assumed his usual morning post, greeting the early arrivals, feeling their moods, dealing with suggestions or complaints, preparing them for the day ahead. He was pleased to see an excellent turnout with few late arrivals. Those with slight handicaps had adjusted to the peculiarities of the boat, and usually were the first seated.

The morning visit to the Lyon outdoor market required a short walk, and he had made arrangements for those needing assistance. The afternoon tour of the city was by motorcoach and would be easier to manage.

Terry was again in complete control of the morning serving, silently directing his staff. The English couples were not to be seen.

"Gerard," Mel called from a table next to the window on the starboard side of the dining room. "Can you settle something for us?"

"I will try, my friend. What is it?" He sat in the offered chair, joining the Weinsteins and the Hunters.

"Is Lyon the second or the third largest city in France? My guidebook says it's the third, but Russell's says it's second."

"Ah, that is easily explained. Marseille is second in the number of people, the population, yes? But Lyon is second in the size of its metropolitan area. Like so many things in life, it depends on how you look at it." Gerard leaned forward.

"Hmm. I can live with that."

"The guidebook also says Lyon was the center of an extensive silk industry," Elizabeth said. "I was surprised to learn that." She drank from her tea cup.

"That was a long time ago," Gerard said, "during the Renaissance, when Lyon was a major trading center. The location between the two major rivers is ideal for a trading post, which is what Lyon has always been. You will see today, on our tour, that the textile industry began here with the Jacquard loom, which allowed the weaving of special patterns. Tomorrow, we will have a demonstration of silk scarf painting on board by a local artist. Lyon is many things."

"I never see it advertised as a tourist destination, but it does seem to have a lot to see," Ruth said.

Gerard continued, warming to his audience. "The arrival of the river cruise boats like Arles is changing that misconception about Lyon. As more people see Lyon, the word spreads among travelers like yourself, and visits build. If you want a special experience, come to Lyon in early December for the Festival of Lights. The entire city is illuminated with every type of lighting available. There are lasers, floodlights, light shows run by computers. It attracts large crowds from all over Europe."

"Lyon was in the spotlight a few years back," Russell said "with the arrest of Klaus Barbie, known as the Butcher of Lyon during World War II, wasn't it?"

"Yes, that trial brought much attention, Russell, but not many tourists. We will see the Palace of Justice today where he was eventually tried for his crimes. We French suffered greatly from the occupation. The heroic resistance is all but forgotten now, unfortunately, by the new generation. But perhaps that is best. We have many German visitors now who were not alive at the time of the war, so we can't blame them."

"That's a very generous attitude," Mel said.

"Life goes on. We French have learned that after two major wars were fought on our soil. But let's talk of happier times. Today you will have the opportunity to visit the market, with magnificent cheeses and vegetables and fruit and flowers. It will be a highlight of your journey, I promise you. Please excuse me. I have to get things moving." Gerard rose to his feet, a quick look at the time, and was off with his usual rapid gait.

Russell poured more coffee into his cup, trying to imagine what it would be like to live under occupation by a foreign army with unlimited control over every detail of life. He wondered what he would have done had he lived in France in 1944. Would he have joined the resistance? Would he have risked his life to deliver a message, or plant a bomb? Could he have endured torture? The late night television comics had created the image of France as a country of appeasers, eager to surrender at the first hint of violence. Being in France, seeing the places where the massacres occurred, where resisters fought back, offered a new respect for the real culture of a complex country.

Following breakfast, Gerard assembled the group on the quay, noting that the two Englishmen were absent, "under the weather, "and explained the route they would be walking over the Saone bridge to the outdoor market of

Lyon where they could wander among the displays of farm produce, a large selection of cheeses, sausages, wines, olives, fresh fish, broiled chicken, even fresh oysters served at a small outdoor stand. He passed out small maps to guide them, and pointed to the light standards that lined the nearby bridge.

"If you look to the very top of the light pole, you will see a crowing rooster. That is the bridge we will cross to get to the market, and the bridge you should cross to return here. Remember the crowing roosters. We will have lunch on Arles, then we will board our motorcoach for a tour of Lyon, especially the old quarter, behind the medieval walls. Lyon is built on two large hills, so a bus tour is much preferred. Everyone ready? Cameras, purses, walking shoes, water bottles? Good. Follow me, please."

The ragged group moved forward, the usual clusters of friends forming. Once again the weather was perfect, a mild 70 degree morning with a hint of a warmer afternoon when they would be on the bus. Kevin scanned his BlackBerry as he and Pamela led the pack. Frank and the Golden Girls trailed behind, and Agnes and Shirley, the oldest travelers, took it one step at a time. Gerard halted the loose formation at the bridge, next to a display of yellow bicycles locked in a rack.

"Let us pause for a minute to let everyone catch up," Gerard said. "This rack of bicycles is a new idea to fight pollution and aid in personal fitness. There are racks like this all over the city of Lyon. You place a coin in the lock slot, and you can remove a bicycle. You can ride the bicycle anywhere in Lyon, and when you are finished, you return it to a rack and attach the lock. A coin like the one you deposited will be released to you, so your ride is free. A simple solution to a complex problem."

"If they tried that in Florida, the bikes would be gone in one day, never to return," Mel muttered. "Not a bad idea, though."

"We are going to cross the Saone now. It joins the Rhone just to the south, there, forming a sort of peninsula or "presqu'île" where the market is located. The Rhone is on the other side of the peninsula." He gestured with an overhead sweep of his arm.

The group was silent, generally ignoring Gerard's over the top information flow, staring at their small maps, struggling to orient themselves while listening to Gerard's animated talk. Most simply followed the crowd as best they could, knowing Gerard would come looking for them if they got lost or turned around in the narrow medieval streets.

"Onward to the market," Gerard signaled.

The open-air market was to the right, just after the bridge. The delicious aroma of roasting meat filled the air. Whole chickens turned slowly on six foot high rotisseries, and sausages sizzled on hot grills. A small cafe with a few tables was packed with oyster lovers enjoying trays of the fresh-shucked

Breton oysters and other varieties favored by the French. The oysters were enjoyed with pale yellow wines, purchased at the nearby stands. Across from the cafe, tables displaying cheeses beckoned, sellers ready with their curved cheese knifes to offer a sample of their product. Weighing scales were on each table, as the French purchased their cheese by weight.

Gerard paused at a cheese display and was joined by the Hunters and the Weinsteins. "This is my favorite cheese," Gerard said. "And this is my favorite vendor, Jacques."

Ruth read the small sign. "Comte?"

"Yes." Gerard explained. "Comte is made from the raw milk of red and white Montbeliard cows in the Jura Mountains of France. The cheese is produced in small, cooperative dairies, known as "fruitières" that produce year round. It is one of the most popular cheeses in France, and it is claimed that there are more than 83 distinct flavors in Comte, including apricot, chocolate, butter, cream, and grilled bread. It has always been my favorite since I was a little boy."

Jacques handed each of the woman a thin slice of his cheese.

"That is wonderful, marvelous. How do I order?" Ruth asked.

"You just point to the cheese you want, then indicate with your finger and thumb the size of the piece you want. Jacque will slice it and weigh it for you. He takes only cash, of course."

"Okay. Jacques I would like the Comte, this much." She indicated the amount with her fingers as Gerard suggested.

Jacques picked up his knife and slowly sliced the firm cheese, placed it on a clean paper, and weighed it. He smiled at Ruth as she nodded her acceptance. He efficiently wrapped the fresh cheese in white paper and presented it with a flourish. Ruth paid for it with Euros, and placed it in the string bag she had just purchased at the entrance to the market.

"I'd like some also, Jacques," Elizabeth requested. "The same size will be fine."

Russell and Mel drifted off while the cheese purchase was made to find themselves next to a large display of freshly baked bread. "That must be the best smell in the world," Russell said. "My grandmother made fresh bread every day, and I could live on it if my doctor didn't find out."

"I know what you mean. The first thing on our kitchen table was always the bread. And a plate with golden butter. There was no cholesterol then. That was invented later," Mel grunted. "Of all the things of the past that I miss, fresh bread is at the top of the list. Let me have a loaf of that, please," Mel gestured.

"I'll take a loaf of that round bread," Russell requested as Elizabeth and Ruth rejoined them.

"Did you get some bread?" Elizabeth asked.

Russell smiled as he was handed the paper wrapped loaf. Mel did the same.

"We have cheese and fresh honey, and now bread. All we need is a good wine," Ruth commented.

"I think we can find a bottle."

Elizabeth strolled slowly as the wine search began, lingering to touch and smell the array of fresh flowers. "If I lived here, I would come here every day and buy my flowers for the house, and my food for the day. Wouldn't it be wonderful to live somewhere where you could walk to a market like this, and small shops with butchers and bakers?" She ran her hand over the top of the blossoms.

"I'm afraid that doesn't exist anymore in the States. We could always move here, I guess," Russell said.

"Who's moving here?" Mel asked, catching the end of the conversation.

'Oh, we were just talking. Why don't we get a table and have some wine? If we like it, we'll get more for later. Ladies?"

"We are in France. I just want a small glass," Elizabeth said.

"We'll get a carafe."

A table was secured next to the wine shop, and Mel asked for a wine recommendation. The waiter returned with a carafe of straw colored wine and poured a sample for tasting.

"Delicious," Mel proclaimed. "A pleasant Bordeaux. Very refreshing."

"To France," Russell said, glass raised in a toast.

"And to new found friends."

"Cheers. Let's try some of the cheese." Ruth unwrapped the fragrant package as Mel tugged at the fresh bread.

"Have some bread."

"What are you thinking, Elizabeth.? You have that profound look," Russell said, sipping the wine. It was wonderful, light and refreshing.

"I was thinking about what we were talking about, about how nice it would be to live where there were markets and shops you could walk to, like a village."

"In America, you mean."

"Yes," Elizabeth said. "I don't think I want to live in any other country. Italy seems so perfect, and the food is so good, but they have corrupt governments and graft. I'm sure their lifestyle isn't so wonderful when you actually live there. And France seems to have a major problem with immigration, even worse than ours."

The market crowd was increasing, chattering in many languages as they slowly drifted past.

"I agree," Ruth said. "I would never give up the freedoms we have. Gerard was talking about the tax structure here and it is insane. There is free health care, but it isn't really free."

"Socialism never works. Something has to give. You want services, you pay now, or you pay later, but you will pay," Mel concluded. He poured more wine, took a piece of cheese.

"There are some new developments in Florida with village-like shopping centers," Ruth said. "Have you looked at retiring in Florida?" She sipped carefully at her wine.

"We have. Too hot for us. And too buggy. And I don't like hurricanes."

Mel nodded his agreement.

"It s hot, and buggy, and hurricanes are unpleasant, but there's no state income tax, and you can get decent housing for a reasonable price," Mel said. "But, it's not for everybody." He tilted his glass for the last drops.

"We're still looking but not very hard. We like our home in Atlanta, and the fact that it has the busiest airport makes travel easy. We also like living in a city with all the benefits of city living. We like the diversity, the differences in cultures, the options cities offer. At least for now," Russell explained.

"What about your kids? Any nearby?"

"No. Our daughter wants us to move near her family, but we won't do that. Too many of our friends moved to be near their children and grandchildren and then found themselves abandoned when their children were transferred or just decided to move."

"That's true," Ruth said. "We've seen that. We also have friends who love their grandkids being close, but end up being free babysitters. When they get tired of it, or complain, their children are highly offended. We love our grandkids, all seven of them, but I can't keep up with a three year old every weekend. Mel and I stayed home with our kids when they were little. We rarely used babysitters. Our kids are always looking to 'get away.' Why did they have kids if they don't want to be with them?" Ruth asked.

Mel poured more wine into his glass.

"It's a new world, hon. You take care of me, I'll take care of you," Mel said, touching Ruth's hand. Elizabeth had noticed Mel's habit before of frequently touching her hand, her hair. "Do we know how to get back to the boat?"

"Russell always knows. Follow him," Elizabeth said as they finished the wine and wrapped up the remains of their impromptu snack.

Back on the Arles, Giovanni and Terry, meeting on the upper deck, spotted the first of the returning passengers. They had been helping Captain Pelletier, who was filling the flower boxes around the ship's rail with soil and bright red germaniums he had purchased at the market when it first opened that morning. It had become a tradition on their excursions down the river. Giovanni signed for the delivery, confirming the correct order, and Terry had his people carry the soil and plants to the stations. Captain Pelletier insisted on doing the planting himself, enjoying the feeling of dirt on his hands instead of oil or grease, for a change. On each trip he would refresh his garden as needed.

"Here they come, Terry," Giovanni said, glancing up. "Quite a few seem to have made purchases. Perhaps they won't be too hungry for your lunch." The passengers drew closer, net bags swinging. The market was happy to supply the tourists with the convenient carryalls for a very reasonable price.

"That's why we have a light lunch planned. A salad, a small sandwich and dessert. That will hold them until tonight. There's your friend, Sonia, the tall blond one with the red scarf," Terry said, pointing at the returning travelers. "She isn't smiling. She looks like she is annoyed, walking faster than usual. Her friend Sally keeps looking backward over her shoulder. Hmm."

Giovanni ignored the remark, concentrating on the new red flowers ringing the deck with bright color, a sharp contrast that complemented the blue and white color scheme of the chairs and canvas awning perfectly.

"Seeing the captain work with his flowers reminds me that he plans to retire to a small farm and become a gardener." Terry offered. "Have you decided when you're going to drop the hook and retire? You are close aren't you?"

"I can retire anytime now, but I still enjoy these river cruises. What would I do in retirement? My children don't need me around and the grandchildren will soon be gone," Giovanni explained. "I'll keep sailing."

"But, if you had a nice wife, someone attractive, intelligent, well off..."

"Like Sonia, you mean?" Giovanni smiled. "You English are so subtle. I do not need a wife in my life after all these years alone. Besides, you know the rules about fraternizing with the passengers. I might lose my pension."

Terry laughed along with his friend. "Speaking of Englishmen, the two blokes were absent from the tour group this morning. They showed up for breakfast after the rest had gone to the market. They had some bangers and eggs, some toast and lots of coffee, then disappeared. They seemed a bit hung over."

"They came to my desk after they left you. They were hung over. I could smell it on them." Giovanni frowned. He did not like people who couldn't control their vices.

"What did they want? Did they try to catch up to the tour?"

"No. They asked about the exchange rate and bought Euros again. I checked the exchanged pounds carefully. They seemed very interested in how I did my job as Ship's Purser. How many people worked for me, things like that. The little one kept looking about while the one with the beard did the talking. Then they went on deck and slept on the stern deck chairs. They may still be there."

"Did their wives go on the tour?"

"I'm not sure. They were at breakfast early. Gerard will know, and he is coming on board now. Bonjour, Gerard." Giovanni called over the side.

Gerard looked around, then up at his friends. He waved as he crossed the narrow gangplank.

"Bonjour," Gerard announced as he joined his friends, taking the steps two at a time. "I see our captain has been busy decorating. The flowers are beautiful, just the right touch of color. How are you this beautiful morning? Can you believe our luck? Another cloudless day."He waved his arms.

"We are very lucky. I looked at the radar report and it looks like this weather will continue for the rest of our trip. How was your market tour? The passengers seem happy," Giovanni said, glancing over the side.

"I believe they had a wonderful experience. I bought some cheese and bread and olives. Here, let's have a taste," he offered, as he unwrapped his packages, spreading his feast on a table. "Almost everyone bought something. I even heard a remark that if they had known there was so much food available, at the market, they would have missed breakfast. The market is full of the early Spring flowers. Just beautiful."

"Did the wives of the Englishmen go on the tour? I know the men didn't." Terry broke off a piece of the offered cheese.

"Yes, they did. They were quite active, buying wine and cheese. I think the gentlemen prefer to drink and sleep." Gerard held out the cup of olives to the men. They both took some.

"That is their option. Everyone else seems to be getting along nicely, like they are all old friends. They still have their little dining groups, but I see a lot of friendly conversations taking place," Terry added.

"Yes, they are compatible," Gerard said, tossing an olive into his mouth. "There was a minor incident this morning between Sonia and that loud woman, Moira, but it passed quickly."

"What was it about?"

"I'm not certain. I saw Moira hand Sonia something, and Sonia handed it back and walked away with her friend, Sally. She seemed offended, but I don't know why. Women are a puzzle. Especially Americans. Well, I must do some paperwork before lunch. This afternoon is the bus tour, an easy day."

"Time to check the lunch set up," Terry said, moving to the stairs.

"And I need to have some cash ready for the shoppers after lunch." Giovanni added. "The flowers look beautiful," he said as the Captain finished his chore.

Captain Pelletier waved back in appreciation, Elizabeth and Ruth standing at his side, admiring his work.

Chapter Ten

The motorcoach was waiting above the quay, idling quietly, as the Arles adventurers finished their light "bistro" lunch, changed clothes for the afternoon heat, and gathered cameras and maps. The stragglers had all made it back to the boat safely and had had time to refresh and change for the afternoon tour. They formed the usual loose formation on the quay, talking quietly, waiting for Gerard. They were enjoying their time with him, and found him to be knowledgeable and professional in his manner, with just a few incidents of overreacting to what they considered minor moments. Americans were different from Europeans, especially the women, whom Gerard found to be very independent and single-minded. They moved according to their schedules, not his or anyone else's. He had had to learn patience when dealing with them. Slowly they boarded the pleasantly air conditioned vehicle.

The special motorcoach crossed the bridge over the Saone, passed the outdoor market, and crossed the Rhone, climbing to the Basilique Notre-Dame-de-Fourvivre. As they neared the top of the hill, Gerard pointed out the ruins of an ancient Roman theatre and a nearby cemetery.

"That old Roman theater you see was built around 19 BC," Gerard said. "In 1989, France celebrated its 2,000th year anniversary here in Lyon. You cannot go inside the fence, unfortunately. The archeologists are still working there. I want you to try to imagine what it was like 2,000 years ago, what it was like at this place where Christians were thrown to lions. It really did happen here." Camera flashes bounced of the windows of the bus.

The bus completed the steep climb and somehow parked in the large lot next to the massive stone Basilica. Gerard pointed out the coffee shop, the gift shop, and the restrooms.

"It looks a lot like Sacre Coeur in Paris," Russell commented as the group exited and spread along the wall for a spectacular view of Lyon and the two rivers intersecting below.

"It does because it was designed that way," Gerard said. "As Sacre Coeur does for Paris, the Basilica of Fourvière provides a magnificent view of Lyon. If you look to your left, you see the Croix-Rousse and the Terreaux district. Below are the roofs of the cathedral of Saint Jean, and lower down the hill and on your right is the place Bellecour, that huge open square. For an even better view, if you don't mind a climb, the Observatory on top of the tower is available."

The group dispersed, some entering the Basilica while others paused for a coffee or postcards at the gift shop. Kevin and Pamela decided to climb the 200 steps to the Observatory and were followed by the Hunters. They climbed slowly, the afternoon sun sending the temperature upward.

"What a view," Kevin said as he reached the top parapet. "Pamela, look."

The view was spectacular as promised, with clear skies offering unlimited visibility. Both the Rhone and the Saone rivers lay below, and the orange colored roofs of the old quarter marked the wandering lanes of Croix-Rousse. Traffic sped by on the motorways, southbound to the beaches of the Mediterranean.

"Quite a view," Russell said. "You can really get a perspective for the value of this location. Any traffic heading south from Paris and the north has to go through Lyon, doesn't it?"

"Yeah, I was looking at a site earlier online and it shows the tunnel that goes through the hills north of here. In summer it forms a bottleneck for travelers," Kevin explained. "I never thought of Lyon before this trip, but it is worth seeing, isn't it?"

"It is. I wish we had more time here. The restaurants are supposed to be the best in France," Russell mentioned. "I'd love to sample them."

"Put it on the calendar for our next trip," Elizabeth suggested.

Russell smiled, nodding his head. "I just might do that."

Kevin waved his BlackBerry. "Anytime you want to, you can borrow this. It has recommendations for restaurants in almost every major city."

"Does it really?" Russell asked.

"Oh, yeah. Let me show you," he offered.

"Tell you what. We'll get together over a beer later, okay? I mean it."

"Are we at the top yet?" a woman's voice called.

"Almost," Russell called back. The familiar faces of Sally and Sonia appeared on the landing. Their faces were slightly flushed from the climb.

"Welcome to the best view in Lyon." Russell waved his arm at the city below.

"Wow. That was one climb worth making. She didn't follow us, did she?" Sally asked Sonia.

"I told you she wouldn't. Sorry. We shouldn't talk behind someone's back," Sonia apologized. She fanned her face with the small map.

"Is someone bothering you?" Pamela asked. "There are laws against that, even in France. But you said 'she,' didn't you?"

"Yeah. Look, we don't want to start anything and ruin a vacation, so don't say anything, especially to Gerard, but Moira has been getting a bit too friendly," Sally said in a low voice, eyebrows raised.

"Maybe she just doesn't have many friends, Elizabeth said. "Her traveling companion seems awfully quiet. It's Kate, right?"

"Kate, Katy. It started friendly, having breakfast, walking together on the tours, but now, every time we turn around there she is. This morning she tried to give us some chocolate from the market. I should say she tried to give it to Sonia."

"Sally, I told you I'd handle it," Sonia said, her voice rising. "We just need to avoid her for a while and she'll get the picture. Please don't say anything, okay?" she appealed to the couples.

"No problem." Pamela said. Kevin nodded his agreement. Russell said nothing, glancing at Elizabeth.

"I think you're handling it right. Just don't encourage her advances." Elizabeth advised.

"I think I finally have my breath back. You can see forever from here." Sonia changed the subject.

Down below, Gerard began rounding up his charges for the next segment of the tour. Mel and Ruth were studying the city below from the Esplanade, having wisely declined the climb.

"Gerard, a question, please?" Mel asked.

"Yes?"

"I know the allies landed in Normandy in June of 1944, and there was another landing in the Rhone valley on the Mediterranean in August of 1944, right?"

Gerard nodded. "Yes, that is right. We will be stopping at the American cemetery when we leave Aix on our way to Nice."

"So where did the two armies finally meet? I mean one is heading east and south, the other north and east, did they meet here in Lyon?"

"No, but just a little to our north, and a bit to the west, near Dijon" He pointed to his left. "You have heard of Dijon? The mustard capitol? The Normandy army turned to the east after they broke out of the hedgerows, and later the Rhone river army came up this valley and turned first west and then east to join Patton and move into Belgium and Luxembourg. There were a large number of Free French troops with the Rhone army. Now let me see if we are all here for the next stop." Gerard consulted his clipboard, glanced at his watch.

Russell and Elizabeth had descended with the others from the Observatory and waited under a shady tree for the head count. "Can I ask a dumb question?" Russell asked. "Is Moira's interest in Sonia more than just for friendship?"

"I suspect it might be," Elizabeth smiled. "Probably nothing overt, maybe just a plea for attention. She's not very attractive or outgoing, and there is a definite tension between her and Katy. I think Katy might be jealous. What does your friend Mike always say? Everyone's in their own movie?"

"Right. When I see the way Moira treats her, I think 'hen pecked.' Can a woman be hen pecked by another woman?"

"I think gay couples experience the same emotions and feelings of jealousy, or envy, or whatever, that all married couples do, regardless of their sexual preferences," Elizabeth explained.

"I never thought of that. There really isn't that much difference between us is there?"

Elizabeth raised her chin. "Be careful. You might end up changing your mind."

"There's Mel and Ruth. Time to board the bus."

The motorcoach maneuvered carefully among the parked cars on the square and made its way onto the Boulevard des Canuts in the old weavers section of the city. Gerard keyed his microphone.

"Well, I hope you enjoyed the view from the Basilica and the Basilica itself. Someone asked why there are so many monuments and churches dedicated to Notre Dame, Our Lady. In medieval times, there were no antibiotics or super medicines to protect the people. What we might treat as a minor disease today could devastate entire communities. Because of that, the peasants lived on isolated hilltops, protected from outsiders and the illness they might bring. Their only defense was to pray. If a village prayed to Our Lady and the village was spared, they built a monument. All the way down the Rhone Valley you will see these attempts to attract divine intervention."

The bus slowed in the tight streets and busy traffic, then moved to the side of the road in front of an unusual multistoried building and stopped with the hiss of air brakes. The door was opened.

"We are stopping," Gerard explained, "for a few minutes so you may see an excellent example of the art technique perfected by French artists centuries ago, and brought to life again with this building. It is called 'trompe-l'œil,' a technique involving extremely realistic imagery in order to create the optical illusion that the depicted objects really exist, instead of being mere two-dimensional paintings. The name is derived from the French for "trick the eye", from tromper - to deceive, and l'œil - the eye. What appears to be a six story building with steps, shops and windows, is a giant mural- an illusion. There are other examples of trompe-l'oeil in Lyon, but this is the best. You have time for pictures, and I suggest you place yourself in them with the painted people."

The effect was truly amazing as the travelers walked up to the mural and saw the incredible detail of the artists work. When a person stood next to the painting, it was difficult to tell what was real and what was not. Shutters clicked non-stop as people went in and out of the scene. Small groups stared at the review screen on the back of the cameras, marveling at the proof of the illusion that had been created.

"Look at this picture of Russell about to enter this car with his hand on the handle," Elizabeth said, offering the camera to Ruth. "It looks so real."

"I know, look at how Mel has joined the line of people waiting outside the shop. Perfect illusion."

"We can never trust a photograph again," Mel said. "You know that same effect was done on the ceiling of the Sistine Chapel in Rome. The curved ceiling isn't really that curved."

Gerard took turns taking pictures for his people, shuttling cameras as needed. The pictures would be a hit from Iowa to New Jersey in the coming winter months. Sometimes Gerard wondered how many pictures of him were scattered across the United States. He had visited the Washington D. C. area and New York City on business, but he would never leave France permanently. He was French in his soul.

"Back on the bus, please, everyone," he called. "We are going next to the old quarter and the St. Jean cathedral. I will point out some other murals as we come to them, but you have seen the best with this one."

The tour of the old quarter, home to the textile workers centuries before, was uneventful except for the sense of history that seeped from the old buildings and slate roofed homes. The tiny cottages where families struggled to survive still stood on narrow streets, glimpsed as the large bus passed on the wider boulevards. The Industrial Revolution attracted farmers to the cities, but the change in the quality of their lives was questionable.

"I know it's Lyon, but some of these places look to be straight out of Dickens' England," Mel commented. "I sense a stop coming up. Another cathedral."

Gerard consulted his notes. "The church you see across the square is the cathedral of St. Jean. It is the cathedral of the Archbishop of Lyon, the "Primate of the Gauls" and the leading Archbishop of France."

The group turned as directed, ignoring most of what Gerard said. They had reached a saturation point with cathedrals and churches. He continued, "The Cathédrale St-Jean Cathedral was built over several centuries, in the Romanesque and Gothic styles. In 1600 King Henri IV came to Lyon to meet his Italian fiancée, Marie de' Medici, en route from Marseille. He took one look at her, approved of what he saw, and they were married immediately in this cathedral. As we French might say, it was 'OO LA LA.' " He paused for the laugh. "Now we will go inside this beautiful work of piety."

"The most unique and interesting feature of Lyon's cathedral is the 14th-century astronomical clock," Gerard gestured. "It is a marvel of technology and intricate beauty. It chimes a hymn to St. John on the hour at noon, 2, 3, and 4 as a rooster crows and angels herald the Annunciation. Remember the roosters on the bridge lights? It should begin in five minutes if you want to hear it."

He continued. "This concludes our tour of Lyon. We will be leaving late morning tomorrow, following an on-board demonstration of silk scarf painting. There will also be a talk about the activities of the French Resistance of World War II in Lyon. If you would like to remain in this quarter and walk back to the boat later, please let me know. For those of you wishing to return now by bus, we will leave as soon as we are all on board. Thank you. Merci."

"What do you think? Go back to the boat or hang around here?" Russell asked.

"I have an idea. Why don't Russell and I have a drink at that lovely sidewalk cafe in the shade, and you two can cruise around the square looking in all the stores?" Mel suggested to the ladies.

"Okay with me if you don't mind," Elizabeth said to Russell.

"Well, I don't want Mel to feel left out."

"What a guy," Ruth said as the men decided on a location. "C'mon Elizabeth. Maybe we can find some treasures."

"We'll be right here."

The men ordered French beer at a café with green umbrellas, and settled in to do some serious people watching from their comfortable position in the shade. "This is one of my favorite things to do when we travel. Just sit still, have a beer and watch the people go by. I love to see new things, but sometimes I want to stop and just watch," Russell mused.

"I agree," Mel said. "When I was a kid, I used to watch the old retired guys in my old neighborhood. They were masters of doing nothing. They'd have a late breakfast at the coffee shop and talk for an hour. Then they'd move to the park, sit on a bench, read the paper, and have a smoke. Maybe later they'd play some bocce, or cards. They never hurried, never got upset. I couldn't wait to get to do that. Now, I'm on committees at the recreation center, the grief committee, the neighborhood association, covenants and variances, or else I'm doing yard work or fixing something in the damn house. The other day Ruth announced that there's mold growing in the dishwasher. Mold? Remember Russell, the house is your mortal enemy, the major killer of retired men."

Russell raised his glass, took a large sip.

"I do know," Mel continued, "that I can never find anyone to have coffee with because they don't have the time. They're retired. How can you not have time for a slow cup of coffee when you're retired? Lunch is totally impossible. Ever see two old guys having a leisurely lunch in a restaurant, a glass of wine? Never. It's always women, sipping white wine, enjoying the insurance money of their husbands, who keeled over at Home Depot trying to find someone who worked there who knew about mold in dishwashers."

"I agree, American men never seem to be allowed to say 'Basta!' Enough! I've spent a lot of time lately looking at the rest of my life, trying to figure out what's next for me and Elizabeth. Being Mr. Fixit is not high on my list."

"Any conclusions?" Mel asked.

"Well, it seems to me that we have all been taught to think about retirement as the final act. You work, have a career, raise kids, maybe grandkids, then all of a sudden, it's all over. Go retire, disappear. End of story. I think there's got to be more than that."

"Yeah, that's a fair statement."

"See, I don't think it's the last act. Death is the last act and that can come later, much later. People are living longer, staying active, building new lives," Russell emphasized. "Elizabeth really pushed me to come on this cruise. I think she's been worried about me since I had a prostate problem that came out of nowhere. I just lost interest in doing anything in the future. Why plan when you may not be there?"

"You don't act like a quitter, my friend. Want to hear my story?" Mel asked.

"Please. I could use some male advice."

"Okay," Mel said, taking a mouthful of beer. "Ruth and I grew up in nice middleclass neighborhoods, very traditional, very orderly. Our mothers were best friends. In fact, they fixed us up when we were in college. I came home one weekend, and there was Ruth, all grown up and looking gorgeous, sitting in our living room. We dated, got engaged, got married. I went to work, she had babies, we were like a television show. I worked hard, made a lot of money."

Russell listened carefully, leaning forward to not miss anything Mel said.

"Then it was retirement time. My brother was in Florida, people from our neighborhood retired to Florida, so we packed up, left all of our friends and memories behind and moved to Palm Harbor. Nice place. Very safe, very orderly."

"So, you're happy with your decisions?" Russell prompted.

"Not the point. A year ago I had chest pains, severe pains. I collapsed, rushed to the hospital, and ended up in ICU with stents in my chest. I thought it was over."

"But it wasn't," Russell said.

"Not by a long shot. I went to rehab, did therapy, did a new diet, all of that. But most of all, I examined my life, the ups and downs, and tried to understand what really mattered to me."

The man sat quietly for a moment, Mel collecting his thoughts, Russell absorbing what he had just heard.

"It's not about money," Mel said. "You spend your life making money, and you find that, you know the saying, after the first million, making a second or third doesn't matter. You can always get money. What you can't get is time, or love- the kind of love like I have, and the kind I suspect you have in your marriage. Here's the big finish: spend all the time you have with the one you love doing whatever it is you both enjoy and don't worry about anything else. We like to travel, and we're going to see as much of this world as we can, as long as we can. L' Chaim. To life."

"To life," Russell raised his glass, meeting Mel's.

"Enough complaining. Getting old is not for sissies."

"Let's have another round," Russell said, turning for the waitress.

The men sat in silence, sipping the cold beer, watching the passersby. Their quiet reverie was broken by the rustle of shopping bags and the smiling faces of their long-term spouses. Life was good for another day.

"Hi. Have you solved all the world's problems?" Ruth asked, sliding into a chair.

"Not all, but we put a dent in some of them. Find something nice?" Mel asked, moving backward to accommodate the women's packages.

"Just some kitchen things for gifts. Nothing too exotic. I'll show you when we get back to the boat. Do we have time for a drink? I'm thirsty for a lemonade," Elizabeth said. Ruth nodded her agreement. Mel signaled the waitress.

"That sounds good. I love the lemonade they drink in Europe," Ruth said. "I found some nice tops for the grandchildren, on sale."

"I like 'on sale'."

The waitress noticed the new arrivals and took their order.

Elizabeth glanced around the square, the afternoon breeze blowing gently. She leaned back in her small chair, lost in thought. Russell recognized the signs of her deep thinking and waited for her comments.

"Are you still with us or are you in a special zone?" Russell asked. "You have that look."

"Sorry," Elizabeth said. "I am having such a nice time seeing the cities and small towns, trying new foods and drinks. There are so many places to see in the world. People are different in speech and customs, but we all have common feelings, and concerns. We like being Americans, but other people like who they are too, and don't want to be like us. Gerard loves being French, and Giovanni likes his Italian roots. I would love to live in Italy or here for a few months to see what it would be like. Ruth, have you ever wondered what life is like for a European?"

"Many times. Mel and I have discussed it. They really do see life differently than we do. For example, Terry is from Leeds, an industrial town in England, but he thinks nothing of hopping over to France for a job on a river boat with an international crew. If you live in London and want to see the latest art exhibit in Florence, it's a short trip."

The lemonade arrived, the glasses tall and sweating.

"I love America for the opportunities it gave our grandparents, opportunities they couldn't get anywhere else, and I would never change, but living here, or in Italy for a while appeals to me," Mel commented.

"Something to think about." Elizabeth said.

"We need to think about it while we head back. Tonight is Fiesta night, for some strange reason," Russell said. "Americans in France celebrate with a Mexican event on a river boat with an International crew. The world is getting smaller, isn't it?"

Elizabeth placed her glass on the table, completely empty of lemonade. "I disagree. I think the world is getting bigger, with so many new places to go and see. Every day there's a new discovery." She rose for the walk back to the boat.

"Follow me, people. The Arles awaits us in all her brilliant white splendor," Russell half bowed, his disposition mellowed by the French beer. He had much to think about.

Chapter Eleven

The Arles bar and lounge area had been decorated with the red, white, and green color scheme of a Mexican cantina for the evening gathering. Waitresses in peasant skirts and bright blouses circulated with glasses of Margaritas for the guests. Gerard and Terry lingered near the entry, greeting people and watching the servers. Sophia was busy behind the bar dispensing the premixed cocktails into salt rimmed glasses. Mariachi music from the CD player blared to add atmosphere to the festivities.

"What do you think, Gerard? Like our little fiesta?" Terry asked.

"It's nice and bright. Happy music. I don't much care for the drink, the Margarita, but I believe our guests like them. They had a busy day today with the walk to the market and the bus tour. Some walked back from the tour also, so there may be some early turn-ins."

"Right. This is not much of a late night crowd, is it?" He scanned the crowd.

"Not really, except for the Iowa people, and the Brits. They seem to go out more, and they have drinks in their cabins every evening. How are your new crew members? Are they working out as planned?" Gerard asked.

"Well, yes, I suppose so," Terry said. "Our new waitress, Brenda, is getting better, but still bears watching. She seems to be spending a little too much time with certain guests. I don't like to see that." He nodded to a new arrival, receiving a smile in return.

"Any in particular?"

"Yes. My people again, the English lads and their lady friends."

"Maybe Brenda just feels more comfortable with her own kind. You know the English and the Americans are different in more ways than language."

"True. I suppose I'm overreacting. Excuse me, got to run," Terry said, hastening into the kitchen after a waiter.

Gerard resumed his duties at the entrance, glancing at his watch, greeting the arrivals, collecting their comments about their experiences. He knew they would all be asked by his company to evaluate the tour, and particularly his performance as a program director. Careers were made or broken based on these reports. He also knew that few people who enjoyed everything would take the time to write positive comments. It was usually the complainers who volunteered their opinions, unfortunately.

Sonia, Sally, and Durgan arrived together, pausing to greet Gerard and pass along their appreciation of the day's events, with Sally doing most of the talking. Durgan waited awkwardly, shifting his feet as Sally talked on. Gerard was uncomfortable with straight-forward American women. Their directness was unsettling to him, and he never was certain of their intent.

He was rescued by the arrival of the Hunters and Weinsteins, two couples he identified as having a genuine appreciation for his country's offerings. He hoped that they would participate in completing an evaluation form. He knew it would be positive.

"Welcome, welcome to our little fiesta," Gerard greeted them. "Sophia has prepared Margaritas for your pleasure. The waitresses have them for you. I trust you had a nice day in Lyon."

"We did. The market was just beautiful," Elizabeth said. "Russell really enjoyed the trompe l'oeil art on that building where we stopped. I have a dozen pictures of him putting himself in the mural." She took an offered glass. "We were talking later about what it must be like to grow up here in Europe, where there are all these distinct cultures so close to each other. Everyone seems to speak more than one language and they go back and forth between them so easily. How many languages do you speak, Gerard?"

"Well, French is my native tongue, but I speak German just as well. I learned English at school, as did everyone else, but I took advanced courses because I wanted to work in the travel industry. I also have some fluency in Spanish and Italian. When you learn other languages as a child, it is not difficult later. If you lived here for one year, you would learn very quickly if you tried," He paused, glanced at the new arrivals. "Excuse me, I must greet our new guests."

Gerard smiled as he welcomed Moira and Katy, both dressed in Mexican style blouses and short pants. Obviously, they had prepared in advance for the special event.

"How nice you look. I love your tops. Are they from Spain or Mexico?" Gerard asked.

"Oh, we got them on a trip to Mexico last year. When we read the itinerary for this trip, we decided to pack them. We don't get many chances to wear them in New England," Moira said. Katy was silent. "I think they're colorful, but Katy thinks they're too colorful, don't you, dear?"

Katy avoided comment, eyes downward.

"Well, I think they're just right for the occasion tonight. Help yourself to a Margarita and mingle with the others."

The tables started filling as the guests sought each other out. The Weinsteins had taken the large table on the port side with the river view for them and the Hunters. They were joined by Sonia and Sally, as Durgan sat with his Iowa friends.

"Well, ladies, how do you like it so far?" Russell asked the group.

"The Margarita's lousy," Sally said.

"Sally," Sonia admonished. "He's talking about the whole trip, not just your drink. It is lousy, isn't it? The drink?" She placed her glass on the table, and pushed it away.

"Too much something. Not like Cancun. They know how to make a Margarita."

"Do you travel a lot?" Russell asked.

"We just started. We went to Cancun to one of those all-inclusive places last year and it was fun. The crowd was much younger, but we still had fun. We decided to get on with our lives," Sally explained.

"You make it sound like we're refugees or something, Sal. We were already getting on with our lives," Sonia said. "We just decided to expand them in a new direction. Anyway, Cancun was okay, but I am really enjoying this vacation. Everything we've seen so far has been great. I loved the gardens at Giverny, and all the beautiful Impressionist paintings. It's like I heard about some things and I knew about art and paintings, but when you actually go there and see them for yourself, it's so real, so different."

"I agree," Sally said. "Same thing with the food. I always heard about French cooking, Julia Child and all that, but I thought it was expensive and just for rich people, you know? But now I understand it's not all expensive, and it's so good. I mean I never had a quiche that tasted like they do here, or soup. A mustard soup, can you imagine?" Sally sat back in her chair,

"I agree. The food is great," Mel said. "Tomorrow promises to be interesting. Did you check the itinerary on the TV in you cabin?"

"No. We haven't turned on the TV today. We're really only there to change clothes or sleep. What's up?"

"Well, something for everybody," Mel said. "There's a demonstration of silk scarf painting on board, which should appeal to you ladies. Lyon was once the center of the silk industry in Europe as we saw today on the tour. Then there is a talk about the French Resistance in Lyon during World War II, which appeals to historians like us, Russell, and then in the evening, we are all scheduled to have dinner with a real French family at our next port. We will be cruising all afternoon and the weather once again will be perfect."

"The silk scarf painting sounds interesting, but I'm interested in the French Resistance movement too," Elizabeth said. "I don't really know that much about what they did, like Russell does, but that plaque at Chalon-sur-

Saone about the massacre on the bridge got my attention. I'd like to know more," Elizabeth said.

Terry poured wine for all, beginning with a white Bordeaux.

"The home based dinner with a French family sounds like fun," Ruth added. "When we pass the houses along the river, or in town, I want to knock on the doors and ask if I could see inside. I wonder how they furnish and decorate their homes."

"Tonight may just be your night, dear."

The dinner was flawless, the travelers relaxed, conversations interrupted with laughing, sharing of pictures and stories. Giovanni circulated, pausing at each table for conversations, while Gerard found himself isolated with Moira and Katy. Terry noted every detail in the dining room, his experienced eye reading the level of enjoyment- and inebriation. The days of heavy drinking, at least by Americans, had diminished markedly. He wasn't sure why, but suspected that drinking to excess was now frowned upon. The English couples had a different outlook, eagerly downing Margaritas, then wine. They sat together, laughing louder as the evening and the drinking progressed. Harmless enough.

As expected, the guests were weary from the days' adventures, and most retired early, just after dinner, except for the British couples who appeared to be ready to go all night. They moved to the bar.

"Here, that's enough of these Mexican things," Barry announced. "Time for a bit of port and brandy, a proper drink. My shout."

"If you insist. I'll get the next round," Tommy declared.

"Your money's no good here. Not while I'm here. After all, it's your doing that got us here, isn't it?"He signaled the waitress, ordered the drinks.

Gladys and Martha sat back, nursing the remnants of their Margaritas, not ready to add to their alcohol level.

"What do you mean, my Tom got us here?" Martha asked. She was dressed in a cotton shift she imagined as a version of a peasant's dress, with a low cut white scooped top and a full skirt, in a soft red. Her badly dyed blond hair was swept up in a stack off her neck. Red hoop earrings dangled. She glared at Gladys.

"Do you know, Gladys?"

"I thought you knew. Barry, didn't you explain to Martha about Tom's winnings?" Gladys asked, her words slurred. She was blond like Martha, but a good twenty years younger.

Barry glared at her, moving forward in his chair. "Shut it, Gladys. You never know when to keep it shut, do you?"

Gladys recoiled, anger in her eyes at the comment from Barry. He could be a real piece of work.

"Well, I thought she knew and I didn't tell her so it had to be you-or Tom-so what does it matter?" She leaned back, crossing her long dancer's legs, the legs that first drew Barry to her. She knew he was married at the time, but that made no difference in her world of cabaret dancing at clubs throughout Europe. He was fun and always had money. It was his idea to get divorced and marry her.

"If I wanted her to know I would've told her. That's Tom's and my business, not yours," Barry threatened.

Terry moved closer, interrupting to ask if another round of drinks was needed.

"Look, love, what Barry means is this trip came about because a gent owed me some money. He came up a bit short, so he offered a free cruise. I didn't want to bother you with all that. You're having a nice time, aren't you?" Tom smiled.

"It's a lovely time, but I thought you were out of that business for good." Gladys whined. She sat down her empty glass.

"I am, I am. This was an old debt, I promise. Barry and I are strictly legitimate importers now. Right, Barry?" Tom raised his glass to his friend.

"Absolutely. Drink up and let's go into town and have a dance or two. Come on, Gladys. Let's have some fun."

Terry sighed inwardly as the couples paid their bar bill with a signature, gathered their belongings and left to continue their party in Lyon. He would inform Giovanni of his new knowledge. He left Sophia to close the bar and went to the front desk in search of his friend.

Rita, the woman in charge of the room maids, was at the desk, thumbing through a magazine. She frequently filled in for Giovanni at the desk during slow hours.

"Hello. Where's Giovanni?"

"Oh, he stepped outside for a moment. I believe he's on deck. We have four people ashore, but the rest are tucked in. Everything's quiet" she said.

Terry took the steps slowly, whistling softly. He looked to the wheel house and spotted the white shirt of Giovanni. A woman stood next to him, peering into the wheelhouse and its green glowing instrument panel.

"Hello? Giovanni?" Terry called.

Sonia and Giovanni turned from the wheelhouse and squinted at Terry behind the light coming from the quay. He moved closer.

"Sorry to bother you mate. I thought you were alone," Terry mumbled an explanation.

"He was just showing me how the boat is guided, and what they do when we go through the locks and all that," Sonia said in almost a whisper. "Are we disturbing someone?"

"No, nothing of the sort. Just a bit of unfinished business I wanted to share with the Purser," Terry said, using the official title. "It'll wait."

"No, no. We were just finishing and I'm tired. You two go ahead. I'm going to turn in. Sally's watching an old musical again. Thank you so much for the tour," Sonia gave Giovanni a brief departing hug. Terry waited as she went below.

"Sorry. Didn't mean to interrupt."

"What do you wish to discuss, Terry?"

"It's about the Brits. I overheard a conversation. It seems that the little fellow, Tom, received this trip in lieu of a debt owed him. A debt for what I don't know, but Martha, apparently his wife, seemed upset about him going back into collecting debts. And, Gladys, the young one with the ample top and long legs, is what the Americans call a 'trophy wife' for Barry. They're off to celebrate some more in Lyon."

"We heard them leaving. I also have some news regarding our British passengers," Giovanni said. "I have a good friend who works for Interpol, just across the river, there," he gestured. "I took the passport information we have on them to my friend this morning and he ran some searches on them."

"Hmm. Are we in danger? Any information?" Terry asked.

"Nothing too dangerous. Our friends Barry and Tom are small time criminals, mainly loan sharking, gambling, and suspected smugglers of small item consumer goods. Fashion watches, knockoffs, things like that. They are listed as importers, an excellent cover story."

"So why would they be interested in our small boat?" Terry asked.

"That is the question. We are small, but so are drugs, bundles of cash, small works of art. Every week we sail between Chalon and Arles, Arles and Chalon, no questions asked as long as we observe the rules of the river. It was some time ago, but I vaguely remember when the cathedral of Saint Vincent in Chalon-sur-Saone was robbed. A 12th century Bishop's Crook was stolen and never recovered, as far as I know. It would be very easy for a thief to bring an object on board wouldn't it?"

"We need to be vigilant." Terry said.

"Inform Gerard of this news, please. He sees everything." Giovanni said.

Chapter Twelve

Russell was up earlier than usual, partly due to the early turn-in the evening before. The bunks were narrow, but comfortable enough for a solid seven or eight hours of sleep. He dressed quickly and quietly, Always leaving a note for Elizabeth. The smell of fresh brewing coffee penetrated to the below deck cabins as he climbed the stairs to the main deck passageway. Giovanni was reading the local newspaper and having a breakfast of coffee and croissants at the front desk as the dining room was preparing for the morning meal. Terry watched as his crew performed the duties they knew so well. He was proud of their efforts and the pride they took in their performance. They were all aware that the passengers left envelopes with money to be divided among the crew-members at the end of the journey. The donations were voluntary, and based on the level of service experienced. It was up to each crew-member to do the best job possible to add to the amount to be shared. Terry reminded his people daily of this obligation.

"Good morning, Giovanni," Russell said. "How's the coffee?"

"Good morning. It is excellent as usual. Can I get you a cup?" He folded his newspaper

"No, no. I can get my own. I'll say hello to Terry."

Russell filled his cup at the station with the strong French roast coffee, and entered the dining room for a croissant.

"Morning, Terry."

"Good morning, Russell. We're having nice omelets on special this morning. Let me know if you want one later. Everything going well?"

"Couldn't be nicer. This is my time of day, you know. I think I'll go up on deck for the rest of the sunrise."

"See you at seven."

Giovanni was waiting at the bottom of the stairwell to the upper deck, coffee in hand. "Going topside?"

"Yes. Care to join me?"

"I have some duties to attend to, but I think I have time to enjoy my coffee. After you, my friend." They ascended the staircase.

Russell pulled out a deck chair and seated himself at a small table on the port side, facing the river. The city lights were still on, twinkling in the sunrise. Cars were moving on the quay, traffic lights blinking red and green as Lyon came awake. The river was still, no barge traffic or pleasure cruisers. Giovanni made a quick round of the deck, looking for left-behind glasses and plates, then joined his early rising friend.

"All done for now. The deck is now clean and ready for your enjoyment," Giovanni pronounced as he sat with his coffee.

"I must say that we have enjoyed every minute so far," Russell said. "The boat is delightful, and the tours have been very interesting. My wife is ready to move here and spend her mornings at the farmers market."

"I'm sure that can be arranged. So you like visiting France?"He sipped the steaming brew.

"Yes we do. My wife loves art and actually knows a lot about it. She educates me. I love history. It has been a big part of my life since I was ten years old, and I now educate her about European history, so much of which took place here in France. It's a fascinating country with so many sides to its national character you could study it endlessly. Quite complex." He sipped his coffee, glanced at the river.

"You are correct. France is a country of many contradictions, many classes of people," Giovanni said. "For years, there was no one language. Each area had its own version of proper French. It was like Italy, a country forced together by Garibaldi in the 19th century.

"Where are you from, what part of Italy?"

"My family home is in Sicily, a small village called Delia, in the south, near the coast. It is very poor. I left as a boy and ran off to sea. That is my home now."

"Home is 'where you hang your hat' we say in America, meaning where you are at any time is your home," Russell explained, leaning back in his deck chair.

"That is a good expression and it is true, for me. I have lived in Italy and France, and Africa, and even in England. Each country has a culture, a character, a way of living life. An attitude, if you will. Italy is romantic, loud with conversations and music and dancing. Full of art and sculpture and ancient sites. Rome is the 'Eternal City.' The people are outgoing and happy," Giovanni waved his arms, hands gesturing. "Or so it seems to the traveler. But to the natives, especially those in my native Sicily, there is a dark side of corruption and crime and heavy taxes. Dealing with the government can be maddening."

"And France? Are there problems here in these beautiful villages and river towns?" Russell asked, as full daylight came up over the river.

"France is in a major crisis," Giovanni said. "The sea of immigrants from North Africa from the former colonies, and the wave of Muslims is bankrupting France. Paris is having riots and car burnings, strikes are every day. Taxes are high and young people cannot get ahead because of them. The French insist on working shorter hours and demand the government take care of all of their needs. It is not good to live in France now."

"How did you end up living in England?"

"That is what you call a long story. England is still the center of the seagoing world. If you work in this business, almost everything goes through England. Also, my ex-wife is from there and prefers being near her family. My children lived with her until they grew up and married. They all live in England," Giovanni explained.

"Are you planning to retire there?"

"Yes, I believe so. I understand the system and the tax laws, and I have no desire to start all over in a new country at my age." He looked at his watch. "Time to get below. The early risers will be stirring."

"I'll go with you. We have a busy day today. I'm looking forward to the talk on the Resistance." They pushed in their chairs, gathered the empty cups for the trash.

"The woman speaker is very good. I have heard her before. If you are a historian, listen very carefully and you will have a better understanding of why France behaves as it does today when it comes to possible conflicts. The Resistance was very real and the scars are deep."

Giovanni led the way down the stairwell, slowing to a stop at the bottom curve. Someone was behind his desk, rummaging underneath the counter. Giovanni moved silently.

"May I help you?" he asked. The young woman jerked upright, startled by his voice. It was Brenda, the new waitress from England. Her face blushed red.

"I was just cleaning up, looking for any cups or saucers," she answered, glancing over Giovanni's shoulder.

Russell followed her gaze and saw Barry emerge from the dining room, coffee cup in hand. He glared at Brenda, then dropped his eyes when he saw Russell, turned on his heel and left the area.

"I maintain my own desk," Giovanni said. "It is not necessary for you or anyone else who isn't authorized to be behind that desk, ever. If it happens again, you will be dismissed, immediately. Understand?" He was coldly furious. Russell found himself pulling back at the show of quiet outrage.

"I'm so sorry. I was just trying to tidy up before all the guests arrived," she explained, hands shaking.

"You have been warned. Now go tell Terry I need to talk to him. Quickly."

Brenda retreated to the dining room, head lowered. "Yes, sir."

"Everything in order?" Russell asked as Giovanni busied himself with a quick inventory of his space.

"Oh, yes. Nothing to worry about. I don't bring out the money box until later. But there are papers, documents that are private business. I shouldn't have left the desk unoccupied, but this early it's usually not a problem. I will make an adjustment to have full coverage."

Terry emerged from the dining room, a look of concern on his pale face.

"Need to talk with me, sir?" He used the formal greeting, sensing a business discussion.

"Yes, please come in," Giovanni invited Terry into his small space.

"I'll see you later. Thanks for the coffee and the talk." Russell excused himself.

Elizabeth reached the passageway just as Russell did.

"Oh, hi. I had given up on you. Are you ready for breakfast?" she asked.

"Yes, but let me get a quick shower first. I'll meet you in the dining room. Start without me, I had coffee and croissants with Giovanni. And a very interesting conversation. I'll fill you in."

"Okay. I'll see you later. I assume you're not going to attend the silk painting lecture later?"

"Good assumption. See you soon. I have my key."

Elizabeth entered the dining room, full of the pleasant smell of fresh baked pastries, strong coffee, and other breakfast foods. The tables were all laid with sparkling cutlery and glasses on white table linens, everything in its proper place, just the way her mother had taught her. She came from a working class family, not from wealth, but was fortunate to have had a mother who believed in living life with a certain dignity and style. Good manners were available to all, not just the rich.

"Good morning. Looking for a seat?"

Elizabeth turned to the voice, recognizing the woman from the Iowa group.

"I'm Debbie. I think we met before?"

"I believe we did. Are you by yourself?"

"Yes, on purpose. I told my husband and our friends that I came on this trip to meet new people, not to sit with the same people I've known all my life. He's off checking on some museum he wants to see, so I thought I'd sit here and meet someone new."

"Well, thank you." Elizabeth seated herself, opening her napkin, arranging her table top. She ordered her usual hot tea. "I'm Elizabeth Hunter. My husband is Russell and he's an early riser, so he is now in the shower, following his managing of the sunrise. He'll catch up. I think we can survive one meal apart," she laughed.

"Isn't that the truth? Larry and I have been married for 42 years. The friends we are traveling with we have known since grade school. We know all about each other, and the kids, and now the grandkids. I'm ready for something new. I've lived my whole life in a five square mile area of Iowa. Where are you from?"

"Originally, Pennsylvania, but we've lived in seven states. We live in Atlanta now, and it looks like we'll stay there. Russell is retired, but is thinking of a second career of sorts, and I plan to fully retire at the end of this year."

"Wonderful. What are you retiring from? Teaching?"

"No. I'm in the business world. I won't miss it at all. Were you a teacher? So many women of our generation were."

"Yes, I was." She added cream to her fresh coffee, stirred it slowly. "So were the other two women in our group, Linda and Pat. We didn't have many choices as young women, as you may remember. Teach school, be a nurse, learn to type, be a secretary. Mostly I taught elementary school and raised kids as my husband did his thing at the bank for 40 years. Now's our time to play. We just hope our health holds up."

"That seems to be everybody's biggest concern."

"I put it right after surviving caring for elderly parents and kids who go from one romantic disaster to another, stopping by the Bank of Mom and Dad for interest free loans, which they never pay anyway. Larry and I sat down with our four last year after his dad passed. He had Alzheimer's. It was terrible for everybody. Larry told the kids, who are in their forties, or close to it, that the bank was closed and we were going to see as much of the world as we can. You should have heard it. They were outraged. Larry told them we were retiring from being parents and focusing only on grand-parenting."

"Good for Larry," Elizabeth said. "And for you. I don't know what our generation did wrong, but almost everyone we know has problems with their adult children refusing to grow up and take some responsibility. They seem to think they are entitled to a successful life without having to work for it, like we did."

Debbie nodded, reached for her coffee.

"When we started out, we had nothing but ourselves and a determination to work together to have a better life," Debbie said. "We would have been ashamed to live off our parents after we married. Now the kids want a house just like they grew up in, and they want it now. Do you know, one of our friends had a big falling out with their son because his new wife wanted a honeymoon on Bali and they wanted us to pay for it? Bali, around the world! She thought it was fair because her parents paid for most of the wedding, which cost a small fortune."

'How long did the marriage last?" Elizabeth asked.

"Not quite three years."

They shared a laugh, acknowledging the irony.

"Good morning. I could hear you laughing out in the passageway. Hi, I'm Russell Hunter."

"Pleased to meet you. I'm Debbie, I believe you met my husband Larry. We're from Iowa. We can move to a bigger table. I snagged your wife when she walked in."

"That's not necessary. I already had something to eat."

"Russell is an early riser. Debbie and I have been talking about retirement and wayward children who refuse to grow up. Her husband told their children that they were getting out of parenting and focusing on grand-parenting. I like that," Elizabeth said.

Russell smiled, head bobbing.

"I love it. There has to be a time when we can get back to why we chose to get married to each other in the first place. We took care of our parents, we took care of our kids, and now it's our time to be together. To quote you, Elizabeth, 'after all these years, you're the only person I can still stand.'"

Debbie laughed at the wisdom of the comment, nodding her head in agreement. "That is so true. Wait till I tell Larry. And look who's here…"

The dining room sound level went up as the other Iowa travelers arrived.

"There she is. Morning, Deb," Larry said in greeting. "Good morning. I think we met before."

"These are the Hunters, Elizabeth and Russell, from Atlanta, Georgia. Elizabeth and I have been having a pleasant breakfast and chat. I told you I wanted to meet some new people."

The other Iowans introduced themselves, then selected a long table at the back of the room for their breakfast meal. Larry waved to them, indicating he would join them later.

"Well that's great. You don't sound like you're from Atlanta," Larry said.

"We're not. We grew up in Pennsylvania. We've been in Atlanta for the last twenty years, but no accent," Russell explained.

"We never left our home town,' Larry explained. "I worked for the same employer for forty years and so did Debbie. We had an apartment, then a starter house we rebuilt, then the big house where our kids grew up. We're looking into selling it, now that it's just us again. We don't need all those rooms to heat and cool. We thought we'd need room for our kids and grandkids, but they only show up when they feel like it."

Debbie broke the awkward silence that followed Larry's remark.

"Are you going to the silk scarf painting lecture at nine?"

"I am, but not Russell."

"I'm going, and I want to hear the talk about the French Resistance later. Larry's off to some museum."

"Well," Larry said, "there's a Museum of the Resistance not far from here, but it might be closed. Bob and Jim and I are thinking of taking a cab over there during the scarf painting talk. Want to join us, Russ?" Larry asked.

"Well, I would, but I don't want to miss the Resistance lecture. What time is that?"

"Ten thirty to eleven thirty. If we get to the museum by eight thirty, we can be back here in time. Giovanni said the museum is supposed to be open at eight thirty, but sometimes they don't open. It doesn't seem to be a popular attraction. It's also very small."

"What's the worst that can happen? We'll still have a nice cab ride. Mind if I go with your group?" Russell asked.

"Not at all. Enjoy yourself. That's why we're here."

"I'll be on deck, Larry. Whistle when you're ready to go."

"I'll come get you."

Russell reached for the coffee.

"Where are your sunrise buddies, Kevin and Durgan?" Elizabeth asked. "Russell has been meeting them each morning, bright and early," she explained.

"I don't know. Sleeping in, I guess. I had coffee with Giovanni, and an interesting talk about living options," He sipped from the cup, thinking of his words.

"And…"

"Giovanni is from Sicily, has lived in a number of countries, and will retire to England where he has a home and his children and grandchildren, even though they aren't close."

"England? That seems strange, with their tax laws," Debbie said. "They're as socialized as you can get."

"I believe you're right. Most of Europe is. But, when you're old, guaranteed health care and retirement benefits may be your top priority."

" I could never live anywhere but America," Debbie added. "But I would like to be some place warmer than Iowa, at least in the winter."

"You need to talk to our friends Mel and Ruth," Elizabeth said, looking at her watch. " Almost time to move."

"I'm off to meet with the guys. Later."

Breakfast completed, the four men assembled on the quay, waiting for the taxi Giovanni had summoned for them. Gerard noticed the group, and decided to investigate, thinking he could be of help in some way. He also was concerned that none of his passengers wander off and miss the noon departure of the Arles.

"Bonjour, gentlemen. Are you going into the city?"

"Hi, Gerard. Yeah, we decided to check out the Resistance Museum, if it's open. We tried to call but didn't get an answer. It's supposed to be very close by."

"Are you taking a cab? It is close, but still a good walk."

"There's one on the way. In fact I think that's it," Larry said, waving at the cab on the street above the quay. The driver waved back.

"Let me tell the driver where you are going," Gerard suggested. "We call it the Museum of the French Resistance, but it is officially The Center for the History of Resistance and Deportation. It is in a building that was once the Military School of Health before Klaus Barbie made it Gestapo Headquarters in 1943 and '44. It is a very upsetting place, I must warn you," Gerard said. He spoke to the driver, head nodding.

"Enjoy your visit, gentleman. Remember the lecture is at 10:30." He waved them off and returned to the boat to assist Terry with the set up for the silk scarf painting talk.

"So, you are interested in the French Resistance?" The taxi driver asked in a heavily accented, but understandable English. He drove quickly, no signaling.

"Yes, we are. We've read about it and we've seen some movies, but this will be our first museum visit," Russell replied for the group.

"If you have read anything then you know about the Butcher of Lyon, Klaus Barbie." He spit out the open window. "He was tried over there at the Palace of Justice, you know. He murdered more than 4000 Frenchmen and women and children. And he killed Jean Moulin, the hero of the Resistance. May he burn in hell!"

"When was that trial, 1946, '47?"

"Oh no, no, no. He ran away to South America after the war. He was brought back here in 1987 and sentenced to life. He died in 1991, the Boche!"

The cab pulled into the empty lot in front of a sinister looking stone building. Russell felt a chill, realizing he was looking at a sight that might have been the last view of the outside world for Gestapo prisoners brought here for interrogation. Larry left the taxi to see if the museum was open. He tugged at the locked door, peering inside. After a short pause, the door was opened by a cleaning man, polishing cloth in hand. The man pointed to a small sign and he and Larry seemed to be agreeing on something with much arm waving. Larry returned to the cab, a smile playing on his face.

"The museum is closed. It is Tuesday, and it is always closed on Tuesday, except for in the winter when it is closed on Monday and Tuesday. At least, I think that's what he said," Larry explained.

"Ah, oui, closed Tuesdays," the driver said. "Back to the boat, yes?"

"Yes, back to the boat."

"Larry, remember that little cafe we passed yesterday on the way to the market? The one next to the bakery?"

"Yeah, the one with the umbrellas with the stripes? It's right over there near the boat."

"Why don't we stop and have coffee and look at the women of France. I really don't want to get dragged into that silk painting thing," Bob pleaded.

"Good idea, Bob. I vote for a stop too. You in, Russ?"

"Let's do it."

The cab dropped the laughing men off at the square across the quay from the Arles, where they staked out a table and ordered coffees and pasties from a wheeled cart. They positioned themselves and the umbrella to screen out the bright morning sunlight.

"I hate to say it first, but sometimes it's nice to just be with guys," Larry said.

"I know. Too much togetherness can wear you out," Bob said.

"The women are probably saying the same thing about being away from us."

"You know, when you first retire and you're home all the time, it's almost like when you first got married. You kinda have to get used to each other all over again," Larry said.

"You got that right. Linda let me know that it was her kitchen, and she didn't want me in it, not even to make a sandwich. Then I realized she thinks it's her house and I'm just an intruder."

"And the maintenance man. Complete with tool belt. I went from Executive VP with my own bathroom and personal assistant to unpaid manual laborer in less than 24 hours, and I'm supposed to love it." Jim said, biting into a Danish he had selected.

"Don't you watch the ads for Home Depot and Lowe's and all those hardware stores? Why, every man ever born yearns to work with his hands, repairing things that are broken, building things he could buy. Man's destiny is a cordless screwdriver of his own," Larry said.

The group's laughter turned heads at the cafe.

"It takes some time to adjust. We finally sat down and came up with new rules as to who does what and when. The hardest part was convincing Pat that I don't have to be busy every minute hammering or raking or shoveling. It's okay to take a nap. I think I've earned it."

"Well, I learned to cook," Larry said. "Nothing elaborate, but I can make a good sandwich, fry eggs, or heat up leftovers. I found that asking Debbie when lunch was going to be ready did not go over well. She took so long to get to it, she drove me crazy. Women eat differently. Different amounts, at different times. Once I asked when lunch would be ready and she said 'you just had breakfast.' I thought, yeah, a slice of toast four hours ago. It's easier to just feed myself when I'm hungry," Larry said.

"That's why I like these cruises and traveling in general. Here you can relax, enjoy the sights, eat good food..." He held up his half eaten croissant.

"Have you taken a cruise like this before? Do you always travel together/" Russell asked.

"Well," Larry said, "we grew up together in a small farm town in Iowa. Played ball together, scouts, high school. We went our different ways for a while, but ended up back in the home town. Now we do a vacation together every year, some place warm. Either in Europe or Mexico or the Caribbean. This is our first river cruise."

"Are you enjoying it?" Russell asked.

Jim and Bob nodded a vigorous "yes," as Larry said "Great."

"Set up camp once, and relax. That's what I love. I don't like a lot of stirring things up in my life. I like that," Bob said.

"And learning something. That's the part I enjoy. That building looked like a Gestapo headquarters, didn't it?" Jim said, changing the subject."I had chills."

"It made me feel uncomfortable, threatened. The Gestapo was real, wasn't it?"

"It sure was for our cabbie. I'm surprised that the French can forgive that."

"It was a long time ago. The old Nazis are almost all gone, and you can't really blame their descendants. They had nothing to do with it."

"That's true," Russell said. "But the memories will never vanish completely."

The men finished their morning treats, watched the traffic pass.

"Time to move on, in more ways than one," Russell said, glancing at his watch. He waved for the bill.

Back on Arles, Gerard sat at a small table on the sundeck, catching up on paperwork, making phone calls, and refreshing his notes when he saw the men returning. They were all big men, compared to the average Frenchmen. They walked with confidence, smiling a lot, comfortable with each other in an informal way. He was aware that American soldiers had liberated his country from the Wehrmacht, possibly, at one time, the most professional, best equipped and trained army the world had ever seen, and he also knew that those American soldiers were not professionals, but mostly draftees. It said a great deal about the fighting spirit of the mixture of cultures that created the people called Americans. He liked them and their generosity, forgiving their ignorance of French culture. It was his role to educate them, and he would.

The scarf painting session ended, and the upper deck filled quickly. Gerard packed his paperwork into his leather bag along with his cell phone, anxious to hear the reactions to the lecture. The returning men searched for and found their spouses, sharing their experiences. Elizabeth and Ruth were showing their new scarf purchases to their husbands.

"Bonjour. I see you have purchased some scarves. I take it you enjoyed the demonstration?"Gerard was all charm.

"Ruth and I did. Russell went to see the museum but it was closed. Did you go with them, Mel?"

"No. I have some problems with exhibits of evil from the Nazis. I find it too disturbing. My family had some tragedies in the war, so I take it personally," Mel answered. "I visited the lounge and looked over the library. There's a nice selection of books that were donated by other passengers. It was nice and quiet. I ran into Durgan there. He was looking at poetry, I think. Honest."

"There are many in France who find the reminders of the war very disturbing. Then there are others who insist we do not forget. So, we will not see you at the lecture about the Resistance?"

"Oh, I'll be at that. I can handle a talk on what was done to kill the Nazi bastards. I might even cheer," Mel added.

"I will cheer with you. Time to move the group along. The next talk starts in fifteen minutes. See you there."

The lounge area filled quickly, Terry ordering his staff to add chairs for the unexpectedly large turnout. He had assumed a small turnout, with the beautiful sunny weather luring the shoppers back to the market area.

Gerard called the group to a form of attention, and introduced the speaker, Madame Guidry. The audience quieted quickly as she began.

"Bonjour," she began. "I am Michelle Guidry, a native of Lyon, and a teacher of history at the university. Today I want to tell you about the role of the Resistance in World War Two, here in Lyon, and also in all of France. I also want to introduce you to a true heroine of the Resistance, Madame Berthe Fraser. Let us begin."

The room was completely silent, as if everyone was holding their breath. No coughing, no moving about on the chairs.

"In the Great War of 1914-1918, France suffered millions of casualties, most of them in the north, in Flanders. It was there that the Germans were stopped by the French and British armies with their network of trenches. It was a war of attrition, and it destroyed the world that existed before 1914. Russia fell in the communist revolution of 1917. The Ottoman Empire of the Muslims collapsed completely, the Austro- Hungarian Empire of the Hapsburgs disappeared, and France and England lost a generation of young men, and the old colonial systems began their decline. The world was turned upside down. It was the War to end All Wars.

Twenty-one years later, Hitler was in charge of Germany, and the world was introduced to the concept of blitzkrieg, lightning war, with a new weapon, the tank, racing around the fortified Maginot line. There would be no trenches stopping the Germans. In six short weeks, the Germans were in Paris, and an armistice was declared on June 22, 1940. The French Republic was established, just north of here, near Dijon, while the rest of France was occupied, including Paris and all of the west of France. Vichy France became the government of the collaborators. The importance of all this is that the war was no longer limited to the soldiers at the front lines, it was now part of daily life for all French citizens. France was occupied, and the people decided to fight back in any way possible."

Madame Guidry paused. "The Resistance movement began in 1940, and Lyon played a major part due to its location near neutral Switzerland, and as the largest city in unoccupied France. The newspaper of the Resistance, Combat, it was called, was written and printed here. It attracted writers like Jean Paul Sartre and Albert Camus, and was distributed all over France by an underground network, using mainly women who would hide the papers in their babies' prams."

Madame Guidry went on discuss the many activities used by Resistance figures, supplementing her talk with a series of slides of the era. She explained that the term "Maquis" referred to the French fighters who operated in the countryside, in the brush called "maquis." Although the Resistance did participate in some key assassinations of Germans, the Nazi policy of massive reprisal by shooting hostages caused a shift to acts of sabotage of communications, transport, and intelligence gathering for the anticipated invasion which came in June of 1944. During the invasion, she explained, French Resistance groups provided vital intelligence, disrupted German movements to the battlefield, and tied down badly needed reinforcements.

"You may have heard of a man named Jean Moulin. He was appointed by de Gaulle to be the head of the movement, and sent back to France from England to try to unite all the different Resistance groups into one national organization. After much discussion, Moulin persuaded the eight major resistance groups to form the Conseil National de la Resistance (CNR) and the first joint meeting under Moulin's chairmanship took place in Paris on 27th May 1943.

On 7th June 1943, Pierre Hardy, an important member of the resistance in France, was arrested and tortured by Klaus Barbie, the Butcher of Lyon. They eventually obtained enough information to arrest Moulin at Caluire on 21st June. Jean Moulin died while being tortured on 8th July 1943. He was 44 years old."

The room was silent as the impact of the talk was absorbed. Some turned away as the slides of the Gestapo torture chambers were shown. Mel and Ruth sat clutching hands, supporting each other.

"Losing Jean Moulin was a terrible loss. But there were others to carry on. This is one of the most prominent, Madame Berthe Fraser," Madame Guidry said as she advanced the slide. It was a black and white photo of a plain faced woman dressed in modest clothing, nothing out of the ordinary. "She was a French housewife who had married an Englishman, and she was from Arras, in Northern France. When the British Army had to be evacuated, many soldiers were left behind. Berthe organized a network to get them back to England. Later she helped downed pilots to escape, and served as a courier, taking messages and weapons across France as needed. In 1944 she was betrayed and captured. She was tortured daily for weeks, then sentenced to solitary confinement for six months. She was freed from the prison after the invasion by advancing troops. She never broke. She was later awarded the King George medal, the Croix de Guerre, the Legion of Honour, and the American Freedom Medal. She was 50 years old at the time of the awards."

The slide projector clicked to a blank slide, and Madame Guidry turned it off.

"Are there any questions?" she asked.

"How big was the Resistance? What percentage of the population joined?"

"We will never know for certain. There is a saying in France that the farther away we get from the war, the more people who were in the Resistance."

A wave of laughter rose from the group.

"What I would hope you have gained from my little talk is the understanding that we French have seen first hand the absolute horror of war, not just once, but twice, and not just on battlefields, but in our streets and our homes. We prefer to use other means to resolve conflicts if possible. I hope you enjoy the rest of your journey. Thank you very much for your attention."

"If I may, I'd like to say, 'Vive la France!'" Russell said.

The group rose as one and repeated the salute, "Vive la France!"

Gerard was waiting as the travelers filed out.

"Thank you, Russell," he said, offering his hand.

"No nation should have to go through what you went through, my friend."

"Not every one thinks the way you do, unfortunately," Gerard smiled. "We will be departing soon, and we will have lunch after we are underway. We will be going through another series of locks as we descend the Rhone on our way to the sea. You will be able to get some wonderful pictures."

Chapter Thirteen

"Is it possible for a boat this size to purr?"Mel asked. "Listen to those engines."

The passengers lined the railing as the Arles slowly slipped into the main channel of the Rhone and continued the southbound journey from Lyon, the twin hills of the ancient Roman city falling behind as only the slightest hiss of water came from the bow. The breeze across the bow made for another perfect cruising day. Deck chairs and tables were arranged in small groupings, some offering sun, while others offered shade. The bow section had become a reading area, popular with individuals enjoying their books and the quiet. The Iowa group and their new friends camped at tables partially protected under a blue and white striped awning. A card game was in progress, and a cluster of women were engaged in lively conversations, sprinkled with frequent laughter, the quiet, reverent mood from the Resistance talk receding in the cheery sunlight. A slight change in course exposed the group to bright sunlight, triggering a repositioning to the new shaded areas. Mel stood and analyzed the situation, staring up at the striped canvas and the frame work supporting twin rolls now deployed.

"What are you looking at, Mel?" Russell asked. "Are you going to add sails?"

"No, but I think we can get more shade and not have to keep moving every time we come to a turn in the river. See those two rolls of canvas, one on the right side and one on the left?"

Russell stared intently at the rigging. "Yeah, I see them."

"It looks like there is still a lot of canvas wrapped around the rollers, which means the awnings may not be fully opened. I'm trying to find out how you open them. There has to be a winch or switch somewhere."

"Why don't you ask that man up front with the captain, the one who's always working on things?" Ruth suggested.

"You see, this is what happens when you empower women. The good ones learn quickly. C'mon, Russell, I have the solution to our problem. Thanks, hon."

Mel and Russell returned with the ship's bosun who carried a chrome key-like device and what looked like a winch. The bosun inserted the key, then the winch, and turned it slowly as Mel guided the deployment of the additional awning, adding more than three feet of shade on each side of the centerline. The passengers moved aside until the action was complete, then settled back in, cool in the new shade.

A round of applause was given as the bosun completed securing the covering.

"Good job, Mel" Larry called.

"This is what I do," Mel said dramatically, arms outstretched, palms upward, in presentation. The travelers laughed in appreciation.

"This really is what Mel does, you know," Ruth said. "He loves helping people. He grumbles about it, but he has a big heart for helping others. I think his success in sales was because he wanted to help his customers first."

The Arles cruised slowly through a series of locks, the boat entering the concrete structure, then slowly lowering as the water in the lock was pumped out. Once at the new level, the huge gates opened, allowing the boat to resume its journey. The travelers, at first fascinated by every detail of the lock procedure, soon became accustomed to the event, ducking under the canvas to avoid the water spill from the overhead lock when the new river level was reached.

The card game ended as the last lock was cleared and the announcement made that the port of Tournon would be reached in 30 minutes. Gerard made his usual pre-stop visit, a slow circuit of the deck with a greeting for each passenger. He gravitated to the shaded area and the friendly group clustered around the tables, plastic glasses of Bloody Marys arrayed before them.

"Bonjour. Are you all rested?"

A contented murmur answered his question. Some times it was nice to just sit and cruise, as they had all discovered. Even Gerard's attempt to help was viewed by some as an intrusion on the mood. The overall assessment of Gerard and his management skills was favorable, with minor objections as to his tendency to push the pace a bit, as well as indulging in a bit of hard selling of optional tours not included in the basic tour package. Many of the Americans resented being "pitched" and began saying so, surprising Gerard.

"Tonight we have a special treat for those of you who have decided to participate," Gerard said. "Tonight you will be divided into small groups for your dinner with a French family. Someone from the family will meet you at the dock, and you will be taken to their home for an informal meal and conversation. All of our host families speak English, and have volunteered to be part of this program. Please ask them about how they live, how they work, how they see the world. Anything you like. They will have many questions for you, also. I will give you your group assignments when we dock. Please come see me in the dining room. I am certain you will have a wonderful visit and meal with our host families," Gerard concluded.

"How are the families selected for hosting?" Mel asked.

"They contact us. They must have good English skills and they must fill out a questionnaire about themselves. We screen them carefully."

"Are they paid for this?"

Gerard was annoyed. "They are compensated for their time and food purchases, yes, but that is not your concern."

Mel stared hard at Gerard. "If it's my money, it's my concern," he replied.

"You will get your money's worth," Gerard said, a defiant tone in his response.

"There goes his tip from Mel," Larry said to his Iowa group. Silent glances validated the statement.

Gerard excused himself as the boat reached the channel leading to the dock, and the travelers returned to their comforts. They were upset with the exchange they had witnessed between Gerard and Mel. The Program Director had much to learn about Americans and their sense of value and correctness. They were generous, but not foolish. The use of high-pressure sales tactics, or condescending comments, was not acceptable.

Arles slipped quietly alongside the dock next to a city park. The well-seasoned crew made docking a seemingly effortless task. Lines were secured, and the short gangplank readied for shore visits.

"Ready for a walk?" Mel asked.

"Yes, but I think we're going to get our dinner assignment from Gerard first. We should have plenty of time before we're picked up. We're really looking forward to this evening. I hope they have good English skills because my French pronunciation doesn't cut it," Russell answered.

"Okay, makes sense. Let's get in line. Anybody know anything about this stop?"

Elizabeth volunteered. "According to our handy little guide, which I have right here, Tournon is 'nestled between the river and the steep slopes of nearby vineyards.' We will have the opportunity to explore the streets of this ancient town tomorrow morning."

"Any special notes about the history of the town, famous sights?"

"If you look to the right, you can see a statue of a man in the park. See it?"

"Got it."

"If I'm right, that is a statue of Marc Seguin, a native of Tournon and the inventor of the tubular steam boiler, which made the invention of the railroad locomotive and the steamboat possible. He, according to this guide, built the first railroad in France, the first suspension bridge across the Rhone, and the first steamboat. Voila!" Elizabeth ended.

"I thought Robert Fulton did that in New York state," Mel said.

"Fulton is not mentioned in our guidebook."

"I'll have to point that out to Gerard," Mel smirked. "Unless he thinks that's none of my concern."

Ruth took a deep breath, glaring at Mel with the secret power of "the look" that all women possessed. Mel recognized the warning and became silent. The passengers dispersed, most returning to their cabins.

The Hunters settled into the cabin chairs, shoes kicked off, deciding to forego a walk. Elizabeth studied the itinerary for the day.

"I think Mel just got himself in trouble with Gerard," Russell said.

"He's in bigger trouble with Ruth. Did you see that look she gave him when he complained?"

"Yes, but Gerard was being a little snippy, don't you think? Mel asked a legitimate question. He deserved an answer?"

"You may be right. I think we're at the point where we may be getting on each other's nerves a bit. Did you have a good talk with Mel yesterday at the café? Ruth said Mel enjoyed talking with you," Elizabeth said.

"Yes, I did. I enjoyed our talk too. Mel told me about their lives, how they got to Florida. And he told me about his heart problem. I told him about my prostate shock, and we talked about getting older and what really mattered now."

Elizabeth opened a water bottle, poured some into a plastic glass from the bathroom. "Want some? No ice."

Russell declined with a shake of his head. "They have had a very ordinary, stable life. A happy marriage, he had a great career, made some big money, while she raised kids, had a job, etc. They transitioned to a retirement community in Florida, and fit right in."

"Did he tell you about the son on drugs?"

"No. That wasn't mentioned."

"Ruth said it was awful. They had to take legal action against the older boy to protect the other kids. They seem to be over it now," Elizabeth said.

"Do we know anyone who has a completely normal family? It seems every family has some dysfunctional member driving them crazy. What the hell went wrong?" Russell asked, getting to his feet. He stared out the small window at the green water.

"That's a question that will be debated for a long time," Elizabeth said. "The differences between our generation and our children's generation are huge. We were raised by the "greatest generation," according to the analysts, and we followed their rules and values. They struggled through the Depression, so they taught us the need for discipline, for hard work, for thrift, for family togetherness, everybody working together."

Russell collapsed in the chair, struggling with his muddled thoughts.

"You're right, I guess. I went to work at 14, dipping ice cream. You were behind a lunch counter at 16, taking orders for the Blue Plate specials. It was just the way things were. We accepted it."

"We've had this conversation before," Elizabeth said, "and we'll probably have it again. The difference, as I see it, is that we tried to give our children more than we had, we tried to make their lives easier, relieving them of financial strain, granting them time to explore and expand. We had the best intentions. But, instead of gratitude for their parents' sacrifices, a sense of entitlement developed. Children believe they are entitled to a free education, a big house, a limousine for the prom, a honeymoon in Bali. Their society agrees with them, and we have to live with it."

They sat quietly. Russell stood, walked to the bathroom, returned with a plastic cup. He poured the water and took a gulp. "But we don't have to like it."

Chapter Fourteen

Gerard used the bar in the lounge as a desk, arranging his papers neatly to aid in his assigning guests and hosts. He had prepared the pairings on the cruise to Tournon, but decided to make a change at the last minute that required some adjustments. He greeted each guest by name and handed them a slip of paper with the name of their host family, instructing them to wait in the lounge. They would be picked up by the host with a car, or by a guide who would walk with them to a nearby location. The group size varied from a party of four to a group of a dozen. There was no explanation of how the pairings and assignments were made.

The Hunters were at the end of the assignment line as it slowly shuffled forward, the conversations punctuated with laughter. Mel approached them, his host assignment in hand.

"How did you do?" Russell asked.

"Well, we're in a group of 12, and we will walk to a local club, with a guide, for an entertaining evening, according to our Program Director. We don't know who is in our group. We might have to cancel that drink before dinner, depending on when we have to depart." Mel looked disturbed with his assigned group.

"Okay. Well, let's see what our assignment is. I thought we would all be in small groups and meet with a family, not visit a club."

"So did I. We'll be in the lounge."

Gerard greeted the Hunters with a smile. "Bonjour. I have your assignment here. You will be met by Madame Deneschaud and have dinner at her home at their farm. You will be accompanied by passengers Sally and Sonia. Any questions?"

"Only four of us? That's great. We'll be able to have a nice talk with our hosts. Is it a big family?"

"No, I believe it is just Madame and her husband, possibly one teenager but I am not certain. They have orchards and also a small vineyard which produces some excellent wine. I believe Sally and Sonia have gone on to the lounge. They know you will be with them."

"Thank you very much."

The Hunters made their way forward to the small lounge, following the narrow passageway.

"That was a stroke of luck, getting assigned a small group with a small family."

"Yes, wasn't it? I wonder if my 'Vive la France' this morning had anything to do with it. That wasn't why I said it. I have a major appreciation for what the Resistance did," Russell said. "I wonder how we would act if America ever was occupied by an enemy force?"

"That's an interesting thought. Maybe you should do some research into what other countries have done when occupied. By the way, do you think Gerard assigns these pairings based on favoritism?"

"How would you do it? There has to be some subjective feelings in play. He likes us and he also seems to like the two ladies."

"And there they are, cocktails in hand. Good evening, ladies. It looks like we are together for the evening."

"Isn't that nice? We are the smallest group, I think. We can't wait to see the inside of a French house," Sally said. "There's wine in the lounge if you want some."

"Hi," Sonia said. "We thought Gerard forgot us when we went for our assignment. At first he couldn't find us on his list, but then he did. His paper was all messed up from changes he made. We lucked out."

"There's Mel. I'll give him the news about tonight. Do you want wine?" Russell asked.

"I'm fine. I'm sure we'll have plenty of good wine later."

The women moved into the lounge away from the entry and the wine bar.

"Merlino? Merlino party? Your host is here. There are four? Yes?" Giovanni called.

"There're four of us, me and the ladies." Frank Merlino replied. "We're ready."

"Hunters, Sally and Sonia. Your hostess is waiting."Gerard called, his eyes on his clipboard.

The group gathered their belongings and moved to the gangplank, carefully crossing the narrow bridge. Madame Deneschaud, directed by Terry, stepped forward.

"Hello, I am Terese Deneschaud. We will be taking my car. It will be a little small in the back, but it is a short drive."

"Why don't you sit in front, Russell? You have the longest legs." Elizabeth suggested. "Is that okay?" she asked.

"Fine with me."

They arranged themselves in the small sedan. "People in France don't have any problem driving small cars do they? No SUVs here," Sally said.

The small car pulled away from the park following the narrow road that paralleled the river. Although it was still daylight, the oncoming cars all had their lights on. Terese drove very fast, the small car nimbly taking the gentle curves.

"Welcome to France and to our little town. I am Terese, and I am Swiss and Italian, a native of Switzerland, not a French native. My husband, Yves, is very French, and we farm the same land his great grandfather farmed. His English is not so good, but he is getting better."

"How did you meet a Frenchman in Switzerland?" Sonia asked.

"He was there in Geneva for a conference on new farming controls. I was working at the conference as a translator. When we met, it was love at first light."

The Americans laughed at the frank and charming variation of an old cliché.

"I like that," Sonia said. "Love at first light."

Terese increased her speed as they left the small village.

"How long have you been married? Do you have any children?"

"Oh, we have three children, only one at home. You will meet her at dinner. Her name is Matilde, and she is fourteen. She may be in a mood, you know?"

"We know about teenagers. I guess they're the same the world over." Sonia said.

"Yes, I suppose. She is a good girl, very smart, but sometimes…We have a daughter in Paris, at fashion school, and a son working in Belgium with a business. We have been married for 21 years. Forever." Terese smiled warmly.

The conversation continued, each person offering a brief explanation of who they were and how they came to be on a cruise ship on the Rhone as Terese navigated the winding road.

The small car slowed as it passed a low white painted wall, the turn signal activated by Terese as she maneuvered into a dirt courtyard behind the wall. She beeped the horn twice. "That will let them know we are here."

The Americans climbed out of the car, adjusting their clothing, gazing around at the straight rows of trees that surrounded the one story farmhouse. A low concrete circle with a wooden cover was between the parking lot and the orchard.

"Is that a well? For water?" Russell asked.

"Yes, it is still in use after nearly a hundred years. We keep it covered but we draw from it with pipes in the ground. This land is very old. My husband is very proud of it, you will see. Here he is, my husband, Yves."

"Bonjour, everyone. Welcome to our home. My wife has much better English, so I will just pour the wine. Come in, please," Yves smiled as he opened the wooden double door. He was wearing shorts and an old shirt, sandals on his bare feet. Dinner with the Americans was obviously going to be an informal affair. They were dressed appropriately casual, as advised by Gerard.

The entryway was a tile floor, with a step down to a cozy living space with a bulky sofa and cushioned chairs, the room dominated by a piano and a standing string bass. Music sheets were scattered carelessly on the piano top. Pillows of different colors were laying about, the setting very comfortable and lived in. Terese collected jackets as Yves offered each visitor a glass of red wine.

"Does everyone have a glass of wine?" Terese asked. "To our American friends," she toasted.

"And to our French friends," Elizabeth replied.

"Delicious," Sally said. "This wine is just delicious. Did you make it?"

"No, I am not a winemaker, but I grow grapes for the winemakers. This wine was made with the grapes from the vines on the hill. We have an apple orchard, and we also grow many vegetables we sell at market." He pronounced "vegetables" with four syllables, "veg-a-ta-bles" in the European manner.

Terese guided the visitors around the small, by American standards, old house, explaining how they had slowly extended and expanded the living space over the years. The stone structure that was the original core had been retained as additions were made. Yves and his brother had performed all the work, including wiring and plumbing.

Chinese lanterns were strung in the trees in the yard, lighting the table set with a platter of cheeses and fruits. A stone carafe offered more wine. "Please help yourself. Dinner will be ready in a little while."

Russell sat in one of the ubiquitous molded white plastic chairs that seemed to have overtaken the world. He noticed that there were no evening mosquitoes or insects of any kind in the warm moist air.

"It is so pleasant to smell the orchards and the fields. And it's so quiet."

"Yes," Yves said. "Our farm is a very peaceful place. Not too large, but enough to provide a nice living for a small family. My great grandfather and his brother began with just this small lot here but the others added to the land when they could."

"You have a son, I believe Terese said. Will he be a farmer like you?"

"No. He is in Brussels, wearing a suit to work in a big building. Farming is not for him. Too hard and ...what is the word, Terese?" Yves searched.

"Unpredictable," she offered.

"Yes, unpredictable. Some years too much rain, some years not enough." He gestured with his hands. "Our daughter in Paris is interested only in fashion and Matilde will probably follow her when it s time."

"You have a piano and a standing bass in your living room. Who plays them?"

"All of the children had to play piano, and our son played the bass for a while but then chose an electric bass. He played with some small bands, very noisy. Now no one plays it. Terese still plays piano and Matilde enjoys it some times. I just farm."

"Do you like it?" Elizabeth asked.

"Yes, very much. It is hard to work all the time, never any time off, but I love it. My brother helps me with the work and we help each other with our home building, but he lives in a town, not a real farmer like me. That is okay with me. We are different," Yves said.

The conversation was interrupted with a summons for dinner.

"This is our daughter, Matilde, who will join us for dinner," Terese said, gesturing to the young girl slouching at the rectangular wooden table. "She has helped me set the table."

The girl jerked upright, outraged at being mentioned without her permission. An eye roll followed. She was silent. She looked like her mother, with dark hair and eyes. Her face was set in a mask of polite acceptance. She was not happy with her duties this evening.

"Matilde speaks very good English, but thinks she doesn't." Terese smiled as another scowl appeared on the teenage face. She was very pretty with clear skin and dark eyes, her hair arranged to cover half of her face. Her oversized Tee shirt and her worn blue jeans were the universal costume of her age group. Bracelets adorned her left arm, and her ears had multiple piercings. The Americans recognized the act and smilingly ignored her, merely nodding at her sullenness.

"Hormones," Sally muttered as Sonia lifted her glass for a sip of wine. Elizabeth and Russell exchanged glances of recognition.

Two large bowls of pasta were placed on the rustic table, followed by a serving of a tossed salad from a wooden bowl Terese carried around the table. A red sauce covered the spaghetti, the smell of olives and anchovies filling the air. A large round bread sat on a cutting board. Yves used a well worn knife to slice pieces for everyone, fragments of crust falling onto the table.

"Please serve yourself. Yves, pass the bread. Matilde, sit up."

The guests accepted the bread and piled the pasta on their plates.

"This is wonderful. It's pasta with puttanesca sauce, isn't it?" Elizabeth asked.

Terese put down her fork, obviously upset. "Yes, that is what it's called, but I didn't think you would know that. I am embarrassed, but that is the name of the dish."

Sonia leaned forward. "Did I miss something? Why are you embarrassed?"

Elizabeth explained. "It's my fault. The name of this dish is pasta puttanesca, an Italian favorite of ours. In Italian, a 'puta' is a prostitute, and the sauce was said to be their favorite because you can make it quickly as the pasta boils. That meant the girls could get back to work sooner. Terese didn't think we would know that, so she's feeling a bit embarrassed, and shouldn't be."

Matilde had her head down, suffering from her mother's error. She was mortified. It was also clear that she understood English very well. She twirled her fork silently.

Sally laughed, breaking the awkwardness of the moment. Russell and Yves joined in, laughing at the simple innocence of it all. Matilde kept her gaze down.

"Believe me, we are not offended. The sauce is delicious and I don't care what it is called. The bread is great too. Does it have a secret name?" Sally asked.

"No, just bread. Yves made it this afternoon. Thank you, Sally."

Matilde pushed her pasta around the plate, then spoke to her mother in French, asking to be excused, her strenuous duty finished. Her wish was granted. She muttered a version of "nice meeting you" and almost ran to her room.

"She is a teenager," Terese sighed.

"We all understand. It's a difficult time, but they get over it."

"Some times," Russell said.

The pasta course was followed by a serving of grilled lamb in a dark sauce with grilled fresh vegetables. Yves explained how he and his brother, Jean, supplied wholesalers with fresh produce for the local markets, and grapes for the winemakers.

Terese questioned the group about what they did with their daily lives and listened, fascinated, to the ways in which Sally and Sonia managed their lives without a man in the house. She was also intrigued by the length of the friendship between the two women.

"So, you have been friends since childhood, yes?"

"Since first grade. We walked to school together each day. After school we stopped at one of our houses for a snack. Our mothers were best friends."

"You were more like sisters than just friends. Did you ever fight, or argue?"

"Not at first," Sally said. "That came later, in high school when we were teenagers like Matilde."

"We didn't really fight, Sal. We just disagreed a little because you were so bossy," Sonia jumped in.

"Well, you were so stubborn."

"I just knew what I wanted."

"Sonia was the most popular girl at our school," Sally attempted an explanation. "She was the prom queen, the homecoming queen. Do you know what I mean? Do you have things like prom queens in France? Help me out here, guys."

Sally reached for her wine.

"I believe I know what you mean.," Terese said. "Sonia was the beauty queen, we would say. We do have the 'most popular' ones. Matilde is involved in that now. She has her special friends who vote for her at school in elections. She is very smart as well. English is one of her best subjects, but she hides it around Americans. So, I think I understand Sonia's life as a teenager."

"It had its good side and its bad side," Sonia said. "It was nice getting all the attention, but sometimes it attracted the wrong kind of attention from the wrong people. It's a long story." She waved a hand, dismissing the memory.

Terese recognized Sonia's reluctance to continue, switching her attention to Elizabeth.

"Were you also a 'prom queen'? I said that right?"

Elizabeth hesitated, glancing at Russell. "I went to a Catholic school where boys and girls had separate classes. My father was very strict about dating, so I lived with many restrictions. I was popular, under those conditions, but the focus was different. Girls weren't allowed to take higher math classes because only boys were worth educating. We were allowed to clean and pray. School isn't a happy memory for me."

Terese nodded. "I understand. Do you have children?"

Russell replied. "Yes, and a granddaughter who is very bright and a delight to be around. She makes me want to be the very best person I can be when we are together. She is our link to the future, our chance at immortality, if it exists."

Sonia and Sally looked at each other, a silent signal passing between them. Terese lifted her chin in their direction, eyebrows raised in question. "And you?"

"We promised we wouldn't discuss our children on this trip." Sonia said.

"Or their spouses," Sally added, her tone firm. "Sorry, Terese, but it's a sore subject with us right now. Do you know what that means? Sore subject?"

"Sadly, yes. Yves and I also have rules about things we won't talk about before friends, mostly about the conduct of our children and their attitudes. Some days we want to pull our hair, yes? Each generation is different."

"You're not old enough to have been here during the war. Was your family affected by it? Were they farming this land then?" Russell probed.

"Yes, my grandfather and my father were here on this land," Yves said. "And then one day in Aix, at the market, my grandfather was chosen as a hostage by the Germans. The Maquis had been active and the Germans decided to shoot hostages as a ...what is the word?"

"Reprisal."

"That's it. As a reprisal for the death of some German soldiers. They were shot in the market square. You will see it when you go there, a marker." Yves lowered his head. "There was no reason to do that. My father and his brother had to manage on their own. It made them strong, and they made me strong. Our new generation knows nothing of the struggles they went through. They have no respect for the past."

"I believe it is time for dessert," Terese said. "I will be right back."

Yves cleared the table as the guests sat back, savoring the rich sauce and the grilled meat. Terese reappeared with an apron full of apples from their orchard. She emptied them onto the table, allowing them to roll along the worn surface.

"Voila, the most wonderful apples in Provence. Please help yourself."

The guests reached for the pale red apples, smelling their fragrance and examining their faded color. Russell was the first to bite into the fresh fruit, the skin popping. "Wonderful," he said. "Just wonderful. Full of flavor, just like apples used to be. I guess these are organic."

"Yes, I think so. We do use some disease fighting methods, but these are very natural apples," Yves explained.

The women had sliced their selections into thin slices and were enjoying the juicy flavor. "Delicious, really delicious," Sonia said.

"Coffee anyone?" Terese held a carafe of fresh brewed coffee and a tray of cups and saucers which she placed on the table. "It is the decaf so you won't have trouble sleeping."

The coffee was poured and consumed, along with the apples and some cheese, as the chatting continued, mainly about France and the standard of living in cities and towns and even villages. Like other countries, the costs went up as the size of the town increased. Cities offered more amenities, but there was a cost.

Yves slowly cleaned off the table as Terese returned to the group with two large ledgers. She placed them in front of the Americans.

"These are the visitor journals we have kept from the start of our joining the program of hosting dinners in our home. We have others in storage. We ask that you leave your names and any comments you may wish to make. Look at them if you like before you sign them."

The journal in front of the Hunters was labeled with the current year, and comments were written in different hands and inks by those who had been visitors on previous visits. At a glance, Elizabeth could see that the comments were favorable, exactly her feelings. The visit had been relaxingly informal, the dinner simple but satisfying, and the conversation interesting with few translation problems. Their hosts were charming and genuine, open in sharing their thoughts.

"How did you get involved in this program, Yves?" Russell asked.

Yves smiled broadly and nodded to Terese. "She is the one. She speaks so many languages and I had none except French. Our son does very well with English because he is in Brussels and English is the language of business. She decided I needed to learn English if our business was to grow. So, here I am, a farmer learning to speak English and understand Americans."

"Have you enjoyed the experience?"

There was a long pause as Yves considered his reply. He cleared his throat.

"I did not want to do this hosting at first because I did not like Americans. I don't like this McDonalds and Disneyland thing. Americans to me meant big, loud people always in a hurry. I did not know any, but I saw them in films and on the news. I did not think they knew France and what it is to be French."

The guests were silent.

Elizabeth spoke first. "And have you changed your mind after hosting so many of us?"

Yves smiled again. "Yes, I have. I realize America is very big, much bigger than France, and we have met people from all over that big country. Like the French, the people are different, depending on what part of America they are from. The people of Paris are not the same as the people of Viviers, or Marseilles, or Lyon. Americans from New York are not like Texans, or Californians. They speak English differently, and they see the world through their eyes, but they all are proud of their country. Not all agree with the government, the same as it is in France. Americans have as little say about politics as we do. The politicians rule the world, while we all are trying to have a nice life, a world without war and suffering. We have children, we work, we die. We are all the same in the end. Now when I think of America, I remember the faces of nice people who have sat here in my house."

The room was quiet as Yves words were absorbed.

"I think we all feel the same way about the French," Elizabeth said. "Our press and our entertainers talk in stereotypes about the French, as if they are one mass of people, all the same. According to them, all Frenchmen are like the Parisians. But they're not. And even in Paris, there are many fine ordinary people who are just trying to have a decent life. It's easy to dislike strangers, but it's hard to dislike people when you actually get to know them. We have all met many nice people like you and your family. Let the governments argue, we'll sit and have a glass of wine. Thank you so much for a most pleasant evening," Elizabeth concluded.

Matilde returned with the guest's jackets, an iPod glued to her head. She grunted a teenaged French version of goodbye. She was so bored. Hugs and farewell cheek kisses were exchanged in the graveled driveway, and Terese ferried the guests back to the Arles along the river road, empty now of even local traffic. At the boat, another round of farewell hugs and cheek kisses were exchanged as another adventure ended for the travelers. Giovanni was waiting at the gangplank.

"Welcome back. Did you have a pleasant evening?"

"It was very nice," Sonia said. "Terese and Yves were charming, and the food was really good. We had a great time. I wish we could do more visits like that, you know, to people's homes."

"I think it was one of the nicest things we've ever done in traveling. I wish we could do it more often," Elizabeth said.

"Good," Giovanni said. "I have met them both, and they are always happy to see new guests. The bar is open if you wish a nightcap. Some of the others who returned earlier are in there now."

"I think I'm ready to turn in," Elizabeth said. "But you can join them, Russell, if you'd like. I know you are wide awake."

"I might do that. I'll see if Mel and Ruth are back. I'll see you later," Russell said. "See you, ladies."

He walked by Sonia and Sally into the crowded bar as Elizabeth picked up her cabin key at the front desk.

The Iowans were clustered in what had become their usual section of the lounge, animated as usual, snifters of brandy in hand. Mel and Ruth sat on the edge of the group, looking weary. Mel waved a limp hello and sat up in his chair as Russell joined them.

"Hi. I see you have survived your visit to a French home. How was it?" Russell asked.

"Excuse me," Ruth said. "I was just about to leave. I am very tired. Mel can fill you in. I'll see you at breakfast." She leaned over, kissing Mel's cheek. "See you later."

"I won't be long," Mel replied. "Can I get you a drink? The bar's open."

"Stay seated. I'm fine. We had some very nice wine for dinner. Elizabeth is also worn out and decided to turn in. Well, how was it?"

"In a word-miserable. And that's the polite word. I need to have a little talk with Gerard." Mel leaned forward, an angry tone in his voice.

"What happened?"

"First of all, we had to walk a pretty good distance into the town. Some of the streets are cobblestone or rough, and we had some older ladies in our group who had trouble keeping up. Then, when we get there, we have this buffet table with warmed over food and some loud music blaring." Mel's voice climbed. "It felt like one of those stops you make on a bus tour where a bad restaurant rushes you through an 'included lunch.' Ruth was, and is, pissed off. So am I."

"So there was no chatting with a French family?" Russell summoned the waitress. "I think I will have a drink. A brandy." He pointed to Mel's glass.

"Not a word," Mel said. "Just a hustle and some bad wine. We left after an attempt to figure out what we were being served. It looked like macaroni and cheese, I swear to God. We walked back slowly, looking in windows, and we did stop at a cafe for a drink, so it wasn't a total loss, but some of the others had a hard time with the walk. Agnes is threatening Gerard with a letter to the company. Her friend Shirley almost fell down the steps at the restaurant."

"That's a shame," Russell said. "We had a delightful visit with a very nice family, or couple, really. Their teenage daughter couldn't have been more imposed upon. We saw their farmhouse, just a short ride from here, had wine made from their grapes, and a simple meal with fresh apples for dessert."

"Did they speak good English? Do you speak any French?" Mel asked.

"Elizabeth speaks some, but I'm hopeless. The woman spoke excellent English, and French, and Italian, and I believe some German. A true European. The husband, Yves, spoke a rougher version of English, getting the words right, but heavily accented. He had some very interesting observations about Americans. They have been hosting weekly visits for a few years now. They showed us their guest logs."

"Now that's what we expected, Mel said, arms thrown outward in emphasis. "A chance to talk with an ordinary family about how they see their lives and the Americans who drop into their living room. I'm not sure I'd open my home to foreigners like they do."

Russell sipped his brandy. It was smooth and warming.

"That's true. I hadn't thought about it, but in a way they do take a risk. We did have a wonderful visit, Sonia and Sally were with us, and we would all do it again," Russell said.

"What did you learn?" Mel asked.

"Well," Russell explained, sipping his wine, "one thing we learned, surprise, surprise, is that not everyone loves America and Americans. We are loud and threatening, insensitive to other cultures and histories, and just plain pushy. We have too much money, and we know nothing about the rest of the world and its problems. We are shallow and without concern for the future. How's that for a start?"

"Hell of a start. All of that from one visit to one family?"

"No, some of that is from my general, admittedly biased observations, but the gist of it came out in our conversations over a three hour period." He took another sip, paused, collecting his thoughts. "Yves and Terese were very honest about what they have learned, and the good news is that they have come to like and enjoy Americans as individuals, ignoring the generalities we all use for other nations and their people. You know, like when it comes to tourists, the English are stuffy, constantly complaining that no place is like England, the Germans are arrogant, the Italians noisy, and on and on. It's a common flaw we all carry in our xenophobia file."

"You're right," Mel nodded. "That's one reason why Ruth and I travel as much as we can. Your viewpoint and evaluation of other countries varies with the amount of exposure you have to the people. History teaches that the first step toward hating and killing is based on ignorance of others, which leads to the initial conclusion 'they're different.' Then comes the fear of 'the different,' followed by it's okay to attack 'the different' and kill them because 'they're different.' A simple solution, don't you think?"Mel leaned back in his chair.

"Simple, sad, and deadly," Russell agreed.

"By the way, Russell, what is your profession? Or was? I don't think I've ever asked you that question."

"You haven't. I worked in the corporate world as a business writer, PR writer, general marketing communications, but ended up teaching basic American and European history at a small community college in Georgia. Nothing spectacular."

"And here I am lecturing you on history." Mel sighed.

"No, no. We're just two old retired guys having a talk about some of life's lessons, none of which we can prove without major challenges."

"My genius children would scream at us for being judgmental, the biggest sin in their world. How you get through life without making judgments, I don't know. Some judgmental skills can save you a lot of grief."

"I agree. My judgment now calls for turning in. Sunrise comes early."

Russell rose from the table, Mel following. "Same for me, except for the sunrise part. Time for bed."

They passed by the front desk where Giovanni and Sonia were engaged in a low level conversation. She was leaning against the counter top, arms extended, fingertips interlocked. Giovanni leaned backward as the men waved and called out their goodnights.

Chapter Fifteen

Russell felt the first rumble of the engines, and reached for the travel clock. It was not quite six in the morning, not quite daylight. He remembered that the Arles was to haul anchor before dawn for the day's run to the port of Avignon, the City of Popes. They would be arriving in the early morning and would first have a walking tour of the city that housed the Pope for most of the 14th century. The afternoon offered an optional tour of the ruins of the Roman aqueduct at Pont du Gard, or could be used for additional sightseeing, the Hunter's choice. Elizabeth was interested in the fine pottery of the area and intended to do some exploring of the local shops. Russell sat up slowly, swinging his feet over the side of the bunk. He did his usual morning routine, dressing quietly, pausing at the coffee pot on his way to the sundeck. The Arles glided quietly on the placid river as he climbed the stairs. Durgan was on the bow, leaning over the rail, watching the bow wave roll out.

"Morning, Durgan" he called.

Durgan turned slowly, turning his body, not just his head, at the sound of Russell's voice.

"Good morning to you. Feels a little cooler today."

"We have been very fortunate with the weather. The cool air feels good. How was your evening? Did you get a good family visit?"

"Not really," Durgan said. "I was with a big group and we went to some local club in town. We walked a lot. The food was just chow, you know. Loud music, noisy."

"Sounds like you were with Mel. He was complaining to me late last night about his group.

"Yeah, I was with Mel and his wife and about 8 others, counting the British guys and their wives. They had a great time, boozed it up. I ducked out early, came back here and read a bit. Mel was pissed at Gerard."

"Sorry to hear that. We had a great time, a trip highlight, really," Russell said.

"Well, win some, lose some. Can I ask you a question? Are you a reader?" Durgan asked, draining his cup.

"Yes, I am. Elizabeth and I were both English majors. We read all the time, almost compulsively. Why? What's your question?"

"Well, I was talking with Sally," Durgan explained. "She backed off a bit so we get along okay now. Anyway, I was talking about how I like having order in my life, how I get uncomfortable with new things sometimes, and she said I was like a guy named Prufrock. Have you ever heard of, let me see…" He pulled a paperback book out of his jacket pocket, squinting in the dawn light. He turned the pages. "Here it is. 'The Love Song of J. Alfred Prufrock,' by T.S. Eliot."

"Yes, I have. It's one of my favorite poems. Studying T.S. Eliot is a requisite for any English major, and 'Prufrock' is discussed endlessly. Where did you get the book?"

"It was in the library. Sally found it. She told me to read the poem. The book is called Modern Verse in English, 1900-1950," Durgan explained, reading the cover. It was almost full daylight on the river.

"Are you enjoying it?"Russell asked.

"I am. I don't usually read poetry. In fact I never read poetry, but I think I get this. Prufrock is thinking about what kind of life he's going to lead, and what it will be like for him to grow old. Was Eliot old when he wrote this?" Durgan asked.

Russell reached for the book, open to the poem.

"No. He was an undergrad at Harvard when he wrote this.The poem is a strange combination, with lots of beautiful descriptive writing, and many sad images of lonely people he sees around him. He mentions seeing 'the smoke that rises from the pipes of lonely men in shirt-sleeves, leaning out of windows.' That's sad to me."

"I was hit by this line, 'I have measured out my life in coffee spoons.' I know I'll think of it every morning from now on when I make my coffee," Durgan said.

"What do you think of Prufrock,?" Russell asked. Do you like him? Dislike him?"

Durgan looked at the water drifting by, gathering his thoughts. "I think he is a guy like me, just looking to have a nice quiet life, nothing to exciting, nothing too unusual. He says, look here, he says 'I am not Prince Hamlet, nor was meant to be'... He just wants to get by. My wife never liked that. She was always pushing me to do more, take chances."

"Well, what do you think of his struggling with questions like, 'I grow old, I grow old, I shall wear the bottoms of my trousers rolled. Shall I part my hair behind? Do I dare to eat a peach?' Does that tell you anything?" Russell pressed.

"I think he's saying that sometimes it's okay to do something different, it's okay to be less rigid. If you're not willing to explore life, you might end up full of 'what if's?' I don't really know," Durgan sighed, leaned over the bow rail. "The line that got to me was about the mermaids."

"You mean, let me see, 'I have heard the mermaids singing, each to each. I do not think that they will sing to me." Durgan read.

"That's the line. I've been a Prufrock all my life, by choice. Slow, steady, dependable Durgan. I think Sally is telling me I need to work on getting the mermaids to sing to me in the time I have left, you know?"

"Durgan, you would have made a good poet yourself." Russell said.

"It's the Irish in me. Thank you."

"Time for breakfast."

Terry manned the dining room entrance as usual as the early risers assembled, led by Russell, Durgan, and then Kevin. He had had some conversations with all of the men and enjoyed their enthusiasm for new sights and adventures. They were not complainers, never refused to try something different at mealtime, and were generally in good spirits.

"Good morning, gentlemen. Ready for a breakfast treat today? We are serving, on request, fresh made waffles with fresh fruit or blueberry syrup. Of course we have our usual buffet also. Any interest?" Terry asked.

"Waffles sound great," Russell replied. "Put me down for a serving."

"Do you have any peaches? Just kidding," Durgan said with a nod to Russell.

"Waffles for me too. With syrup. I love this cruise life."

"Me too. We're going to be climbing around an aqueduct this afternoon and I'll need the energy. Just don't tell Pamela. She's very strict about her diet."

"You're not ordering for Pamela, are you? Eat what you want," Durgan advised. "Have a peach."

"What?" Kevin asked, confused.

"Just kidding. Russell and I have a little joke going."

"Oh. You're right. I can eat what I want. It's just that she has these rules..."

"Your choice," Russell said.

Terry scurried to the kitchen with the special order as the men chose the port side window seating and poured coffee as Kevin removed papers from his small backpack. "These notes are from the Avignon website. I was looking at it last night. Fascinating stuff. Did you know there were once two Popes serving at the same time? One here and one in Rome?"

"I believe I have heard about that, but I don't remember any details," Russell said. "Refresh me as I dig into these waffles with blueberry syrup."

"Okay," Kevin read. "City in Provence, France, administrative center on the River Rhône, 80 km/50 mi northwest of Marseille. Tourism and food processing are important, yada yada business facts. An important Gallic and Roman city, it has a 12th-century bridge (only half of which still stands), a 13th-century cathedral, 14th-century walls, and the Palais des Papes, the enormous fortress-palace of the Popes. It's been around a while."

"Excellent, Kevin," Durgan said. "I assume we will be seeing the half a bridge that is still standing somewhere on our journey."

Terry paused to glance at the picture of the Pont d'Avignon.

"By the time you have finished your breakfast," he said, "we will be tying up at the quay just 100 meters from that very bridge. It is the one mentioned in the French children's song, 'Sur le pont d'Avignon.'"

"Really?" Kevin exclaimed. "I know that tune. I have to get some shots of the bridge. Pamela will be thrilled."

"Where did you dine last night, Kev? Did you get to visit a home?"

"Yes, we had a delightful time with an older couple who live in an apartment that goes back hundreds of years," Kevin said, digging in to his waffles. "It was originally carved from stone, I believe. The couple who live there explained how the French health care system worked for the elderly and retired. He asked us to call him 'Papa.' I thought it was fascinating, but our other guests didn't. We were with that guy who calls himself 'Just Plain Bill,' and his wife Vicky, remember him?"

"Refresh my memory."

"At the arrival reception in Paris, he asked for American beer instead of wine, or 'overpriced grape juice' as he charmingly named it. Gerard was quietly furious," Kevin said.

"I remember now," Russell said. "His wife is very nice, little, quiet."

"Yes, Bill let it be known that this trip was all her idea and he would prefer to be home fishing on a river. Pamela was ready to kick him. He's a jerk and showed it last night when he tried to impress our hosts."

"Why do you think that?" Russell asked.

"Well, their apartment is small, maybe 1000 square feet. Bill announced he had a garage bigger than that for his two cars-one of which is a huge SUV- 'the BIG ONE,' unquote."

"What else could it be?" Durgan added sarcastically.

"It was embarrassing," Kevin explained, "but our hosts had heard all this before. They ignored it and just got nicer. We ended up sipping some excellent cognac. Bill decided to 'throw it down,' his words, and he got ripped. Papa and I shared a few secret smiles as the evening progressed. The old man knew what he was doing."

They were interrupted by Elizabeth's arrival. She pulled out a chair and joined the men.

"Good morning, guys. Umm, waffles. They look great." Elizabeth said. "Pamela's right behind me. She just stopped at the desk."

Terry materialized and quickly took the new waffle order.

Pamela arrived, and Kevin rose to pull out her chair. She sat with a sigh of satisfaction.

"Thank God you found a full table. If that Bill character gets within ten feet of me, I swear I'll jump overboard. Or maybe throw him overboard."

"What happened? Did he bother you? When?" Kevin was agitated, searching for the offender, Durgan on alert as well. Russell sat, observing.

"Stay calm, dear. It's okay," Pamela said. "He won't be bothering anyone today. He was just now at the desk pleading with Giovanni for a raw egg and tomato juice. I think he will be sleeping in a bit today."

"Rough night out?" Elizabeth asked.

Kevin spoke up.

"I was just explaining to Russell and Durgan that Pam and I ended up with Bill and Vicky on a visit to an older couple who live in a small ancient apartment in a building originally carved out of stone. Bill was his best ugly American self, insulting them in particular and France in general. The old gent, Papa, wisely fed Bill some potent cognac. I suspect Bill will be indisposed for most of the day."

Terry arrived and coffee was poured.

"He was so obnoxious. What do you do when someone you're sort of with makes a total ass of himself? I must have apologized to our hosts a dozen times. No wonder the French hate us when they meet people like him," Pamela fumed.

"I think they know the truth. Our hosts said they had been hosting visitors for more than two years, almost three. I think they have probably seen more than one Bill and Vicky," Elizabeth commented.

"Vicky was fine. She just sat there quietly, suffering in silence, the good wife."

"Sorry to interrupt. Waffles?" the waiter asked, holding the warm plate.

"Those are mine," Elizabeth said. "Is there any fresh fruit with them?"

"I will bring you a plate immediately, Madame. I also have some fresh blueberry syrup."

"I'll have the syrup. Even better."

"That looks so good. I think I'd like some waffles as well," Pamela said. "And the blueberries."

Kevin sat back in his chair, a startled look replaced by a small smile.

"Good for you, Pam. Go for the waffles."

"Well, we are on vacation, and we are supposed to crawl around a ruin this afternoon," she said, chin raised, spirits up."Loosen up, Kev."

"My thoughts exactly," Kevin smiled as his hand touched hers. "Got to keep the energy levels up." He smiled.

Pamela's face flushed. "Drink your coffee."

The Arles glided to a stop along the quay as the last of the passengers finished their breakfasts, the early finishers recording the faultless docking with their cameras. The crew scrambled to make the mooring lines secure, and the now well seasoned travelers slowly assembled on the dock for the morning tour.

Chapter Sixteen

"Welcome to Avignon," Gerard announced. He held out his notes, turning to catch the morning sun on another beautiful day. "We will soon be joined by a local guide who will provide a detailed history of the city. The important point to remember is that it was the home of the Palais des Popes from 1309 to 1377, and Avignon was the papal seat, not Rome. We will be touring the palace today and you will see the Pope's bedchamber and kitchen."

The group milled quietly, adjusting clothing, checking their cameras and water bottles, studying the small maps Gerard always provided before a tour. The mood was the usual: smiling anticipation of the next event. Gerard completed the head count, allowing for the no-shows that had reported to him that they would not be participating in the tour. Just Plain Bill was absent, as were the two British men, but Vicky was present, attaching herself to Sally and Sonia.

"I hope you don't mind if I walk with you for the tour. You always seem to have so much fun doing things." Vicky explained. "Bill is under the weather and I just couldn't stay in the cabin all morning and miss this tour. I'm Catholic and I never heard of having two Popes at the same time. My sister won't believe me unless I get some proof with pictures or something."

"You're welcome anytime. What's with Bill? Did you have some bad food last night on the home visit? Ours was great," Sally chirped, her usual cheerful self.

"I'm afraid it wasn't the food. Bill has another problem, with drink. He's hung over. I'm kind of used to it."

Sally glanced at Sonia who inhaled deeply and lowered her head, shaking it from side to side. "We understand, don't we Sonia? We've both been there with men that drank too much."

"I'm sorry. I didn't mean to bring up bad memories," Vicky apologized.

"It's okay," Sonia reassured her. "You did the right thing, leaving him in the cabin, not missing out on something important to you to take care of him. Let him puke by himself."

Vicky smiled. "That's what I figured. He'll be mad, but so what? I came here to see France."

"Good for you. And if he gives you any crap later, we'll all have a talk with him. I hate abusers." Sonia declared, "And here is our guide, I think."

"Attention, everyone," Gerard called. "Please welcome Madame Cluny, our local guide for Avignon." There was polite applause, with a small bow from Madame. She wore a long flowing light tan dress, with a colorful scarf around her neck, and a large brimmed straw hat shading her slightly lined face. Worn sandals were on her feet.

"She will be taking us on a tour of the Palais des Popes and a portion of the old town this morning. After the tour, you are free to return here for lunch, or explore on your own more of Avignon. There are many wonderful cafes available, and many lovely shopping opportunities. Please stay close together and note how to return to the boat. Follow me, please."

The group surged forward, clusters of friends forming as usual, the sun once again delivering a beautiful day free of rain and the dreaded wind called the Mistral. The travelers had been warned of the punishing wind of Provence. When a high-pressure system forms over the plateau of the Massif Central, and a low-pressure area forms over the Mediterranean, the cold mountain air begins to flow downhill, accelerating dramatically as it roars through the gap of the Rhône valley.

Madame Cluny guided the group through the narrow streets, the shop owners just beginning to open the shutters and yank up the protective metal grills in front of the shop windows. Awnings were cranked down in anticipation of a sunny day, and brooms swept entryways as the day began. Cries of "bonjour" echoed in the streets as the shopkeepers welcomed the tourists and their cash.

"The French are certainly into shoes, aren't they? Especially sneakers, or walking shoes," Elizabeth observed. "There are styles here I've never seen any where else."

"I know," Ruth added. "I love the styles and they are so comfortable. I wish I had more room to pack a few pairs home with me, but, we travel light."

"So do we. We learned on our first trip to Italy. Friends of ours warned us not to take more than one suitcase and one small handbag each and we listened to them. They were right. Never take more than you can carry comfortably."

The group paused as the Papal palace came into view. Madame Cluny climbed the steps to face the tourists and began her talk.

"Avignon has been home to seven popes. The walls built in the years immediately succeeding the acquisition of Avignon as papal territory are well preserved. The "Palais de Popes"with walls 17–18 feet thick, was built on a natural spur of rock, rendering it all but impregnable to attack. The group surged forward, following their guide. She continued her dialogue.

"Avignon, which at the beginning of the fourteenth century was a town of no great importance, underwent a wonderful development in the form of an imposing fortress made up of towers, linked one to another. The Palace of the Popes belongs to the Gothic art of the South of France, while the execution of the frescoes inside was entrusted almost exclusively to artists from Siena in Italy. Are there any questions?"

"Will this be on the test?" Mel muttered. Russell tried not to smile, but lost it. The tour guides did a wonderful job, but after days of touring, the facts and dates all ran together.

Ruth glared, not amused. Mel looked away, shrugged it off.

Vicky raised her hand.

"Yes, Madame?"

"So how was all this business with two Popes resolved?"Vicky asked. "Who became the right Pope, like we have today in Rome?"

"That is an excellent question. When we had two Popes, it was bad, but it became even worse when we had three Popes at one time. In 1414 at the Council of Constantine, the decision was made to name the new Pope Martin V, and place the seat of the papacy in Rome, where it has been ever since. There is a book for sale in the gift shop that explains this period of Catholic history. I will help you find it if you are interested," Madame Cluny smiled.

"Thank you. My sister won't believe this without a book."

"Let us move inside. The day is getting hotter already."

Madame Cluny led the group through the entrance, bypassing the ticket line, into the courtyard. "You can visit more than 20 rooms, in particular the Pope's private chambers, and see the frescoes painted by the Italian artist Matteo Giovannetti."

The tour began in the old guardroom, where Madame Cluny pointed out the Pope's coat of arms with three golden bees, hanging on the wall, followed by a look at the Pope's audience hall, before moving into the "Courtyard of Honour."

"We will move along to the room that was the banquet hall where the Pope entertained his guests, and then into the Pope's chambers and the Great Audience Hall."

The quiet shuffling continued through the cool chambers.

"I'm surprised at how all the rooms are empty. I thought they'd at least have some reproductions of the furniture used, and table settings," Elizabeth commented.

"You're right. It's just a big old stone room, isn't it?" Ruth agreed.

"The Consistory hall, Madame Cluny continued, "was where the Pope used to meet with his cardinals. The Grand Tinel or Banqueting Hall is a huge space with beautifully fitted wooden paneling built into the shape of an inverted hull," Madame Cluny explained. "It is believed that this was originally swathed in blue cloth covered with a liberal scattering of golden stars." She passed through the open doorway into what had been the Pope's private chambers, and waited for the group to join her before continuing her dialogue.

"The Pope's bedroom," she continued, "as you can see, has walls entirely decorated in tempera with foliage on which birds and squirrels perch; birdcages are painted in the recesses of the windows. "

Madame Cluny guided the group into a large room. "This is the Chapelle St-Jean, known for its beautiful frescoes, attributed to the school of Matteo Giovanetti The frescoes colors are still vibrant after almost 700 years."

The crowd moved slowly, savoring the sight of a timeless masterpiece. Conversation was hushed as the art overwhelmed the audience. Sunlight filled the open hallway.

"And now we have come to the end of the tour. Just ahead is the palace gift shop and bookstore where you can buy souvenirs and gifts for your friends and family. Thank you for your attention. Are there any questions?"

Mel and Russell scanned the crowd, silently willing them to be silent. They had both reached the point that comes on every tour when the facts being quoted become meaningless, and great art becomes just another beautiful thing.

The travelers glanced at each other, then broke into polite applause for the efforts of the guide. As they shook her hand in gratitude, many handed her a separate tip of Euros, a common practice on tours. The crowd dispersed, eager to be on their own for further explorations.

Mel and Russell sought out the toilet facilities while their wives visited the gift shop.

"So, how do you like the palace?" Mel asked.

"Well, it could use some furniture and some decorating, but I got the general idea," Russell said. "The Popes lived well, the people struggled. Nothing much has changed. Lots of stone, cold rooms, great art, bookshop, end of tour."

"I agree. Enough already. I think Ruth is ready for some serious shopping this afternoon, but I'm going to get some deck time on the boat and do some light reading after lunch. I'm feeling a bit worn down. She said something about a pottery shop when she was talking at breakfast with some of the other women."

"I think we're going to have lunch in town, but I think Elizabeth might like to join the ladies later for the pottery search. I can only say 'that's nice' so many times in one day. I'll mention it to her. Thank you, Melvin."

"It's what I do." Mel's arms spread wide, palms upward.

"And you do it so well."

Outside the palace, Frank and the ladies were consulting a travel guide, searching for a restaurant for lunch rather than returning to the boat. A rubber tired "tour train" of open cars pulled through the streets by a small motor idled in the square. Other groups of tourists were buying tickets and selecting their seats for the town tour.

"So, are you staying in town or heading back to the boat?" Ruth asked Elizabeth as they emerged from the palace gift shop with their purchases.

"I believe we're going to wander about and find a spot later for a long lunch and people watching. Russell has been studying the guidebook and I think he's found a cafe that sounds interesting. And you?"

"Mel wants to have some quiet time on the boat for some reading, and I told Sonia and Sally I'd go look at pottery with them later this afternoon. There are some great stores here, according to Gerard."

"That sounds reasonable. It's nice when you realize you don't have to spend every minute with someone."

"If you did, retirement would be very difficult, if not impossible. We all have different interests and Mel and I give each other a lot of room. Keeps life interesting. Here's a table. Why don't we wait here for the guys?" The women pulled out the metal backed chairs, their gift bags on the tabletop.

"Ruth, do you ever feel a bit overwhelmed when you realize how much of your life has passed? " Elizabeth asked as they sat. "I mean, when you hear yourself saying you've been married almost fifty years, does that seem impossible?"

"Yes, it does. Maybe not that the time has passed, but that it passed so quickly. I wake up some days and I think I'm just entering my forties, almost done with raising teenagers. Then it hits me that my grandchildren are becoming teenagers."

Elizabeth nodded. "I rarely think of age as an excuse for not doing something, like some of our friends do. We're going to keep active, learning, exploring, and traveling as long as we can. You can't stop aging, but you can stop complaining about it and enjoy what's available. At least, that's what I plan to do when I retire."

"You have the right attitude, Elizabeth. Retirement is a special state of mind, and we see people who love it, and people who are miserable with it. It's a matter of choice and mind set. Mel and I live our lives the way we want to now, not the way our children or other relatives want us to. We're much happier since we made that breakthrough. Mel does enjoy working at the community center with people."

"Thank you. Russell and I came to the same conclusion a short time ago. We're ready now for the good times, if we can stay healthy. I've been worried about him since his prostate scare. He changed somehow. I'm trying to get him back to his old self. I don't want to retire and just sit."

"There they are," Ruth gestured as she spotted the men standing in the shade of the palace. The day had become very warm. "I agree," she told Elizabeth.

"What happened to our group? Where did everyone go?" Ruth asked.

"Some went back to the boat, some took the trolley ride, and some are just wandering the streets, waiting for their wives to tell them what to do next," Mel said.

"Well, Mr. Congeniality, we are returning to the boat and the Hunters are going wandering, okay? After lunch you are on your own as I will be shopping with the ladies. How's that for a plan?" Ruth smiled.

"Paradise," Mel replied with a wide smile. "I'm going to find a deck chair, some shade, a glass of something alcoholic, and a good book to doze off with."

"Enjoy," Russell said. "We are off to the Cafe of the Artists for a leisurely lunch and some serious idle moments watching the French and others pass by."

"Which direction is the boat?" Mel asked, scanning the street.

"Right this way. At the bottom of this hill, you turn right. We will go straight. See you this evening."

The friends strolled slowly along the old streets once walked upon by the various Popes of Avignon and their courtiers. The sense of history was present everywhere among the faded buildings with their tiled roofs and wooden shutters. The Weinsteins waved as they turned onto the side street leading to the river and the boat. Mel was moving very slowly.

"What did you say was the name of the restaurant you've selected?" Elizabeth asked as they strolled.

Russell reached into his back pocket and extracted a thin, well-creased flyer for Avignon. "It is the Cafe des Artists on the square of something I can't quite make out, but it is close by on a street just inside the old wall next to the river. It's just a short walk from the boat. If we don't like it, there are more cafes very near by."

"And you selected this one because..."she paused, the question hanging in the humid air.

"I like the name."

"Sound reasoning." She smiled.

"It has always served me well."

They continued their slow walk, comfortable with each other as always. Their early dates had been mostly walking, talking about their dreams, their desire to escape from their tired world of struggling to get ahead in even the smallest ways.

"Have you noticed anything unusual about how the crowds move here?" Elizabeth asked.

"No, not really. What have I missed?"

"Well, the streets are filling up with people, but no one is moving quickly, moving in and out of the group, pushing ahead. Everyone seems to adjust to a slowdown by slowing down, and waiting. No one seems to be in a hurry."

"Maybe they're all tourists with lots of time, like us."

They passed another shoe store.

"Some must be locals with jobs. Surely someone is late for something."

"I salute those who refuse to rush," Russell said. "Just another thing I admire about the French. This is our turn, by the way. The river wall is dead ahead, and there are cafes on both sides of the street. Look for a sign, or say something if you see a cafe that looks good."

The Hunters glanced down the tree-shaded street, scanning the colorful umbrellas that marked each cafe's site. All the storefronts were open for business with a flow of slow moving shoppers drifting along on both sides.

"I think I see the cafe, left side, black and yellow umbrellas, next to the steps going up the wall to the street," Elizabeth said.

"Good eyes. I believe you're right. Yes, you are. There's the sign."

A white coated middle-aged man smiled at them as they approached the small desk. He made a slight bow.

"Bonjour, and welcome to the Cafe des Artists. Table for two?"

"Bonjour, and yes, a table for two, preferably outside."

"Of course. Follow me please."

The host led them to a small tabletop under an umbrella with a view of the open square where shoppers were beginning to gather for an early lunch. Sunlight sparkled off the glasses at each place setting, the white of the napkins almost vibrating in the overhead sunlight. Flocks of pigeons circled and landed in random patterns on the square, searching for food.

"All we need is an accordion playing softly and Gene Kelly and Leslie Caron will dance by," Russell mused as they were seated.

"It is perfect, isn't it? Just like a postcard."

"I always stress the need for in depth research for things like picking a restaurant in a foreign land. And the name is nice too."

Elizabeth sighed the long amused sigh of the contented spouse, pleased to know she made the right decision those may years ago when they first met and dared to share their dreams. They were always comfortable with each other, always offering support and encouragement as they moved forward in life. In all the years, they had never been bored with each other.

They studied the menus carefully, grateful for the English translations provided, sipping the chilled house white wine Russell ordered, while nibbling on the excellent bread with sweet butter. A soft breeze began as if on cue as they raised their glasses in a toast.

"To us."

"To us. Umm, delicious. What are you having? Or are you still deciding?"

"I think a salad. Something local, maybe this salad with all the garlic. Sounds so profoundly Provence," Russell explained. "You know, with a little encouragement, I could become a real snob."

"Not with me, but maybe with your second wife."

Russell winced, shaking the menu.

"I think I'm going to have a salad also. And the bistro beefsteak. Rare, if possible," Elizabeth put down her menu with a grin.

"I always knew I'd marry a woman who liked red meat. I will have the garlic salad and a bowl of seafood chowder and two or three loaves of this bread. How's that?"

Russell nodded to the waiter, and they placed their order, recharging their glasses from the wine carafe. The waiter took away the empty bread basket, promising to return with more of the crusty loaf.

"So, my dear, are you ready to come clean with our traveling companions as to your true identity?" Russell asked.

"You mean the part about my being a psychologist?"

"That's the part."

"I don't see any need to, do you? When people hear the word 'psychologist,' they start looking for an analysis or advice for 'a friend' or relative. We agreed that this trip was strictly a vacation, with a little bit of retirement planning mixed in, but mostly a vacation, remember? Besides, if I'm going to retire, I need to get used to not working inside people's heads anymore."

"You're right. But, knowing you as I do, I can see you taking mental notes every time we are with the group. Any special people so far that got your interest?"

The young, dark haired waiter appeared with their food as Russell's question waited for an answer. The service was correct and efficient. They started on their salads.

"Well, obviously, Mel and Ruth have worked it out, except for Mel's running battle with Gerard. Sonia has a story to tell, and probably Sally does too. Durgan the widower is interesting, and the Iowa people have mixed results from small town living. Based on what we learned from last night's visits, Just Plain Bill and his long suffering wife, Vicky, must have a heck of a story going on, but I haven't found any possible axe murderers. Oh, yes, Kevin and Pamela seem to be rediscovering each other without their kids."

"In those bunk beds?" Russell asked, grinning.

"You know what I mean. They just need to rediscover themselves."

Russell smiled. "I've been meaning to talk to you about that. The doc says I'm coming along nicely, and should be fully recovered by the time we get back home." His face had reddened. He kept his eyes down, feeling awkward and hating his embarrassment. He sipped the cool wine.

"Well, that's good news. I assume I'm included in the welcome home party?" Elizabeth asked.

"Of course. I just, well, I wasn't sure how to tell you. This is embarrassing for me. I've always been able…"his voice trailed off, the words failing.

"Russell, I love you. I will always love you. I understand how you must feel, how you don't want to disappoint me. But there is more to us than that. We have something rare. Sooner or later, you have to face the basic reality of aging. Nothing will separate us as far as I'm concerned. Stop apologizing or worrying. We'll work it out." She squeezed his hand. He wiped at his eyes with his white napkin.

"Damn sun is bright," he said. "Did you notice anything else about our little world of happy travelers?"

"Well, this trip is not inexpensive. It's not a week in a condo at the beach. And, many of our fellow travelers have taken similar trips. They are curious, not afraid of being in a foreign country, and in general, well educated. They probably have less money problems than most people, and lead active lives. They are definitely not just sitting around waiting for the end while watching daytime television. I don't think you could call this group 'typical retirees' in the usual sense."

"Hmm. That's true. But, money issues aside, the issues of aging still apply. We all have to deal with the same realities. Unfortunately," Russell sighed.

They continued with their lunch, watching the passing crowd and trying to guess their nationalities. The Americans were the easiest to identify by their loud voices, light colored clothing, water bottles, and walking shoes. Digital cameras in pockets had eliminated the camera slung across the chest of previous years, and few women carried big purses, the lessons of pick pocket prevention being heeded. Few Americans smoked, and a pale group of darkly dressed and made up scruffs passing by with a smoky exhaust from their cigarettes, defiance on their clenched fist faces, were identified as definitely European, most likely Bosnian.

Elizabeth silently cut and consumed thin slices of her rare beefsteak while Russell drained the last drop of seafood from his bowl, wiping it clean with the delicious fresh bread. He poured the last of the wine between their glasses, and sat back with a smile, content.

"It feels so good to just slow down and be absorbed by the current world. I am ready for a break from the tour routine and the statistics and dates. No more cathedrals, please. You know we just have one more night on the boat, then we switch back to the bus for our trip to Aix and then Nice," Russell said.

"I will miss the boat. It is such a pleasant way to travel and meet people. And convenient, no daily repacking and leaving suitcases outside hotel rooms at 5:00 a.m."

"I like the entire feeling of being part of a special community. I love the sun deck and the small bar and the whole feeling of traveling in style, without hassles. I'll miss it."

"Are you ready to go back home?" Elizabeth asked.

"Almost. I still want to see the rest of the towns and sights, but I'll be ready when the time comes. I just dread that long flight home. But it is in daylight, so maybe I'll be able to enjoy an afternoon nap going back."

The waiter removed the dishes, brought coffee and suggested dessert options, which were declined. The sun had shifted, requiring an adjustment of the umbrella. As the waiter made the adjustment and Elizabeth was no longer facing into the sun, she noticed a woman wearing a red silk scarf sitting outside a cafe across the narrow side street. She squinted slightly, seeing something familiar in the woman's posture and clothing.

"Russell," she said, "That woman at that table over there looks like Sonia, don't you think?"

Russell looked as directed, eyes sweeping the cafe. "The one with the red scarf? By herself? I think you may be right. Do you see Sally?"

"No, she's alone. But not for long. Look who's here," Elizabeth smiled as she watched a silver haired, well-tanned man in casual European clothing approach Sonia with a slight bow before joining her at the table.

"So, she is not alone. I wonder who that is?"

"Try to see him in a white uniform," Elizabeth suggested.

"My God, you're right. It's Giovanni. I guess he gets some time for sightseeing too."

"What a happy coincidence," Elizabeth laughed.

"You know, I've always believed that if you wanted to have an affair with some one and not be found out you should meet in the most public of places. Then it could be a coincidence, but when you happen to meet in an obscure location, it looks a bit strange. Like now, when he seems to be holding her hands."

"It's really none of our business, is it?"

"None at all. We need to slip away before they see us. The bill is paid. Are you ready?"

The Hunters quietly left the cafe as a group of students appeared, laughing and waving political signs supporting the female candidate for president of France in the coming election. Their leader, bullhorn in hand, began a chant as they crossed the plaza in front of the Hunters. Recognizing them as Americans, the leader asked in English, "Are you American?"

Russell replied they were and was asked if they were enjoying their visit to France. "Of course," he replied very congenially as the bullhorn was raised to catch his answer. "We love France and its wonderful people."

A scattered applause and whistles greeted his answer. The bullhorn was raised again. "Do you know we are going to elect a new president in a few days?" the leader asked.

"Yes, we do," Elizabeth answered.

"And who should that be?"

"Why, Madame, of course," she spoke into the amplifier as cheers erupted from the students.

The people at the cafes were smiling and laughing at the light hearted display of political maneuvering and good humor, applauding the American for her clever response. Elizabeth glanced around the square, surprised at the sudden thrust into the spotlight, and made direct eye contact with Giovanni, who nodded politely. Sonia sat with her head averted. The student demonstrators moved on.

"I just made a direct hit on Giovanni. I think we need to say hello."

The Hunters threaded their way through the lunch crowd, acknowledging waves and smiled greetings. The mood was very warm and accepting, no language skills needed.

"Hi," Elizabeth said as Russell nodded. "I wasn't sure it was you in those civilian clothes. Hello, Sonia."

"Hello, we were just discussing some shopping places. Would you like to join us?" Giovanni offered.

"Thank you, but we've just finished lunch and are about to do some more walking. Elizabeth was told there are some great pottery outlets here, so we may give that a look."

"That's just what we were talking about," Sonia interjected. "Here's a flyer about this shop just down the street from here, I think. Giovanni was giving me directions."

Elizabeth took the flyer and glanced at the pictures. "I think I remember passing this place."

"Yes, it is just a short walk down a side street. You turn at the statue of a pirate and follow until the end where the shop is. Very nice pottery at reasonable prices. I think a group of women are planning on being there, maybe a drink after?"

"Thank you. We'll check it out."

"You may see Sally and Vicky there. I'm supposed to meet them at, oh my God, ten minutes ago," she said, glancing at her watch. "I've got to run. Thank you for the coffee and the advice, Giovanni. I'll see you at the boat later. Elizabeth, see you there?"

"In a while. We're strolling today."

Sonia left in a swirl as Giovanni sipped his drink. "Are you sure you can't join me for a drink? It would be my pleasure."

Russell hesitated, turning to Elizabeth.

"I have an idea," Russell offered."Why don't you catch up to the ladies, see the pottery, maybe have a drink with the ladies, and I'll have a drink here. I'll track you down in, say a half hour."

"Oh. You realize you'll miss out on seeing a lot of great pottery?"

"I can live with that," Russell grinned. "Don't talk to any men with tattoos."

Russell kissed Elizabeth's cheek and seated himself at the table, deciding on a glass of Pastis, matching Giovanni's selection. He added water to his glass of the liqueur and watched the color change to a golden hue. He sipped the drink, the refreshing anise flavor rushing to his mouth.

"Good?" Giovanni asked.

"Very good. I have come to genuinely appreciate the art of the subtle aperitif instead of a heavy cocktail. Especially on a very warm day. Delightful," Russell said.

"You would make a good European. You have the right attitudes, an appreciation for life and its nuances."

"Thank you. I am realizing it more and more, now that I am retired and my time is my own. Life is different when you don't have to account for every minute. Not wasting time is a curse in my country, I'm afraid. I've been trying to adjust to a new way of living," Russell said.

"My friend, you cannot waste time," Giovanni advised. "Time is always there. You can just choose to use it differently, as you prefer. There is nothing wrong with sharing a drink and watching pretty girls pass by. It is not a waste of time. Think of it as a sensible use of time."

"I'll remember that. "

They sat quietly, sipping Pastis, watching the passing parade.

"May I ask a question?" Russell leaned forward.

"Of course. What do you want to know?"

"Do you remember when you and I came upon the new English waitress behind your desk?"

"Yes, you mean Brenda."

"I left when you met with Terry, and you both seemed very concerned. Is there a problem with her?"

"You are very perceptive. We try to watch all of our staff very carefully. We have direct responsibilities for 42 people, and we want their time with us to be as perfect as possible. Terry, Gerard and I are watching her closely. We have considerable quantities of cash on hand, both dollars and Euros, and we must be on guard."

"I understand. I will tell you if I see or hear anything involving Brenda."

"Good," Giovanni said. "You know, when you said you wanted to ask me a question, I thought it was going to be about Sonia. I admit she has caught my eye. She is a very attractive woman, as is your wife Elizabeth, and Ruth, and others I have met. I find American women to be very interesting, very strong in their feelings. I am sure you are wondering about my being here with Sonia." He finished his Pastis.

"Well, that's your business." Russell smiled, leaning back in his chair. He was very curious.

"Yes, it is, but I want to reassure you there is nothing romantic between us. I do not get involved with passengers when I am working, and it could cost me my job if a complaint were filed. If I see someone after a cruise is over, that is different, but the truth is Sonia is the one who is not interested in anything beyond friendship. That is what she was telling me today. She did not offer details, but she has had bad experiences with men, I suspect."

"Too bad," Russell said. "She is a strong woman, not to be taken lightly. Maybe she needs some time to adjust if she has just lost a husband or maybe she isn't sure what to do and needs to avoid getting close to someone again."

"My thoughts also. There is time if it is to be, but I also do not want any serious involvement with a woman at this time. I like my freedom, even if it is lonely on occasion. I would appreciate if you didn't mention this meeting with the other passengers," Giovanni said.

"I give you my word. And some advice. Never hold hands in public. It draws attention," Russell said.

"What? Oh, I understand. The reason I was holding her hands was she was showing me how she had damaged her hands with chemicals she used to treat women's hair. I was telling her of a French cream that helps damaged hands. That is all."

"I believe you, "Russell said slowly, "but a casual observer may not see it that way."

"What can I say? The truth is always the truth."

"Thank you for the drink. I think I need to find the ladies." Russell stood, adjusting his clothing.

"My pleasure."

Chapter Seventeen

Russell walked slowly through the plaza, feeling that special feeling he always felt when traveling alone. He was in his own private world, not responsible to anyone at the moment. He could stop anywhere, he could explore any interest, he could just observe, letting his mind open up to new sights, smells, sounds. He loved life, and learning. Learning to read at an early age first fueled his natural curiosity, and started his life long journey into exploring the past and thinking about the future. Meeting Elizabeth had been his greatest fortune. She shared his curiosity, even surpassing it in some areas of knowledge. She was ready to go anywhere, anytime, insatiable about learning. Together they had overcome the working class poverty of their youth, and built a wonderful life, happily sharing their accomplishments.

The diagnosis of cancer after a routine screening test had shaken him to his core. He had always been so energetic, up at dawn, running for miles before sunrise, a stack of books next to his chair or on his nightstand. Elizabeth was amazed at his good health, noting that he never had a headache or even a cold, a fact he laughed off as a result of his genetic pool. Then the world turned upside down. All the energy, all the exercise, all the great thoughts were ineffective. He was helpless for the first time in his life, and slowly he felt himself shutting down, waiting for the worst. Why plan when there was no future? Why study the past when he would soon be part of it? He drifted into a dark area, sinking deeper daily. Finally, at Elizabeth and his doctor's urging, he chose a procedure to eliminate the cancer, and hopefully not destroy his quality of life. To his overwhelming delight, the procedure was a total success. He would be watched closely, with quarterly testing to monitor his status, but he appeared to have survived, with high expectations of a return to normal.

His biggest challenge now was to regain the confidence and spirit he had taken for granted for so long. Elizabeth was right as usual. Each day of their trip, he felt his old self returning. It was time to get over the past and embrace the future.

Turning the corner of the side street, Russell saw the pottery shop sign further along, and the bright yellow umbrellas of a café across the narrow alley. He would treat himself to a second Pastis while he waited.

The sound of women laughing came from the pottery shop as the small group of ladies from the Arles slowly emerged onto the sunny street, bags holding their recent purchases in hand. Russell immediately saw Sonia and Sally, together as always, leading the way, with Ruth and Elizabeth close behind, followed by the Iowa ladies, whose names he could never keep straight. Agnes and Shirley slowly emerged into the bright sun, hands raised to block the glare. The group slowly drifted across the narrow lane to the café with the yellow umbrellas.

Russell waited, knowing Elizabeth wanted time to talk with the group and hear about their experiences with retirement. She had scheduled her retirement date to be a few days after her 65Th birthday, less than a week after their return from the river cruise. Elizabeth was looking forward to being finished with the corporate world, but had some misgivings, as most people do. Leaving an active life, interacting with many people every day for an unstructured life spent mostly with one person, was a major transition to face. She was interested in hearing how other women had adapted to their new world, what problems they faced, and how they managed them. She and Russell had always enjoyed good, open communications, talking about plans, and dealing with difficult decisions in a calm, rational matter. She wanted to maintain that in their retirement years. She wanted an organized life, as stress free as possible, with time to explore various interests they shared.

Russell's problem became a major challenge to these plans when he began showing symptoms of depression. Elizabeth was hoping the exposure to other successfully retired men on the trip, some of whom also had to overcome health challenges, would help him regain his eagerness for life and its experiences.

A sharp cry came from the sidewalk café where the women had gathered. Russell turned at the sound, looking down the narrow street, seeing the women moving quickly, Sally jumping to her feet. He ran to the café. The women were all standing in a circle, Sally at the center, leaning over the small figure of Agnes, slumped in a café chair.

Russell called to Elizabeth at the edge of the group. "What happened? Do you need help?"

"It's Agnes," she said. We were just talking and she just dropped her glass and fainted, I think. Sally's looking at her now. She's awake."

"Giovanni's at the café. I'll get him."

Russell rounded the corner, almost colliding with the onrushing Purser.

"I heard a cry," Giovanni said.

"It's Agnes. Sally's giving her first aid." The men reached the café to find Agnes sitting in the shade, drinking water, being fanned by Shirley. Giovanni moved through the crowd.

"Is she all right?" he asked. "Do we need an ambulance?"

Sally turned at the sound of his voice. "I'm glad you're here. I think it's just a heat reaction. Her temperature feels high, and she's a bit dehydrated from all the walking on cobblestones. She should probably be looked at."

"Of course. There is a small clinic nearby. If she can walk, we can take her there."

"Let's get some water into her."

Chapter Eighteen

On the Arles, Terry stretched the kinks out of his back, swaying gently, enjoying the sunshine and clean air on the sundeck. A slight breeze came out of the south, from the Mediterranean. Lunch had been served, the dining room once again cleaned and prepared for the next event. His crew had performed with a minimum of supervision. They would only get better as the touring season progressed. Tomorrow they would make their last port of call, arriving at Arles in the morning after a night cruise. The usual breakfast would be served, the guests would leave for their morning tour of the small city, and his crew would prepare for a small lunch onboard. In his experience, most of the travelers had lunch in town when possible, preferring to mix with the locals. In the evening, they would celebrate the Captain's Farewell Dinner with a cocktail reception, followed by dinner and some entertainment provided by a local vocalist and keyboard player. He had alerted his set up crew to be prepared to move furniture should the passengers decide to dance, as sometimes happened.

The next morning, the travelers would depart, boarding the motorcoach for the rest of their journey to Aix-en-Provence and Nice. The Arles would be thoroughly cleaned and re-provisioned for its journey back north with a new group of travelers, and the memory of this first group of the season replaced with new faces and names. Life would go on.

Terry's gaze shifted as taxis appeared at the top of the landing area, returning the tour group from the Pont du Gard aqueduct in Nimes. The aqueduct was ancient, built in AD 19, a masterpiece of Roman engineering that delivered water from Uses to Nimes, thirty miles away, without the use of pumps or motors. It was an astonishing accomplishment.

Terry watched the guests returning, Gerard talking to a circle of drivers from the taxis. By the gestures of waving arms in classic Gallic postures, it appeared the conversation was not cordial. Kevin, the one with the BlackBerry, saw Terry and waved.

"Welcome back. How was your visit?" Terry asked.

"The aqueduct was great. Unbelievable, in fact. We had a great time, once we got there. I'll fill you in when we get on board."

The lady pottery shoppers were next to appear, shopping bags swaying with their purchases, one lone man at the end of the short column. Terry recognized Russell, strolling with a smile of pleasure on his face as he watched his wife with the other women, giggling like schoolgirls. It was a happy sight.

Kevin huffed up the winding stairs, gripping the hand rail. His face was flushed, his fair white skin showing some sunburn. Pamela trailed behind, also with signs of mild sunburn.

"Good to be back on board. That was a hot one," Kevin offered.

"Yes, your face looks like you got some sun. How was your tour?" Terry asked. "Can I get you some water?"

"We just need some shade for now. The taxis we were in had no air, and it was a scary drive on narrow roads. Plus, we did far more climbing around the ruins than we anticipated. It reminded us of hikes we used to take when we first met and camping was all we could afford."

"But that was our choice, Kevin. You wanted to get all those shots of the aqueduct. I didn't think it would be so hot at this time of year."

"I thought you were going on a tour bus. What happened to that?" Terry asked.

"Well," Kevin said. "it seems that we didn't have enough people signed up to pay for a bus, so Gerard said we could cancel or go by taxi. We voted for taxis, and Gerard made the calls. The drivers didn't want to run the AC because it uses gas, I guess, and our driver, at least, wouldn't budge. Coming back was much warmer than going there. We need showers and cool air."

"I think something else happened between Gerard-and the drivers. They were arguing about something when we got there." Pamela explained. "Probably the price."

"Well, at least you are back in one piece. And so is Gerard. Bonjour, Gerard."

"Bonjour, Terry, Kevin, Pamela. I apologize for the inconvenience caused by the drivers today. They decided to become difficult when it was time to return, but I set them straight," Gerard nodded, anger still in his eyes.

"It is not easy being a PD, is it Gerard?"

Gerard smiled, laughing at himself and his loss of control. "These French can be so obstinate."

Terry laughed at the self-confession, glancing over Gerard's shoulder, noting the arrival of another taxi. He watched as Giovanni, in his off duty attire, and Sally, helped two elderly women from the car. He struggled for their names.

"Excuse me. What are the names of the two women Giovanni is helping? I can't remember."

Gerard squinted. "That is Agnes, the one he is assisting, and her friend Shirley, with Sally. Agnes does not hear well, and Shirley has difficulty walking. I have been watching them carefully. Agnes seems to be having a problem."

Giovanni held Agnes's arm as he led her across the short gangplank onto the boat, Shirley following closely.

"I better go see if I can help," Terry said as he went below.

"I need a shower. Now." Pamela stated, arms raised away from her body.

"Why don't you go do that, and I'll come down later and clean up. I'll sit here and have a drink. Look, there's Mel. I'll go say hello." Kevin stood.

"Okay. See you later," Pamela said."I have our key."

Mel looked up from his novel, watching the arrivals as they settled into the deck chairs, ordering cool drinks, examining purchases and reviewing pictures taken. He would miss them when the trip was over. They were a very upbeat group, not dwelling on their advancing age, as so many of their neighbors back in Florida did. He refused to take part in conversations about which pills people were taking for which illnesses. He treasured a card his wife received from their old friends in New York. It was an announcement from Marvin, a former business partner, of his 80th birthday. It read, "I'm 80. I'm here. What's there to complain about?" Mel framed it. When he returned to Florida, he was going to resign from the grief committee. Enough with the negatives already. He had plans for the future.

Kevin smiled at Mel, "Hi, you look comfortable. Good book?"

"This? Pretty good. Good enough for reading on a vacation on a boat in France. Learning is nice, but on vacations, I like the light stuff, nothing that makes my head hurt. How was the aqueduct trip?"

"Terrific," Kevin said. "We had a transportation problem, not enough people for a bus, but overall, it was really fascinating. The Romans built it so long ago, thousands of years ago, and it is still standing." Mel gestured to the empty chair and Kevin sat down.

"I wonder if the Romans were a superior group of people, far advanced for their time? Like, if they were alive today, would they be exploring space in fabulous vehicles? Would they be the smartest people on earth?"

"I've wondered about human intelligence and how it occurs," Mel said. "It would seem that if we have evolved physically over the centuries, getting bigger, stronger, sturdier, than shouldn't we have seen a steady improvement in intelligence, each generation being smarter? The Egyptians ruled for 5000 years, built the pyramids, tracked stars. What happened? How did we lose their knowledge and end up with the Dark Ages?"

"That's very interesting," Kevin said. "What propels us forward, and what holds us back? I guess things like warfare, natural catastrophes, disease outbreaks..."

"And don't forget religious disagreements," Mel added. "It's an intriguing concept to understand."

"I'll run it by Pam. She usually has a different way of seeing things. It certainly changes how you view things when you travel, doesn't it?"

"It does. It's good that you can run things by your wife, you know. As long as you have that, you'll always have respect for each other and you'll never be bored," Mel advised.

"Right. Pamela and I have talked to each other more on this trip than we have at home in six months. I didn't realize how much time raising kids takes. I'm not complaining, I love our kids, but it is work. You and Ruth must talk a lot. And the Hunters seem to be the same. They just seem so relaxed with each other."

"I'll tell you a secret about why I married Ruth. She was the first girl I met who argued with me. Most girls agreed with everything a guy said if they were looking for a husband. Not Ruth. If she thought she was right, she stood her ground. I was fascinated by knowing a woman who really didn't need me in her life if everything had to be my way. I never forgot that lesson. End of lecture. As far as the Hunters, it's all about sex with them."

Mel watched Kevin's face, waiting for the shocked look. "Just kidding, Kevin. Got you."

Kevin laughed the nervous laugh of relief. He was embarrassed when he thought of people older than him having a sex life. He wondered what his children thought about their parents. He'd talk to Pam about it.

"Hi, guys. We're back." Ruth announced.

"Hi. I was just leaving. See you at dinner."

"Bye, Kev," Elizabeth called as chairs were rearranged. "Well, Melvin, did you enjoy your quiet afternoon?"

"It was great. How was shopping?"

"Okay. Mostly ordinary stuff, but some unique pieces. Nothing worth hand-carrying home. But we did have some excitement with Agnes. She had a major dizzy spell. Sort of fainted. Thank God she was sitting at the time. Sally took care of her. She was a nurse, you know. It was hot, and I think the walking in the heat got to her. Giovanni came by and they quickly got her to a clinic, I think."

"They just got back. I remember her. She loved to tell Gerard she couldn't hear him when he made his announcements on the bus. I think she made a game of it. Feisty lady," Mel said. "Shirley, too."

"What about you? Did you find anything, Russell?" Mel teased.

"As a matter of fact, I had a drink with Giovanni while the women shopped. Nice guy. We talked about the European concept of retirement, among other things."

"What's so different?"

"Depends on the country," Russell explained, "but basically it's the involvement the government has in your life, with pensions and health care and benefits. It's socialism versus capitalism. One of the big problems the US has is we are a capitalist society trying to implement a socialist program while pretending it isn't one. I have no further answers."

"Now you know the secret of aging well," Mel said. Let someone else find the answers."

"So, nothing on the social agenda tonight other than dinner, and a night cruise to Arles, right?"

"That's it. And a little talk by Gerard about our final day in Arles. At last we get to see where van Gogh lived, and ate and drank his absinthe, and painted. I will miss this little boat. It has been such a pleasant way to travel," Elizabeth said.

"Well, let's make the most of it. I need to freshen up. Ready, Russell?"

"I like the sound of that," Russell grinned. "Later, guys."

"Is Elizabeth blushing?" Ruth asked.

"She should be so lucky," Mel leered, Groucho style.

Russell stretched out on the bunk as Elizabeth washed her face and hands, then brushed her teeth. She walked out of the bathroom wiping her face on the small hand towel. "Are you awake?" she asked.

"Of course. Just resting my eyes from the glare of the sun of Provence. What's up?"

"We had a nice little talk at the café before Agnes had the attack."

"Good. Did you get any insights to living with a retired spouse?" Russell asked.

He raised up on the thin pillows, head against the wall.

"Yes and no," Elizabeth said. "The biggest problem seems to be deciding territorial rights. Most of the women feel that the home is theirs. They have been doing the cleaning and cooking and general home management for all of their married life, and they don't welcome intruders."

"Even if the intruder has been paying all or a significant amount of the bills?"

"It's not about the money. It's about a newcomer interfering with an established routine. Worse is when an attempt is made to change a procedure. Debbie has a set time of the day for her cup of tea, her family phone calls, her meal planning, and she does not like Larry, her husband, interrupting her to ask when will lunch be ready?'

"Aha. I see. What else?"

"There are some minor things, like who reads the paper first, who does the crossword first. But mainly it's a question of who is in charge and who should be quiet and adjust."

"Sounds like when you first get married. I was telling Kevin that a good marriage is one where a rhythm is established, where you sort out responsibilities and schedules for all the things involved in running a house." Russell said.

"Right, except after almost 50 years, both parties seem to think they have everything in place. You really need to approach retirement with open eyes and a new plan of behavior," Elizabeth said.

"That's why you got those big psychology bucks."

"Seriously, Russell, couples need to talk, to communicate. It's a new way of life and needs new rules of behavior. One of the other ladies said her husband drove her crazy at first because he just "hovered" over her. She couldn't peel a potato without his questioning what she was doing and why, and wondering if there was a better way."

"What did she do?"

"She sent him out to a golf course as often as possible. Oh, this is funny. Debbie said she told Larry after a long rainy day indoors that he had called her name more than 100 times. 'All day long all I hear is Debbie, Debbie, Deb. Tomorrow, I want you to call me Camilla.'"

They both laughed, enjoying the cleverness of Debbie in dealing with a tense situation.

"The guys were talking about how hard it was to get something to eat on a woman's schedule. I guess it takes major adjusting by both parties when two people share everything every day. Think we can do that?" Russell asked.

"I think we're compatible, don't you?"Elizabeth replied.

"We always have been. I mean lately it's been…you know."

"Why don't you move over and we'll talk about it," Elizabeth smiled as she eased onto the narrow bed.

"I love when we talk…"

Chapter Nineteen

The Arles approached its namesake port as the sun rose over the Rhone, another cloudless day ahead for the travelers. Russell and Durgan were in their usual early morning positions, enjoying the sensation of the boat gliding softly through the green hills and chalky cliffs of Provence.

"Last stop," Russell said. "Elizabeth is beside herself, knowing we will finally see where Vincent did his thing, one masterpiece after another."

"Yeah, Sally was all excited last night at dinner. I don't think she's ready to go back home yet," Durgan said. "By the way, I told her about what you said about that poem, the Prufrock thing. I read it again, a couple of times."

"Any new insights? New thoughts?"

"Well, my wife, Kit, Kathleen, she used to tell me I was too shy, too cautious. I guess she saw me as a guy like Prufrock. I just never enjoyed being in the spotlight, the center of attention. I guess I disappointed her."

"Everybody's different. I was always in the spotlight, first one to recite in class, first one to volunteer for anything exciting," Russell said. "It's hard for me to not be on stage now. I like an audience."

Durgan shifted from the rail, sipping his coffee.

"Sally said that, yesterday, after the pottery store, the ladies were talking about being home all day with their husbands after retirement, and comparing notes. Some of them were complaining about their husbands driving them crazy because they don't know what to do now that they're not big shots anymore."

"Elizabeth mentioned that. I believe one complaint was that some men just hover over their wives, always asking what they're doing, when will lunch be ready."

"Sally said one girl had a routine in the morning where she finished cleaning up the breakfast dishes and had a cup of tea while she read the paper and how her husband kept pestering her. She gave him a list of times when she wanted to be alone," Durgan laughed.

"He should have given her his times off, too. That's not a bad idea, come to think of it. How are you getting along, being alone?" Russell asked.

Durgan cleared his throat and looked at the river passing underneath.

"Oh, there's good days and bad days, he said softly. Mostly nights, and Sundays are lonely. But I think it's easier for me to adjust to being alone than it would be to get used to full time togetherness again. Don't tell anyone I said it, but, I don't really need a woman full time in my life anymore. I can shop for groceries, I can cook, do laundry, all that stuff."

"Are you dating?"

"What you mean is, do I miss sex? That's usually why men date. Women date because they're looking for another marriage, a guy to help take care of them, be a companion, and I'm finished with that. Sex is okay, but not worth all the effort it takes anymore. I could be wrong, but that's the way I see it," Durgan concluded. "At least for now."

"I have male friends who are now alone. Most of them would agree with you," Russell said. "Some hit the booze hard, at least at first."

"I tried that, but it just made things worse. Now I walk a lot, watch sports, fish a little. Read. I'd like to learn more about surf fishing, I don't know," Durgan said. "I'm okay, now."

He turned to the stairwell as Kevin appeared.

"Morning, guys."

"Morning," the men said, turning at the sound of Kevin's voice. "You sound pretty chipper."

"Yeah," Kevin said, eyes downward.

Durgan and Russell exchanged glances, smiling. Kevin joined them at the rail.

'Say, guys, something strange happened yesterday after we got back," Kevin said. "I'm not sure if I should report it to Giovanni or not."

"What happened?"

"Well, when we got back from the trip, Pamela went to our cabin to get a shower, and when she got there the door was open and that waitress, the English girl, was in our room. The maid cart was outside."

"You mean Brenda, I believe. What was she doing?"

"Nothing much. Pam said she thought she was looking at our wall safe, where we keep the passports and stuff. Of course it was locked."

"Did Brenda say anything?" Russell asked.

"No, just muttered something about looking for the maid and left in a hurry. Nothing seemed disturbed," Kevin said.

"Those safes are electronic, aren't they?" Durgan asked. "You need the code to open them, right?"

"Well, yes, but there are ways to override the code and reset the combination. People do forget their codes. And, after every cruise, the safes are all reset for the next group to use," Kevin explained.

"That must take some time."

"It does, but a boat this size would most likely have an electronic override device to speed things up. Giovanni probably has one in his safe or in his office."

Or at his desk, Russell thought.

"I'll let Giovanni know, Kev. Might as well be cautious."

"Thanks, guys."

The men watched as the Arles slowly glided into the dock. The crew quickly secured the bow lines, then moved to the stern and repeated the process. The gangway was lowered and secured as lines for electrical and water service were taken aboard.

"Well, Kevin, this is our last port. What does your magic device tell you about Arles?" Russell asked.

"Let's see. Here it is. I'll read it to you. 'Arles is an extremely ancient town, having been established by the Greeks as early as the 6th century BC. Rome took the town in 123 BC and expanded it into an important city, with a canal link to the Mediterranean Sea being constructed in 104 BC.'"

"Sixth century? And now we're in the 21st, that's some 1500 years ago. 1500. Can you imagine that? America is only a little more than 200 years old," Durgan shook his head.

"I know. The concept of time in Europe is totally different than our viewpoint. No wonder the Europeans look at us as babies when it comes to international relations. What could we possibly know with our limited years of experience? Listen, there's more:

'The city reached its peak during the 4th and 5th centuries, when it was frequently used as headquarters for Roman Emperors during military campaigns. It became a favorite city of Emperor Constantine the Great, who built baths there. Emperor Constantine III declared himself emperor in the West and made Arles his capital in 408.'"

"Constantine was the Emperor who converted to Christianity, wasn't he?"

"Right," Kevin answered, reading from the small screen. "It became a center for Christianity in France and numerous synods were held here over the years. Then there is a lot of info on different invaders and rulers through the centuries, medieval times with burnings of heretics, and so on and so on. The modern city seemed to get a big boost with the arrival of the railroad," Kevin finished.

"What about Vincent? Anything on him?"

"Yes, it says, 'This, meaning the railroad, made it an attractive destination for the painter Vincent van Gogh, who arrived there on 21 February 1888. He was fascinated by the Provençal landscapes, producing over 300 paintings and drawings during his time in Arles."

"Really? 300 paintings?" Durgan questioned. "I had no idea he painted so many."

Kevin nodded, reading from the screen.

"Many of his most famous paintings were completed there, including the Night Cafe, the Yellow Room, Starry Night, and L'Arlesienne. Paul Gauguin visited van Gogh in Arles. However, van Gogh's mental health deteriorated and he became alarmingly eccentric, culminating in the infamous ear-cutting incident in December 1888. The concerned locals circulated a petition the following February demanding that van Gogh be confined. In May 1889, he took the hint and left Arles for the asylum at nearby St-Rémy-de-Provence."

"That's where he killed himself, I believe," Russell mused.

Kevin continued, eyes on the page.

"And, finally, it seems that the Provençal poet Frédéric Mistral was born near Arles. The fierce wind that blows through the Rhone river valley was named after him. Now you are both experts on Arles. God bless the Internet." Kevin smiled as the Arles was secured to the dock.

"You know, that device of yours is really handy. Everything you need to know is right there," Durgan said. "With one of those, you're never cut off from anything, are you?"

"That's right. No matter where you live, if you can connect, you can be part of the library of the world," Kevin said.

"It is amazing," Russell added. "All that knowledge on command, quite literally in the palm of your hand. You know, Elizabeth has been trying to get me to be more willing to work with technology. Thank you, my friend. I will dazzle her with my knowledge. It is my daily goal to amaze and amuse her. I usually do well at the amusing part," Russell grinned as the men descended to the dining area.

Terry was at his post, the delightful aroma of fresh coffee and breakfast foods filling the room. "Morning, gentlemen. Enjoy the sunrise?"

"Oh yes," Kevin smiled. "Russell's made me a believer in early rising."

"And Kevin's convinced us to take a new look at using computers," Russell said. "A serious look."

"Terry, any word on Agnes?" Durgan asked "We heard she had a problem yesterday with the heat."

"Yes, she did. Sally, your friend, has been looking in on her, and I believe Giovanni has been in touch with a doctor in Arles where we will be in just a short time." Terry excused himself as he greeted new arrivals.

"Good. She is fragile. We'll be back for your terrific breakfast."

Russell turned to Durgan. "Well, Durgan, it seems you are now an official friend of Sally, according to Terry."

"That's all we are-friends. We had a drink the other night, and after 15 minutes I wanted to just hand her my resume and move on. It was like a job interview. I'm not interested, as I said before."

"But she did introduce you to T.S. Eliot and Prufrock," Russell said.

"True. But I'm still not ready, you know?"

Terry resumed his morning routine, monitoring the efficient service. The morning serving was well attended, as usual, the refreshed travelers ready for another tour after an early night turn in. The ages of the passengers ruled out late nights in clubs and bars for almost all. This group came to see and to learn, and today was going to be the high point of the entire trip. Today, they would see Vincent van Gogh's world as he saw it all those years ago.

The diners peered out the windows at the arrival of a black Citroen. They watched as an older man, well dressed in a dark suit and red tie, carrying what looked like a medical bag, got out and crossed the gangplank to be met by Giovanni.

Giovanni touched the brim of his hat, shook the man's hand, and led him through the passageway to a forward cabin shared by Agnes and Shirley, the elderly ladies. They knocked and then went inside.

The buzz of conversation rose as the diners speculated about the new arrival. Some knew of the collapse of Agnes on the previous day, but most did not.

"We just heard about the lady who got sick yesterday. Is she the one who always says she can't hear, or is it the other one who has trouble walking?" Larry asked Mel as they moved through the buffet line.

"It's Agnes, the 'can't hear you' lady," Mel explained. "She came back yesterday looking flushed. I think the heat got to her. This weather has been great, but it is warmer then usual for this time of year."

"That's too bad. Maybe she just needs a long rest out of the heat."

"Yes, she needs a day off."

Breakfast continued with talk about the two tours scheduled for the day. The first was about the Roman history of Arles, complete with a local guide, and the second, a briefer tour of the world of Vincent van Gogh, which included seeing the actual scenes he captured on canvas for all time. That opportunity was the reason most of the group had selected the tour. Elizabeth and Russell had already charted a walking tour based on the small maps they carried, and Kevin and Pamela were hunched over his BlackBerry, planning their day in Arles.

Mel leaned forward and pulled back the long sheer curtain from the side window. On the dock, an ambulance arrived with lights flashing, but no warning siren. The attendants opened the rear door and rolled out a wheeled stretcher.

"Looks like someone is going for a ride."

The group watched as the attendants struggled to get through the narrow passageway. Breakfast was over and the first tour about to start. Gerard had been in the cabin with the doctor, and appeared now to address the anxious travelers.

"Bonjour, my friends," Gerard began. "I regret to tell you that our fellow traveler, Agnes Brennan, has been taken ill and needs to be in hospital. A local physician is with her and will be with her, providing the best possible care. We will be leaving to meet our guide at the Roman amphitheater in fifteen minutes, after Agnes is transported. Our day will continue as scheduled. Thank you."

"What's wrong with her? Is it serious?" Questions were shouted out as the wheeled stretcher with Agnes strapped to it, her face covered by an oxygen mask, made its way through the passageway and out to the waiting ambulance. Gerard waved off the questions, saying only that she was in excellent hands. Slowly the knot of the curious onlookers broke up as the ambulance departed, lights flashing silently, and the tour group reformed on the dock.

"Attention, please, attention," Gerard requested. "We have a short walk to meet our guide, Madame Depuy. She is a native of Arles and an amateur artist of some note. She will guide us through the Roman sites of Arles, and will help us find sites painted by van Gogh.

I will be in touch by my cell phone with Agnes's doctor, and will keep you informed of her progress. It appears that she has suffered a slight stroke. I want to express my appreciation for the assistance provided to Agnes by our passenger, Sally, a former nurse who sat with her until we could get her to a doctor and hospital. Please follow me to our guide."

The group huffed up a slight rise to an open park area with the usual game of Petanque in progress, the metal boules colliding with a pleasant sound, the men squatting to throw in their turn.

"On our left, over there, just down the hill, next to where the cafe now sits, was the site of the building where van Gogh first lived when he came to

Arles. He called it his 'Yellow House' and painted many versions of it. He also did a portrait of his bedroom there. The original house was destroyed by an accidental bombing in World War Two. To our right is the ancient wall that has surrounded Arles since Roman days. We will pass through the gate where Emperor Constantine himself once walked," Gerard explained.

"He was the first Christian pope," Russell said to Elizabeth. "He loved this place and built many baths here. He was also born here."

"You've been reading again, haven't you?" Elizabeth asked, eyebrows arched.

"Just a little. Actually, it was Kevin and his BlackBerry."

They passed through the city gate in the old wall.

"Are you impressed? I mean, really. Don't you think it's nice to have access to a world of information like that?"

"You're right. It would be nice. Look, I don't object to learning new technology, just people cutting themselves off from each other with gadgets." Russell said.

"Maybe it's time for you to change your mind," Elizabeth suggested.

"Can I do that? At my age?"

"You have my permission." Elizabeth smiled, suspecting Russell was about to make a major change in attitude. She knew he was not rigid in his thinking, but cautious of changing any long held values without good reason. It was a quality of his she most admired. He was willing to change when he saw the need. They both realized aging really began with inflexibility, a refusal to move forward with new ideas.

"I just remembered I need to pass something along to Giovanni. I'll catch up to you at the arena. I have a map," Russell said. He walked quickly back to the boat.

Giovanni was at his lobby desk, doing paperwork as Russell approached. "I need to talk with you, briefly."

"Please be seated, my friend."

"You asked me to tell you if I saw or heard anything about Brenda. I did." Russell relayed what Kevin had told him about Pamela finding Brenda in their cabin and her reaction and explanation.

"It may be nothing more than she said it was, but ..."

"Interesting," Giovanni said. "Rita has been telling me her cleaning girls have noticed Brenda in the cabin area. She has also been asking them about the safes and what we do when someone accidentally locks one."

"Do the maids know what you do? How you open them?"

"They know to tell Rita, who tells me, and I fix it. I use an override device, and they may or may not know that." He paused, eyes looking upward. "Do you remember when I found Brenda behind my desk and warned her?"Giovanni asked.

"Yes, I do. It was early in the morning."

"I had received a call for help in opening a safe earlier, and I had done so. I placed the device under my desk temporarily because it was early and I had people to help."

"Who had the problem with their safe?"Russell asked.

"It was in the cabin of Barry, the Englishman and his wife," Giovanni said.

The narrow streets of Arles were a uniform color, a dusty tan, the same tone as the small buildings with the souvenir shops displaying racks of T shirts and hats, with rotating carousels of post cards. Directly ahead were the broad stone steps that led to the Roman Stadium, still in use after all the centuries since its construction. Faded posters in the nearby shops advertised recent bull fights and other gatherings. Gerard halted the group at the foot of the steps where a woman dressed in a long gauzy yellow dress with a flowered sash waited. On her head was a large floppy straw hat, dark shaded glasses prominent on her fair face. She looked like a profoundly dedicated eccentric artist.

Gerard approached her, hand extended. "Bonjour, Madame," he said.

"I was hoping he was going to kiss her hand, like they do in the movies. I always wanted to learn how to do that," Mel muttered. Ruth narrowed her eyes in her "don't start" look.

"Ladies and gentlemen, allow me to introduce Madame Depuy, a native of Arles, famous for its beautiful women," Gerard gestured to Madame, "its ancient Greek and Roman past, and the paintings of its adopted brilliant artist, Vincent van Gogh. She will be our guide for our tour today. Madame."

"Thank you Gerard, for the lovely introduction," she said. "I welcome you to Arles, the city by the Marshes, according to the Romans. It is here that the Rhone divides, forming a delta before it enters the Mediterranean. It was founded by the Greeks, and used by the Romans as a rest area for the Roman Sixth Legion veterans. Emperor Constantine was born here, and was responsible for much of the sites we will visit, like this stadium, an amphitheater, and, of course, the baths. Arles was one of the first Christian towns, since Constantine was a Christian convert, and was the site of many church gatherings and conferences, or synods. You can read all about this in this pamphlet Gerard is now distributing. We will begin with a look at the stadium. Any questions? No? Please follow me and watch your step."

Russell appeared just as the group began to move.

"Did you see Giovanni?" Elizabeth asked as Russell drank from his water bottle.

"Yes, all taken care of. I let him know about the incident with Pam in their cabin, the one I told you about."

"Good. It may be nothing, but it would upset me to find someone in our room other than a maid.

The line formed dutifully behind Madame Depuy as they entered the shade of the stone walls, each visitor stopping for the handout from Gerard. Russell and Elizabeth waited patiently for the line to move, Elizabeth snapping photos.

"Hey, look who's here," Russell said.

The Hunters waved to the approaching figures of Sonia and Sally, smiles of relief on their faces at having caught up with the small group. "We just got started. Madame Depuy is taking us inside." Russell explained as the women climbed the steps, slightly out of breath.

"Thank you for watching for us. We were told to just go straight to the old stadium and we'd find you, but no one said how far it was. This was easy."

"What happened to Agnes? Gerard mentioned you helped take care of her, Sally." They moved slowly into the cool darkness, following the pack.

"Well, she's definitely had a stroke," Sally said. "She had sunstroke yesterday in town. She was dehydrated and definitely tired from the walking, but she seemed to recover after Giovanni got her back and in her cabin. We poured a lot of water into her, and she had a light dinner brought to her and Shirley last evening. I wanted her to go to the hospital, but she refused."

"So when did the stroke happen?"

"Not sure, but some time after we docked, probably while breakfast was being served. She and Shirley had decided to sleep in and have a late breakfast. We went to check on them and Shirley said Agnes was in the bathroom. I called to her and there was no response so Sonia and I opened the door. She was on the floor. Sonia got Giovanni and he called the hospital, or the ambulance, I don't know." Sally paused, sighing deeply. "Then the doctor came in and took over."

"Where's Shirley? Did she go with her in the ambulance?" Elizabeth asked?

"No. She needed medical help herself. I tried to comfort her, but she was freaking out, so I took her to the library and gave her water and calmed her down."

"Then Rita came by," Sally continued. "The woman who manages the room cleaners? Giovanni sent her to care for Shirley. She's with her now. They told us to leave and do the tour. I guess we were getting in the way. I can't even think."

Ahead of them, Madame Depuy and Gerard were guiding the travelers, pointing out details of the stadium. Gerard was glancing around nervously, looking for his missing members.

"Maybe you two need to find a cafe and have some coffee and gather yourself. These ruins have been here for about 2000 years, so I think they'll wait." Russell suggested.

"C'mon. There's a little cafe I saw just down the street from here. You need a break," Elizabeth urged. "Russell can explain to Gerard, and we can catch up later."

"Elizabeth is right. I'll take care of Gerard, and I'll find you." He entered the cool dark chamber, moving quickly to locate the group on the arena floor.

Madame Depuy was explaining the Provencal version of bull fighting, where brave souls attempted to grab a money bag suspended by a string between the bull's horns rather than taunting and eventually killing the bull with a sword in the Spanish style.

"Both methods of fighting are demonstrated, but I believe the bulls prefer ours," Madame commented with a smile. "In medieval days, when the town fell under siege from invaders, everyone moved into the stadium, which was protected by the towers you see ahead of you." The group shuffled forward.

"Gerard, may I speak with you please?" Russell asked.

"Yes, I was beginning to worry about you. Where is your wife? Is she alright?"

"Elizabeth is fine. She's with Sally and Sonia. They hurried to catch up to us. Sally is very distraught about Agnes and she and Sonia are having a break with Elizabeth in a cafe. I told them I'd let you know and then come back for them. Where can we meet you in, say a half hour, or so? Any particular location?"

"I am happy that they are all well," Gerard replied. "I am worried about Agnes and her friend. We are going to the amphitheater from here, so you can probably find us at the church on the town square in forty-five minutes. Here, I'll show you on the map."

Gerard pointed out the meeting place and traced directions there with his pen. "It is a five minute walk. Take your time and wait for the ladies to be comfortable. I don't want another passenger in hospital." He handed the map to Russell.

"Any word about Agnes?"

"Nothing yet. We have notified our American office and they are contacting her family in the States. Shirley is being looked after here."

"Okay. We'll meet you at the church in about thirty minutes. Please let Mel and Ruth know where we are, okay?"

"I will tell them."

Russell left the stadium and moved down the narrow street, eyes scanning for anything that looked like a cafe. He found them on the first corner, crowded around a tiny table barely big enough for four coffee cups.

"Hi, ladies. I see you found a spot. How's the coffee?" Russell asked as he pulled up a wire backed chair, edging into the circle.

"It's okay," Elizabeth said, nodding to the waiter.

"Coffee for Monsieur?"

"Please, merci. I talked to Gerard and asked him to let the Weinsteins know we're okay and will meet them later at a church. I have a map and Gerard says it's very close by. There's no new word on Agnes, other than the US branch office is trying to reach her family. Does she have any, do you know?" He looked to Sally for an answer.

"Shirley indicated she has a daughter and grandkids, but she is a widow. So is Shirley. They grew up together, like me and Sonia. Best friends."

"What will they do for her, for Shirley? Will she go on, or wait here with Agnes?"

"I guess that's up to the travel agency. I'm sure they must have policies for incidents like this. We have a friend who owns a small agency and he had a client die on a trip to Italy," Elizabeth explained.

The waiter arrived with coffee for Russell.

"What did he do?"

"Well, the wife of the dead man was on the trip, so he and the wife stayed in Rome while the group went on, led by an assistant. The wife had to sign papers and wait on paperwork for days to get the body home. It was very difficult. I imagine Agnes's family will fly here to be with her, while Shirley will either go on or perhaps be flown back early. Too early to tell."

Cups clattered on china saucers.

"She looked very bad. I don't think she will make it, based on what I saw. Her mouth was drooping, and she couldn't raise both arms..." Sally's voice trailed off.

Gloom settled over the table as the waiter returned asking if more coffee was wanted. He totaled the bill and left it on the table next to Russell, who turned it over, counted out the Euros, and stood up.

"Do you want to continue, or do you feel like going back to the boat?" he asked the ladies.

"I want to go on. We've been looking forward to this tour since we booked the trip a year ago. There's nothing more we can do for either of them. Except pray," Sonia said.

"I agree. Life goes on. She may pull through. Some old people can be very tough, you know," Sally added. They started walking toward the square and the high steeple visible over the dull slate roofs.

"It may put a damper on tonight's farewell dinner and celebration," Elizabeth said as the group resumed their walk into Arles. "And tomorrow evening we'll be in Nice for the last night with early departures the next day."

"Maybe we should plan on a special farewell dinner then, just us and the Weinsteins, or anyone else you want to invite," Russell suggested. "It sounds callous, but other than Agnes, it has been an extraordinary vacation. Who knows if we'll ever meet again?"

"That's fine with me, the farewell dinner in Nice. You pick the place, okay? Some place close enough to the hotel for walking." Sonia said. "Okay with you, Sal?"

"Okay with me. There's a square ahead with a church. There's always a church in these towns. And there's Mel and Ruth and that's Gerard." She waved.

They quickened their pace, stopping to try to answer the questions coming in a stream from the travelers. Mel waved them forward. "Gerard explained where you guys were. You missed a tour of St. Trophime, a Romanesque church."

"More's the pity," Russell said. "Did she get into van Gogh yet?"

"That's next. We just walked out of there. The amphitheater before that was great. I can't get over how old these places are. We rebuild our neighborhoods every twenty years."

"That's because we have to," Russell said. "Stone lasts."

The tour group was assembled in the open square if front of St. Trophime with its intricate facade, taking pictures of the church and each other. Madame Depuy and Gerard were huddled in discussion, pointing to a small map.

Gerard called for attention, holding his map above his head.

"We are now going to walk to our next stopping point at L'Espace, the hospital where Vincent van Gogh was treated, and where he painted his view of the gardens on the grounds. Please follow closely."

Mel and Ruth strolled along with the Hunters, questioning them regarding their conversations with Sally and Sonia. "So it doesn't look too good for poor Agnes. I like her. She's feisty. She let Gerard know when she couldn't hear his comments," Ruth said.

"I thought that Shirley would be the one to have a problem, not Agnes. She seemed much more fragile," Elizabeth said. "They both were determined to get the most out of this trip."

"You know," Mel said, "when we decided to take this trip, the first thing I did was look at travel insurance plans to make sure we had medical coverage, just in case. When we were younger, that was the last thing we would have thought of when we traveled. Now..."

"Mel, it's something we all have to face as we age. Much as I hate to admit it, the body requires maintenance and parts begin to wear out. We try to maintain a healthy lifestyle, watch our diet, exercise and keep our minds active," Russell added. "The rest is unknown. But we do take trip insurance."

"That's about all you can do. Unless you're religious, and prayer starts to be a big part of your life. I know it's big with our grief group."

"Oh, I almost forgot," Elizabeth said. "We talked with the ladies, Sally and Sonia, about getting together in Nice tomorrow evening for a farewell dinner celebration. We'll find a restaurant and handle reservations. Would you like to join us? It would be an early dinner because we all have early return flights in the morning."

Mel and Ruth exchanged a glance and nods. "We'd love to. Just let us know where and when. Maybe about 6, 6:30?"

"That sounds good. We'll book something through the hotel concierge and let you know. Also, if you want to invite someone else, that's fine. I think I'll invite Durgan too, if he's not busy."

"Let's keep it small," Mel suggested.

They entered a lovely shaded courtyard next to a pale yellow two-story building. It looked familiar. The garden was in full bloom.

Madame Depuy formed the group in a small circle in a shaded section of the interior garden. She waited until she had their full attention.

"Now we begin our tour of the Arles as seen through the life and painting of Vincent van Gogh, the greatest of all the Impressionists. This courtyard where we are standing was painted by Vincent when he was here as a patient at L'Espace. He was taken there after he cut off a portion of his earlobe with a razor after threatening his friend Gauguin, the painter, during a psychotic episode. It had nothing to do with remorse over a woman. But to begin correctly, a few facts about Vincent's brilliant but troubled life."

The group drew tighter together to hear Madame's' soft voice. A breeze lifted the leaves on the small trees. Small clusters of tourists silently snapped photos of the scene in the background.

"He was born in the Netherlands in 1853, the oldest son in the family, Theo being 4 years younger. As a young man he worked at an art gallery, but his spiritual nature led him first to religion, and he became a missionary among the coal miners of Belgium. His radical views of the role of the church in daily affairs led to his dismissal and he turned to painting as a spiritual link to a better life. In 1885, he completed his first masterpiece, *The Potato Eaters*, done in the somber, dark style of the Dutch painters. That style changed later when Vincent visited Theo in Montmartre in Paris and was introduced to the works of Monet. I believe you have all been to Monet's home and seen his gardens at Giverny, yes?" She paused as the travelers nodded agreement.

"There, in Paris, he met the artists Gauguin, Toulose-Lautrec and Pissaro, she continued. "He adopted the swirling brush strokes and the use of vivid yellows, blues and greens in his new style, which he brought here to Arles in 1888. During his 15 months here, he completed 187 paintings. Let us walk and see what he saw."

The travelers circulated through the grounds, trying to imagine van Gogh standing before a canvas, brush in hand. There were sites scattered around Arles that were the exact locations where Vincent captured their beauty for all time, including *Starry Night Over the Rhone, Jardin d'Ete, where they were standing, Studio of the South, Bridge near Arles,* and the magnificent *Cafe Terrace on the Place du Forum, Arles, at Night.*

"You passed the site of the Yellow House where Vincent first lived. It was destroyed by a bomb during World War Two, probably during an attack on the railroad bridge across the river near where your boat is now. Vincent lived there, very frugally, on money sent by brother Theo as he struggled with his art. During his lifetime, he sold only one painting, *Red Vineyard at Arles."*

A hand shot up.

"What caused his madness?" Mel asked. "One story I've heard related it to his drinking absinthe, which had wormwood as a component." Others in the group nodded, having heard the same story.

"Yes, that is one theory. He had a very poor diet, and he did drink a lot in the local cafes where he was a regular patron. Today, the medical people say he was mentally disturbed and probably bipolar, with massive changes in mood. In 1889, Vincent, at the request of prominent citizens of Arles, was admitted to the asylum at Saint-Remy where he painted 150 more paintings. He was released in 1890 and went to visit Theo near Paris. He stayed at the Ravoux Inn in

Auvers-sur-Oise. On July 27, he went to the fields, painted his last painting, and shot himself in the chest, somehow returning to the inn to die. He and brother Theo are buried side by side in Auvers at the local church."

The crowd waited quietly, reflecting on the death of a genius.

"What was his last painting?"

"There is some controversy over that, as there is for many events in his troubled life. For years it was believed that it was *Wheatfield with Crows*, a brooding scene with threatening clouds, a scene a suicidal man might create. But, now there is a theory that the final scene was actually a more cheerful depiction of a peasant's home called *Daubigny's Garden*. We will never be certain. What we can be certain of is the genius of Vincent van Gogh and his contribution to the world of art. Of all the creatures on this planet, only humans can and do create art. Vincent felt it maintained a special connection with a creator. Perhaps he was right. Any other questions? No? Thank you all for your attention. You can now continue on your own. Just follow your maps. The trail is well marked."

"Thank you, Madame," Gerard said as the group applauded and moved forward to hand their guide some Euros in appreciation of her efforts.

"You have a map indicating where you can see the other locations painted by Vincent," Gerard went on. "You will find they are close by, except for the Bridges at Arles, which is a short walk south of here. As you walk, try to imagine, if you can, a red haired man with a full beard, scurrying along with an easel, a folding camp stool, with his brushes and paints in a canvas bag. He is hurrying to catch the special light of Provence."

Gerard paused, watching the faces of his guests.

"Lunch will be served on board Arles if you choose, or you may stay in town for lunch and continue your tour. The rest of the day is yours for whatever you wish to do. Tonight is the Captain's Farewell Dinner, a special occasion, with musical entertainment following dinner. Tomorrow after breakfast we will say farewell to Arles, both the town and our lovely river boat, and board our motorcoach to Nice, with a stop in Aix-en-Provence, and a visit to the American Cemetery near Draguignan. Unless there are more questions, you are free to explore on your own. Thank you."

The crowd dispersed slowly, each group studying the small map as they made their choices for the afternoon.

Russell caught Sonia's eye and he lifted his chin in a silent question. She smiled and mouthed "we're okay" in reply. He turned to Mel. "What are your plans? Are you going back to the boat or continuing the walk?"

Mel glanced at his watch. "I think we're going back to have lunch on the boat and write some postcards. We'll finish the walk later when it's not so hot in these narrow streets. How about you?"

"We're going on," Russell said. "We really want to see the cafe that was the subject of *Café Terrace at Night*. That picture has been a part of our life for more than 40 years. At least a print of it has been. When we first got married, Elizabeth found some prints by van Gogh and saved her pennies to buy *Cafe Terrace at Night* and *Sunflowers*. She matted them herself, and hung them up in our tiny apartment. They have traveled with us to many different states. We always talked about some day coming here and seeing where Vincent painted. This has been a dream for us. We're going to explore Arles through Vincent's eyes."

"Enjoy yourself. We'll see you tonight."

Gerard watched his people disperse, some returning to the boat while most wandered the streets, consulting their maps and guidebooks. He called his home office, anxious for word about Agnes, even though it was far too early for any significant report. On past tours he had had passengers injured, usually because of falling on cobble stoned streets, but never a major medical problem like a stroke or heart attack. He had come to enjoy Agnes and her complaints about not being able to hear, or the temperature of the coach. She tried her best to overcome the handicaps of her advanced age, refusing to be limited, her curiosity not to be denied. He wondered about his own future, years ahead, when he might face medical issues. What would the world be like then? Would he have someone to share his life, his dreams?

The Hunters followed the map, stopping to gaze into the windows of the many small shops. Elizabeth enjoyed the differences in fashion between American and French viewpoints. After the overwhelming sensory explosions of shopping at an American mall, the open friendliness and customer attention of the small stores was a pleasant reminder of how small town shopping used to be. No flashing lights, no booming music, no uninformed clerks useful only for pointing to rows of merchandise.

"Elizabeth?" Russell said softly as they scanned the latest shoe styles being offered. "I think I see something familiar."

She turned to look as he directed, the yellow awning immediately catching her gaze. "Is that the Cafe he painted? The Cafe Terrace at Night?"

They stared at the sight they had seen so often in the painting.

"I believe so. The Forum is just behind us, and according to the map, that's the cafe." They walked to the building, its walls the same yellow color as Vincent had captured a century before. In the center of the long wall was the proclamation "Cafe Van Gogh." More than a dozen wooden backed chairs sat at tables set for four in two rows paralleling the street. White coated waiters and waitresses were busy setting up for the noon crowd, their actions choreographed by years of repetition.

"I can't believe we're here. It looks just like our old print, except for the name."

"Well, it wasn't the Cafe Van Gogh when Vincent painted it. Do you still have that print? I thought it disappeared in a yard sale years ago."

"I couldn't part with it. It's in the garage, next to the Christmas ornaments." Elizabeth had somehow scraped together enough money to buy the print, and material to frame and mat it. She insisted on adding beauty to their lives, even when they worried over every penny. They were a true team, valuing their sharing life together more than any material possessions.

They stood quietly, recording every nuance of the cafe, imagining the many souls over the years who had sat at these very tables, on these well used chairs. Small groups of tourists paused to take pictures of the scene, then moved slowly along.

"Let's come back later for a cocktail? Okay?" Russell asked.

"Absolutely. Let's find the other views where Vincent painted, and have lunch somewhere small and special, then we'll come here for some serious people watching while we sip something nice, like a well chilled Pastis."

"Sounds perfect. Let's find the Jardin d'Ete. I think it's down this way."

"Elizabeth?" Russell said softly.

"Yes?" she answered.

"I love you."

"I love you too," Elizabeth said, quietly.

They joined hands as they walked on the cobblestoned street.

Back aboard the Arles, Giovanni was on duty at the welcoming desk, greeting the returning guests.

"Bonjour, Giovanni. Any news about Agnes?" Gerard asked as he crossed the gangplank.

"Bonjour, my friend. No, there is nothing new about Agnes. She has been admitted, and is being looked after. They are trying to reach her family. Shirley is in her cabin and will continue on to Nice today and back to America, I believe. It's only one more day. The nurse, Sally, is with her now. And Sonia, possibly."

Gerard noticed the stacks of money in front of Giovanni.

"I see it's time for the crew envelopes. So much cash on your desk."

It was customary for the travelers to place cash in an envelope to be used as a collective tip for the crew at the end of a cruise.

"Yes, people have been stopping by to make their contribution. Some do it in Euros, some in dollars."

Giovanni looked over Gerard's shoulder, scanning the passageway. They were alone. "Our British friends were just here. The seemed very interested in the exchange rate, and these stacks of money. They asked if it was our custom to offer this currency exchange service after every cruise."

Gerard frowned. "Perhaps we should arrange for a local policeman to be present. They, the British people, have told me they will not be going on to Aix and Nice with us tomorrow, and they were not on the tour today, not even the women."

"What about Brenda?" Gerard asked.

"I learned that yesterday she was discovered in a guest's cabin by the guest, and she has been talking to some of the room cleaners," Giovanni said. "A few questions about the safes and how they work, how the codes are changed, how we can open them if we have to. When Terry and I confronted her this morning she pled her innocence, saying she was just curious about how safes worked. Terry will dismiss her today, probably already has."

"Let me take a brief walk around the boat," Gerard said. "Just to be safe." He climbed the stairs to the sundeck, scanned the now empty chairs, and stopped at a familiar smell of cigarette smoke. It was coming from the stern of the boat, where supplies were loaded and trash removed. It was the only designated place for smoking and was used mainly by the crew. Gerard moved silently to the railing above the open deck.

"That's a nice pile of cash on that table," a familiar voice with a British accent said. "How much do you reckon is sitting there?"

"Ok, I'd say a few thousand, maybe. Hard to tell. But it's unprotected, no security. I doubt there's even a gun on board. Don't want to alarm the travelers."

Gerard peered over the railing, confirming visually the identities of the voices. It was indeed Tommy and Barry, the British travelers. He moved back from the edge. They were standing at the railing, leaning over the side, cigarettes in hand.

"Add to that the take from the room safes, and you'd be doing all right," Tommy said. "I know a few lads with connections to the Marseille group who might be interested in a quick hit."

"But it would be difficult to hit all the safes at once, even with a power outage. Those you could do one at a time after you identify the high rollers," Barry said. "Brenda located the opening device, but even with that, it's not worth all the time it would take. Too bad about her getting caught. Good looking lass, but a bit stupid."

"She better keep her mouth shut," Tommy threatened.

"She has nothing to say. We asked her to find out about the safes, so what? She won't mention the money we paid her. She's already on her way back to wherever it was she came from," Barry said. "It's like I told you before, we came for a nice cruise, a few days off at no cost to us, thanks to you. A pleasant little boat ride, right? Along the way, we look for a chance for a nice score, and if we find one, we make it available for a price to someone local. Simple."

He flipped his cigarette into the water. Tommy followed. "Let's get the ladies and find a good pub. I think they're in the lounge."

"Gladys loves flipping through magazines."

Gerard returned to the front desk where Giovanni summoned Terry for a meeting.

Chapter Twenty

The Hunters moved slowly, hand in hand, returning to the Cafe Van Gogh as the afternoon shadows slid over the narrow street. They had found the markers for the van Gogh sites, standing where he stood in 1889 when he created his masterpieces. Elizabeth had photographed each site, from multiple angles. She had recently taken to photography, and was very adept at composing shots. Digital cameras had eliminated most of the mysteries of earlier photography, and the inconvenience of carrying rolls of film. The ability to edit later further simplified getting excellent quality pictures.

The Cafe van Gogh held a few late diners, or early drinkers, enjoying the quiet afternoon, leaning back in their chairs, watching the passersby. Their dark clothing suggested they were natives of Arles, or European, at least. Clouds of blue cigarette smoke filled a corner of the outdoor area.

The hostess greeted them cheerfully, telling them to sit anywhere, menus in her hands. They selected a table in the forward row, away from the smokers, slowly settled in, and ordered Pastis. Lunch had been sandwiches and cheese obtained at a local patisserie, with a special pastry for dessert, eaten picnic style near the monument to van Gogh. They had enjoyed the warm sun and the soft wind as they shared a simple meal.

"Well, it seems we are at the end of the line for this cruise," Russell said as the waitress placed the glasses of the pale straw colored liquid in front of them, along with a pitcher of water and a bowl of crushed ice. Russell added ice and water to each glass, watching the Pastis turn green, smelling the rich anise scent. He took a small sip, marveling at the refreshing taste of licorice and alcohol.

"I know," Elizabeth said. "It went so fast. There's still tomorrow, but no more boat. I'm looking forward to seeing Aix-en Provence, but I wish we had more time in Nice. I guess we can take a short walk, and meet our friends for an early dinner."

"There never seems to be enough time for a good vacation in Europe. Maybe we should think about a longer time period after you're retired. There is that 16-day river cruise across Europe we looked at," Russell said, adding more water to his glass of Pastis.

"I'd like that. Why don't we get it scheduled when we get back? These trips fill up fast. I'll be retired by early fall, or sooner if needed. I'm ready to be finished with it all."

They sipped the cold drinks.

"Are you sure?" Russell asked. "You had a lot of retirement questions coming on this trip. Have you gotten the answers you were looking for?"

"More or less. There are so many things to consider. Our parents retired based on what their employer's policy said. At this age, you have to retire. They stayed in the same house most of their lives, and when they retired it never occurred to them to move anywhere. They were just glad not to have to work any more."

"Or, for some, they had to go find a new job because they didn't have enough money to fully retire on just Social Security," Russell said. "I suspect that was the case more often than not."

"You're probably right. What I see is a series of choices about where to live, and how to live, as in should you stay in your home or a buy a condo or move in with your children-and there are two schools of thought on that-and then what you want to do with the rest of your life, based on your interests."

"And don't forget health care," Russell added. "For most of our lives we are happy, healthy creatures, seldom sick, full of energy. Then, wham, our friends start dropping from lung cancer, or heart attacks, or some other uncontrollable event. Instead of taking a river cruise, you struggle worrying about co-pays and prescription plans. That's the true down side to aging. The maintenance costs go up sharply."

"The other part, and I think it's the hardest part, is when people lose their spouse, especially when it's been a long marriage, or commitment. All the retirement plans evaporate. Being alone and fighting off aging is too painful to think about," Elizabeth said.

Russell added water to his glass.

"I know we talked about this before," Russell said, "but I think men have it harder than women when it comes to dealing with being alone. Look around you. There are quite a few couples, women, sharing a cabin, traveling together, widows or recently divorced, in our group. But only one single man, Durgan. And he's here because his wife made him make her a promise, knowing he would never do it on his own. Men live together and share quarters in the military, but as civilians, that doesn't happen. I guess there are clubs for men to go hunting or fishing, but generally men age alone."

"Remember that survey I did on depression in men?" Elizabeth asked, sipping her drink.

"Yes, I do."

"I learned that men internalize their feelings," Elizabeth said. "They don't reach out for help from other men. They don't join support groups or talk to psychologists. When they lose a spouse, they retreat inward and wait for their own death. It seems they lose interest in a world without their spouse, even when they were in a marriage that didn't work."

They sat quietly, thinking.

"But the men you covered then were really much older then our generation. Don't you think we will handle things differently? Don't you think the guys we've met on this trip will continue traveling and exploring on their own?"

"They may. You're right, they're different than their fathers were, but keep in mind that this group is not typical retirees. They already have some sense of adventure and curiosity. And they have the money to continue the lifestyle. So, the question is, will they? What will you do if something happens to me?" Elizabeth asked.

Russell looked down at his glass, swirled it briefly. "I would grieve deeply. I would seek help, professional counseling from a trained psychologist. I would find a way to go on because I know you would want me to, as I would with you. But life for me would never be the same. I love you, Elizabeth. Everything good in my life has come from you. If we have to have a reason to exist, I was put here to be with you."

Elizabeth placed her hand on Russell's. "Thank you."

Russell nodded, emotion shutting down his voice.

"Can we talk about something else?" he finally croaked. He swiped his napkin at his eyes.

A smile appeared on Elizabeth's face. "See why I want to retire? It isn't easy being serious all day, listening to other people's problems. The key to enjoying retirement, the same as enjoying life, is to never stop being involved in the world. I believe you have to keep reaching, learning, working on whatever is your passion. If you are fortunate, you have someone to share it with. If you don't, then you have to push yourself along and make the best of what you have, whether that's a very little, or a lot."

"It sounds like you've saying we all need to 'listen to van Gogh,' in some way or other."

"That's another way to look at it. Did you hear him today?" Elizabeth asked, smiling.

"I certainly felt his presence. I really did."

"Did it make this trip worthwhile?"

"Absolutely. Look at what all I have learned. You're a good teacher."

"As Mel would say, 'It's what I do.'"

"Cheers." They touched glasses.

"I wonder how Agnes is doing?" Russell said.

"Agnes is having a bad time now, but at least she has been to Giverny, and dined in Paris, and cruised the Rhone Valley. She isn't a quitter, and neither are we. To us!" Elizabeth raised her glass in a second toast.

The waitress appeared as the glasses touched, a broad smile on her round face. "You are celebrating? An anniversary perhaps?"

"We are celebrating us, and our life together," Russell said. "Would you mind taking our picture?" He handed her the camera.

"I would be happy to." She motioned them closer together, said "smile," and pressed down the shutter button, waiting for the flash. "One more for insurance," she said with her delightful accent. She handed back the camera to Elizabeth, the review screen displaying the shot.

"That is one great picture," Russell said to Elizabeth.

"We've never looked better."

Chapter Twenty One

Terry and Gerard stood by the bar, chatting with Sophia, discussing the details of the final evening of the cruise, as the wait staff adjusted chairs, checked silverware, and lined up glassware.

"Well, my friend, we have completed the first cruise of the new season on M/S Arles. I hope they all go like this one, with the exception of Agnes and her illness. We have had perfect weather, an excellent group of guests, no squabbles, and overall a happy time. Do you agree?" Terry asked.

"It has been excellent as you say," Gerard replied. "There have been a few minor objections, but there always are. Not everyone likes all of the food, the temperature on the bus is always too hot or too cold, and some would like bigger cabins, but, I declare this trip a success. No one has been left behind, no one has been robbed, and there have been no fights between passengers. The potential problem with the British folks has been resolved, and both Brenda and the two couples have left the boat and the tour. Tomorrow, the rest of us leave you, on our way to Nice."

After the meeting between Giovanni, Terry, and Gerard, the decision was made to insist that the now unwelcome guests leave the Arles immediately. Knowing they had been discovered, the men had not challenged the decision.

"And we will prepare for the return to Chalon next week with the next group," Terry said. "It is an interesting life. I enjoy it, and the people we meet on our journeys. The Americans are so full of life, so almost frantic when they arrive here, but then they start to relax as the days pass. I watch the way friendships form, how the dining arrangements happen. I wonder how many friendships continue after the holiday?"

"We try to provide everyone with a list of email addresses if they want," Gerard said. "Most request a listing."

"I've seen a few people exchanging addresses," Sophia said, slicing lemons for the bar. She motioned to Gerard to approach her as Terry turned to meet the guests.

"Here is my address, my phone and email information. I live in Aix. I enjoyed meeting you, Gerard."

"Thank you. I will be in touch," Gerard beamed.

The first arrivals strolled into the dining room. Vicky wore her most attractive smile, walking in front of a somewhat subdued "just plain Bill."

The tables filled quickly, the usual groupings claiming their places. The small table usually occupied by Agnes and Shirley was notably vacant. The talk was about Agnes, and her status, and speculation as to the fate of Shirley.

Captain Pelletier, in full uniform, stood and addressed the travelers as the waiters delivered wine and other drinks. Salad plates were already in place on the tables.

"Good evening, ladies and gentlemen. It seems that just yesterday I was welcoming you to the Arles, and now we are at the end of our river journey. I hope you have enjoyed it." He paused for the applause.

"Our chef has prepared another outstanding meal for your dining pleasure, and Terry has selected two excellent wines. Please begin with your salads. I will be brief with my announcements. Our traveling companion, Agnes Brennan, is resting comfortably in hospital in Arles. She has been diagnosed as having suffered a somewhat severe stroke, which forbids her being moved at this time. Her family has been contacted, and I believe someone is flying here now. Her friend and companion, (he glanced at his notes) Shirley Anderson, will continue with us to Nice and the return flight to the US, where she will be met by family. She is in good health, but understandably upset by what has happened to her dear friend. She is resting in her cabin." The Captain paused, letting the impact of his news set in with the well dressed crowd. The room was totally silent. He continued.

"We have enjoyed having you as our guests, and we trust that you have found our country interesting, and our people to be good and gracious hosts. After dinner, we will have local entertainment with songs by Pascal. We will also have a small area for dancing, should the spirit move you. We hope it does. The motorcoach will leave here tomorrow morning after breakfast for the rest of your journey to Nice, with a stop in Aix-en-Provence and the American cemetery afterward. Enough talk. As a famous chef once said, 'Bon appetit!'" He raised his glass in a toast.

The passengers responded to the offered toast with raised glasses, followed by applause. They were sincere in their appreciation, pleased with the efforts of the crew to meet their needs. The reports to the agency would be favorable, the cruise being even more enjoyable than first imagined.

The Hunters and Weinsteins found a table for six near the port side windows, saving two places for Sonia and Sally, who arrived just after the Captain's toast.

"Sorry we're a bit late. We stopped to look in on Shirley," Sally said.

"How is she?" Ruth asked.

"She's out. There's a nurse with her, and she's been sedated. I guess Giovanni arranged that with the hospital. The poor dear is in shock about Agnes. She blames herself for not getting help earlier, but there was nothing she could have done. They have been friends since childhood."

"Yes, Shirley told us that a long time ago Agnes was a singer, a jazz singer, working in small clubs. Her first husband was a musician, a piano player," Sonia offered.

"She said Agnes had a hard life with him, then divorced him and raised her kids herself until she remarried. He died just a year or so ago. Shirley lost her long time husband just before that, so they have really supported each other. She also said Agnes was very beautiful in her younger days."

"I can imagine that. She has soft features, high cheekbones. I can see her using her natural feistiness to get ahead as a singer," Elizabeth commented.

"Everybody has a story. I have always wondered what my father wanted to be when he was a young man. What did he dream about becoming when anything was possible, at least in theory?" Russell mused.

"My father came home from work one day, put his feet up, said he was tired, and died from a massive heart attack, right in our living room. He was 52," Mel said.

"How terrible. What did he do? For a living, I mean." Elizabeth asked.

"He was a cutter, a fabric cutter in a dress factory. A good job, paid well, and he was very skilled. But I don't think it was his dream when he was a kid."

"I wonder how many of us ever realize their dreams," Russell said. "I guess doctors do. It seems that every doctor I have ever met decided to be a doctor at an early age. I'm not too sure about urologists though."

Russell's comment got a laugh, Mel smacking the table.

"As a matter of fact, there are a lot of father and son urologists in practice together. I know this because of my recent extensive research into this area of medicine," Mel added.

"That will do Melvin. We are about to be served," Ruth said firmly.

The dinner proceeded faultlessly, each completed course swept away silently by the well trained staff. The wine glasses were kept full, and fresh bread was replenished quickly. A gentle buzz of conversation hung over the tables set with sparkling white linens and small floral centerpieces. The setting was one of understated elegance, a comfortable, cozy feeling for people to exchange addresses to continue the new friendships.

As the meal ended, the sound of a keyboard came from the bar area. A familiar tune floated in the air as the passengers tried to recall the name of the song. A baritone voice confirmed the song to indeed be the French classic, "La Vie en Rose." The guests slowly moved to the back of the room, securing seats on the lounge chairs or leaning against the bar, as Pascal welcomed them.

"Bonjour, my friends. I am Pascal, and I am here to entertain you with my songs and my keyboard. If you have any requests, I shall try to perform them. If you want to dance, we have a small area, so there will be no tangos, please." He added a riff, and segued into "April in Paris." He wore a striped nautical sweater with a red neck scarf.

The Iowa folks were the first to fill the dance floor, slow dancing to the early rock and roll classic, "Smoke Gets in Your Eyes." Larry dropped some bills into the tip jar next to the keyboard in appreciation. Most of the group had been teenagers in the fifties, when rock and roll had suddenly exploded on America and then the world. They had been there to welcome the new music and the creation of the teenager, the new social creature who demanded a new world. Overnight they created a new language, new styles of dressing, new hairstyles, new attitudes about what would be important to their generation. And most of all, there was the music with the big driving beat, the shouted lyrics, the percussion that made sitting still all but impossible. The worst sin of all was to "be square."

Russell signaled to Mel as he walked to the bar. "Let's see what kind of Scotch they have. You like Scotch?"

"Is the rabbi Jewish? How about Glen Livet? Neat, no ice."

Russell placed the order with Sophia and leaned on the polished rail.

"So what did you want to be?" Mel asked as his drink was placed before him. "When you were a kid?"

"Oh, back to that. I never really knew. I never said 'this is what I want to be, a fireman or a business tycoon, or a chemist.' I just knew what I didn't want to be. I wanted to explore the world, to see all those places I read about. I was the kid who went to the barbershop and actually read the National Geographic magazines." Russell raised his glass to Mel in a silent toast. He continued.

"I didn't want to spend my life in a boring job where you do the same thing every day, hanging on for a pension. Mostly, I had no idea what types of jobs were out there. All I knew were the jobs in my small town, and I didn't have any interest in them. When I got to college I discovered a deep love for history that had started when I was in fifth grade. After college, I tried the corporate world, but it wasn't for me. Then I applied at a community college and got lucky. No big bucks, but I enjoyed the job. We've had a terrific life together. I guess I didn't realize my complete dream, but maybe I did get a piece of my daydreams."

"That's a good answer," Mel said.

"How about you?" Russell asked, sipping the mellow scotch slowly, the smoky taste on his tongue.

"I always dreamed of being a salesman of women's underwear," Mel said with his most earnest voice.

Russell barked out an uncontrolled laugh, completely taken in by Mel's deadpan response.

"I should have seen that one coming. Well, you reached your dream."

"Face it, "Mel said. "Most people, with a few exceptions, like for doctors or maybe entertainers, have no idea of where their talents lie, so it's hard to select a career. I think life is random, not predestined. Some people trip on success and some keep falling in holes. We just climb out and try again. If you are extraordinarily lucky, you find that one person who is made for you. If you do that, you win. If I didn't have Ruth, I'd have nothing. I mean that," Mel concluded, placing his empty glass on the bar. He looked to the table as Pascal invited everyone to dance to "Sea of Love."

"I must dance this one with Ruth," Mel said. He looked hard at Russell. "It's a long story, full of begging and desire. I did most of the begging."

"Right behind you," Russell laughed as they walked to their spouses' table, bowed politely, and offered their arms to lead them to the crowded floor.

"We can barely move," Ruth complained as they squeezed into the crowd.

"Yeah," Mel leered. "Just like old times." She slapped his shoulder.

The Iowans had moved closer to the open doorway, seeking the cool air. The entertainment continued as Pascal honored requests, the passengers enjoying the nostalgic music, memories flooding back with each new song. When he announced his last song, Larry handed him a handful of Euros, buying another half hour of songs. For the grand finale, Larry requested a polka, in honor of the Slavic heritage of the Iowans. Furniture was pushed further out of the way as Pascal played the "Beer Barrel Polka" As the music swelled and the dancers broke into a heavy sweat, Sophia emerged from behind the bar, pulling Gerard by the hand. He held her close and began a high stepping polka, the passengers clearing the floor for the new dancers. Gerard and Sophia twirled and leaped in a dance of joy, eyes sparkling, accompanied by the sound of clapping hands. When the song ended, they bowed in appreciation and more applause. "Thank you," Sophia shouted. "It is almost like I am home. Thank you."

Gerard was beaming, face flushed from the dance.

"Hell of a finish to a perfect cruise," Russell said.

"That was fun," Elizabeth added, patting her brow. "It has been a great trip. This is a nice finish for the boat."

"I need some air. Why don't we go up and sit under the stars?" Ruth suggested.

"I'm with you. Let's take some drinks with us. My turn," Mel said. "Sally, Sonia, what would you ladies like?"

"I think we're going to check on Shirley first. Save us a seat if you can."

"Okay. You'll find us."

The sundeck had a larger crowd than usual as the travelers tried to hang on to their time on Arles as long as possible. The Iowans had their usual camp forward near the wheelhouse, complete with drinks and snacks. The music had set a mellow mood, and smiles lingered on happy faces.

Mel found his party snuggled behind the main stairwell, deck chairs in a rough circle. He placed the drinks on the table and leaned back onto the soft cushions. They sat in a welcome silence, experiencing the warm mood and the night air, listening to the river lapping at the boat, fish jumping in the shadows. That afternoon they had witnessed a school of river fish attacking a baguette of stale bread the crew had thrown to them. They were astonished by the size of the school and the violence of the attack as the bread was ripped into pieces. The crew assured them that the fish in the river never attacked humans, and were safe to eat, in spite of the discharge from the nuclear reactor upstream near Lyon.

Sonia appeared and found her friends, sliding into her cushioned chair. She placed her wine on the table, letting out a sigh.

"Is Sally coming? How's Shirley?"

"She'll be up in a minute. Shirley's awake. All she wants to do is to go see Agnes, but she can't. She's going directly to Nice early tomorrow and taking an early flight home. They changed her ticket and all that. She'll fly business class. Gerard was very nice, very helpful. He's feeling awful for what happened."

"It wasn't his fault."

They sat in silence as they waited for Sally.

"Hi, gang. I'm here," Sally announced. "Just popped up for a nightcap." She waved a wine glass. "Shirley is doing fine. She's going home tomorrow, directly from Nice. Gerard made all the arrangements. I think he's taking this harder than Shirley."

Mel nodded. "I wasn't too pleased with him before, but maybe I need to give him a special tip. His job isn't easy."

"Good thinking. I think I'll do the same. What do you think, Elizabeth?"

"I think he has a difficult job and works very hard at it. Sometimes he's a bit overeager, but he's working with people from a culture that is quite different from his own. How many of us could work with a group of French citizens visiting our country?"

"You're right."

"Well, I don't know who gets the credit for the entertainment tonight, but it was great," Sally offered. "I wish we would have had music every night. I love to listen to rock and roll and dance to the 'oldies.' Probably because I'm an 'oldie.' Remember how we went to a dance every Saturday at the school? How about 'Cry Me a River?' Sonia?"

"Sally, I wish you'd get over that. It was just a fluke, a one in a million chance. I'm over it," Sonia said, sipping her wine.

"Sounds like a story here," Mel prompted. I remember, "Cry Me a River," Julie London, about 1956, 57. Great song."

Sally spoke up. "It was one of our favorites, me and Sonia. There was this boy Sonia knew, a nice boy, a good dancer, and he and Sonia always danced to that song. He'd find her or she'd find him whenever it played at the dance."

"And did he become a boyfriend?" Mel asked.

"Well, no," Sonia answered. "See, that's what makes this whole thing so strange. Last summer Sally and I were going to a wedding. We were dressed nice, you know, summer dresses and pumps, the works."

"We looked great, if I do say so," Sally interrupted. "But I had to find my brother Bobby to give him some keys to our cottage, and anyway, he was at a picnic at a church grove. It was on our way to the wedding. See, a few years ago, one of the classes from the fifties, I think it was 57, decided to have a picnic each summer for any class members in the area. Our classes all scattered after graduation because there wasn't a lot of work locally. Well, the reunion idea caught on and other classes decided to attend, and now they get over a hundred people at this picnic every August. There's a catered barbecue, a couple kegs of beer, and a CD player with music from the fifties. Anyone from a fifties class who's in the area can come. They charge a few bucks for the food and beer. The fun part is, you never know who will show up."

"And last summer, as we were standing there in our heels and dresses, because we were on the way to the wedding, Buzz showed up," Sonia continued the story. "He was the guy I danced with to Julie London. I hadn't seen him since high school, almost 50 years."

"Right. And the first thing you did was ask him why he stood you up. Imagine, after all that time, she asks him why he stood her up back in high school," Sally said to the circle of friends, leaning forward to catch every word.

The group was smiling, some laughing at Sonia's incredible memory feat, and her long maintained anger at the event.

"Women never forget a slight," Mel said.

Sonia sighed. "Well he did stand me up and he told me why. He remembered, too. We were dancing and he had finally worked up the nerve to ask me to go to a movie. Buzz was a little shy, a nice guy, skinny, not a football player or anything, but funny and different from most of the guys I dated. He was real smart."

"I need to explain something here," Sally butted in. "Sonia was a cheerleader, homecoming queen, prom queen, you get the picture? She only dated the top jocks, the heroes. Guys like Buzz were a little intimidated."

"Sally," Sonia threatened. She raised her wineglass.

"Hey, it's true. Guys got tongue tied around you. Poor Buzz."

"Well, anyway, after he finally asked me out, he said he had to go to his car for something and he left the dance. I waited and waited, but he didn't come back."

Sonia sipped more wine, sighed, and sat quietly.

"And?" Mel asked, waving his open hands to get a response.

"He never came back. No call, no explanation. A few days later, on my birthday, someone left a 45 of 'Cry Me a River' on our porch. I'm sure it was Buzz. Then we graduated a few weeks later, he left town for good, and I went to work for my aunt at the beauty shop. The reunion picnic was the first time we saw each other since that night at the dance."

"That's quite a story," Ruth said.

"Wait, there's more. Tell them why he stood you up," Sally insisted, the wine taking effect.

"Oh, they don't care, Sal. It was so dumb."

"I'd like to know," Elizabeth said. "What was the reason?"

Sonia looked at her empty glass, twirled it, and said, "He told me that when he went to his car to get something for me, it was the 45 by the way, he met two guys in the parking lot, two brothers who were hoods, JDs, you know? Black leather jackets, boots, all that bull. They told him to get in his car and get lost. They said their friend Marlin was dating me and he didn't want any competition. Marlin was a real JD, you know, juvenile delinquent, DA haircut, switchblade?"

"Were you dating him?"

"No. I went out with him once, but I didn't like him. He would call me but I never went out with him again. I don't know how many nice guys Marlin ran off. That was a problem, trying to date nice guys."

"You were a victim of the 'Prom Queen' syndrome," Elizabeth explained. "That's an invented name for a condition that many very attractive women face. Their appearance, and the status that goes with it, does intimidate the ordinary, regular men. They all assume a really special woman would never be interested in them. So, you have these beautiful women sitting around wondering why they can't meet anyone nice, a ready target for the men who know how to take advantage of the situation, the manipulators who use the insecurities of the woman to control them."

"Did you know Frank? Sonia's husband? You just described him." Sally said.

Sonia twirled her glass, head down.

"Did you forgive Buzz after he explained what happened?" Elizabeth asked.

"Yeah, I wasn't really mad at him," Sonia said. "It's just that that was the first thought I had when I saw him. I always liked him. We sat down and talked and I told him how I'd married Frank, a guy from another town, he didn't know him. I had two sons, got divorced, and I took over my Aunt Antoinette's beauty shop, and that's what I did for all of my life." She reached for her wine, slowly raising it to her lips. "Sometimes I wonder what my life would have been if I had ended up with a guy like Buzz instead."

"Is Frank still alive?"

"Yes, unfortunately. I'm sorry, but he was a bastard. He treated me like dirt, called me names, 'beauty queen', things like that. Then he started drinking and slapping me around. I kept quiet because of my kids. But, as they got bigger, and my shop turned into a real moneymaker, Frank's drinking got worse. One night he was really drunk and hit me in front of the boys, who were 14 and 16. They grabbed him and threw him down the steps off our porch. Broke his collarbone. I filed for divorce the next day."

"So you raised the boys on your own?" Ruth asked.

"I did. Except for Fabe. He was the cop who showed up when the boys beat up Frank. We became friends when Frank decided to stalk me."

"He stalked you? What a jerk!"

"It wasn't called 'stalking' then, but he would sit in his car outside my shop for hours, watching people come and go. It was scaring my customers. Then he poisoned my dog. I couldn't prove it, but I knew he did it. Then one day he disappeared and all the nonsense stopped. He always sent the child support checks on time. I think Fabe had a talk with him," Sonia smiled. "Or maybe Marlin. He always did like me even though I never went out with him again."

"So, Fabe is one of the good guys," Mel noted.

"Was. He died last year. Cancer. Sally actually helped nurse him. We dated, but I never let him move in. Now it's too late."

"How did Buzz do in his life? What has he been doing? Any old sparks there?" Russell asked.

"Oh, Buzz was fine. He retired from a career with the Post Office in California where he was a budget manager. Something with computers. He's been happily married for years, a grandfather, you know. Still a regular nice guy."

Sally reached for Sonia's hand, squeezed it gently.

"Now tell them the good part. You know, about the song?"

"Sally, that was just something that came out without thinking. They're not interested."

"Yes, we are," Ruth almost shouted. The group laughed as they realized they were all very interested in Sonia's story conclusion.

"Sal and I had to leave, to get to the wedding. As we stood up, the CD player was turned on and they asked for any requests. Buzz looked at me and said he could still dance, and would I like him to see if they had 'Cry Me a River?'"

Sonia paused, looked at Sally, and continued.

"I said no. I said I didn't think so. I told him, you know, I think I finally understand how a woman could sing those words. Sooner or later, you learn to stop crying over men and what they do to you. I'm finished with that. I kissed his cheek and said goodbye. He said he'd always think of me when he heard our song. He was sweet."

"That's sort of when we decided to take this tour," Sally said. "We're going to live our lives the way we want to. If a nice man comes along, fine. But we can survive on our own."

"Russell's right. We all have our story, don't we?" Mel said gently. "Thank you Sonia, Sally. I wish you both the best."

He lifted his glass. The others followed.

"Thanks for your patience," Sonia smiled. "My life's been mostly boring."

"I still think you should check out Giovanni one more time," Sally muttered. "I would if I were you."

"Sally, I am not interested, okay? Where's Durgan, by the way?"

"Somewhere with the Iowa guys and wives. He's not interested. I think it's too soon for him. I do have his home address though."

She put her empty glass on the table.

"So much for going it alone, huh Sal?" Sonia laughed.

"Well, that's it for me," Elizabeth said. "Time for sleep."

The group got to their feet, the evening ended. As they moved to the staircase, Russell stopped and said "You know, I think I'd like to take a walk to where the Yellow House was, just over that hill," Russell said.

"You mean the one where Vincent lived? The guide said it was bombed in the war," Mel stated.

"I know. I just think I'd like to see if I can feel his presence. I'd also like to see what he saw at night when he looked outside his small room.

"I'm turning in, but go look if you want to," Elizabeth said.

"I'll go with you, Russ. I could use a walk," Mel said. "Okay, Ruth?"

"Enjoy yourself. I'm turning in. Night, Russell."

The men crossed the narrow gangplank and started up the short rise as the women returned to their cabins. The night was very dark, with only dim street lights scattered about.

The gate in the protective medieval wall leading into Arles was to their right, past the small park. On the left, just before the corner where the Yellow House had been, was a small cafe, next to a small dark courtyard. Neon signs advertised French beverages. A smattering of locals sat at the tiny bar or in convenient booths. Mel and Russell passed it by.

"This is the spot," Russell said. "It matches the sketch in the guidebook. This is where Vincent first lived in the Yellow House."

Mel looked at the sky. "There's light reflecting off the clouds from the town. I bet that didn't happen when Vincent lived here. That's probably why he could see the stars as he did."

They turned to walk back to the Arles, and stopped at the top of the rise, then descended to the riverbank.

"Look," Russell said. "Look at the curve of the river, the curve of the wall past the boat. Now imagine how this looked when there was no electricity. This is what Vincent would have seen. This is where he must have stood when he walked to the river at night."

"Let's go get the girls. They have to see this spot," Mel insisted as they walked back to the Arles. They went to their cabins and convinced the women to join them for a very special sight they had to see.

Russell said. "You've got to take a short walk, just up this little hill and then down to the water. You may never have this chance again, and you'll never forgive yourself if you let it slip away."

"Right," Mel said, understanding Russell's announcement. "C'mon, you have to see this. Trust us. Just throw something on."

The group crossed the gangplank and made their way to the crest of the hill, then down toward the riverbank where Russell directed them to halt and face the curve of the river. "Just imagine that it is 1899, there is no electricity, no bright lights flooding the sky, lighting the low clouds. All you can see are the stars over the Rhone."

They stood in silence, each of them in their own thoughts.

"Oh my God," Ruth said.

"Do you think this is where Vincent stood to paint 'Starry Night Over the Rhone?'" Elizabeth asked.

"Yes I do. His house was just down there, a stroll away. This lines up with what I remember of the painting," Russell said.

"We need to take another look at that one. Kevin can probably call it up on his computer thing," Mel said. "Even if it isn't the exact spot, it's close enough for me to feel a definite connection. Vincent was here."

The sound of water slapping against the Arles came from the river as they studied the night sky, seeing what van Gogh saw, trying to place themselves in his troubled mind. Above them stars twinkled faintly in the cloudless sky, transporting them to another time.

"I'll remember this moment forever," Elizabeth said.

"We all will," Mel added. "It's why we choose to travel."

The couples quietly walked to the Arles, holding hands, not wanting to break with words the spell they were feeling. They descended to their cabins on the lower deck, and said goodnight, knowing a bond had formed.

Chapter Twenty Two

The crew of M/S Arles was standing in one line, just 13 in number after Brenda's departure, smiling at their departing guests as they crossed the gangplank to the dock for the last time. The travelers' suitcases had been packed and placed outside the cabin doors at 6:00 that morning, and had been loaded on the waiting motorcoach. Following breakfast, the happy passengers gathered their carry-on bags and said farewell to what had become their floating home for seven wonderful days. Each passenger shook the hands and exchanged hugs with the crew, the waiters and waitresses, Rita and the room cleaners, Sophia, the bartender, Terry, the dining room manager, Giovanni, the Purser, and Captain Pelletier. The emotions were genuine, as many bonds of friendship had been established during the brief time. After one final burst of picture taking, the full motorcoach left the dock, the Arles crew waving them on their way. In a few short days, another group would be boarding the boat for the trip northward to Chalon-sur-Saone.

Gerard waited for the bus to clear the city limits of Arles and enter the countryside, heading eastward into the morning sun, before making his announcements.

"Bonjour," he said. "Welcome back to the highway. It's not as much fun as the river is it? Did you enjoy your time on the Arles?"

A smattering of applause answered him. It was early in the day.

"Today, we will stop in Aix-en-Provence, have a tour, and then you are on your own for lunch. We will move on to Nice after a brief stop at the Rhone American Cemetery where 862 American soldiers, killed in the invasion of southern France in August of 1944 are buried. In Nice we will go to our hotel on the Bay of Angel's. We will have a brief meeting when we arrive to discuss a few final details, then dinner will be on your own. Any questions?"

"Yes, what about Agnes? Any news?"

Gerard nodded. "She is in hospital being treated. A family member will be joining her today, I believe. Shirley, her friend, is on her way home, with an escort. If you would give me your email addresses, I will send you more news as I get it later. Okay? Any other questions?"

Gerard replaced the microphone in its cradle and sat in his front row seat, glancing at his watch. They were on time.

The comfortable coach glided through the sunny countryside, passengers reading guidebooks, looking at the photos they took that morning, and talking about their impending return home to the US the next morning. A small number had opted to stay an extra three days in Nice.

Gerard got to his feet as the bus entered the ancient city of Aix. It was a city built on natural hot springs, famous for its water and its art. The Romans had built elaborate baths and fountains, and the world of art was blessed with the works of Paul Cezanne, the Impressionist. It was also home to many universities, with a high student population.

"Bonjour. We are now in the city of Aix, the city of fountains. If you look to our front, you will see one of the most famous fountains, La Rotonde. It was built in 1860, and the three statues on the very top represent Art, Justice, and Agriculture. The water flows from lions, swans and dolphins. It is 12 meters in height to the top of the statues.

The street we are on now is the Cours Mirabeau, a wide boulevard and the main street of Aix. It is lined with cafes, including the famous Les Deux Garcons, a favorite of Cezanne, Emile Zola and Ernest Hemingway. Remember this location and the name of this fountain. We will be coming back here to our bus after our walking tour. The bus will be here by the fountain. Now we are proceeding into another part of the city for our tour."

The large coach maneuvered through the narrow streets to an empty parking lot. The passengers climbed down the steps and assembled on the macadam. The sun was rising and so was the heat of the day.

"I ask you to follow me, please," Gerard said. "We will be stopping at the cathedral St.Sauver. As you walk, notice the footprints on the sidewalk. They are there for the program 'In the footprints of Cezanne,' the famous artist. His studio is behind us, in that direction. Following our cathedral tour, we will visit the famous farmers market. Then you are on your own to explore and have lunch as you choose. You need to be back at the bus at the Rotonde by 1:30 for our departure. Follow me, please.

"I really don't want to see another cathedral. Can't we see Cezanne's studio instead?" Russell complained.

"Maybe it's too far."

"Or closed," Russell said, remembering the Resistance Museum in Lyon.

The group surged forward and came to the stone facade of the church.

"We will be entering here. I want to call your attention to the intricate carvings above the arches..."

"I've had enough," Russell said.

"I can't hear," Elizabeth said as she strained to hear Gerard's comments.

Again the group moved, filing into the church.

Russell held back and called to Elizabeth. "I need to talk to you."

"What? We're going inside." She was annoyed.

"I'll be at that cafe, over there, when you come out," he said.

"Suit yourself." She entered the cathedral as Russell claimed a table at the cafe.

He sat back in the sunlit square, enjoying the warmth of the morning, sipping his espresso. Their long awaited vacation had been better than expected, with few problems. Elizabeth was having a wonderful time, as usual not missing a thing. Her insatiable curiosity had been one of the first qualities he had noticed in her, and it made her different from all the other girls. He was immediately drawn to her. The vacation to the heart of French Impressionism had been her idea, an idea she had carried all of her life. She had inherited her love of art and adventure from her mother, a recent tragic victim of Parkinson's disease and dementia that left her unspeaking and non responsive for the last few years of her 86 years of life. It was heartbreaking to watch a vibrant, brilliant mind disappear into that lost world.

Otherwise, Russell was feeling content. He was alive, recovering daily, with a wonderful wife and partner, his mind still sharp. His health was once again excellent, with the prospect of many years of life ahead. What he needed, he now saw, was a new goal, a new focus of interest for this new and somewhat bewildering period. Kevin had gotten his attention with his comments on using technology to stay connected to the world. He liked using his computer to explore, and just needed some brushing up on basic usage. Maybe his talented granddaughter would be willing to educate him. Digital photography was another possibility. Elizabeth loved taking photos, and was accomplished at framing and composing beautiful pictures. Maybe that was something they could really develop together. Like a Lewis and Clark trip. He felt the rush of ideas filling his mind, thoughts piling on top of thoughts. He reached for a napkin, tapping his pockets for his pen.

Russell looked up at the sound of voices exiting the side door of the cathedral. He had paid for his coffee and rose to reconnect with Elizabeth. She was talking animatedly with Ruth, while scanning the square for him. They had developed a sense of each other's location that automatically kept them close. They made eye contact as he moved to her and the group.

"How was it?" Russell asked.

"I should have had coffee with you," Mel said.

"Oh, it wasn't so bad," Ruth said. "The stone work was remarkable. Think about how long these churches have been standing."

"Will they still be standing ten years from now?" Mel asked.

"I would hope so."

"Then that's the next time I come to Europe and see another church. Next time we visit ancient saloons and cafes. Maybe an ancient Baskin-Robbins."

Elizabeth laughed at his irreverence. Turning to Russell she said, "You and Mel should travel together. How was the coffee?"

"Excellent. I am addicted to espresso. I had a nice visit with myself."

"You're good at that aren't you? Russell has always been good at entertaining himself," she explained to the Weinsteins.

"What's next? Follow the footsteps of Cezanne? Or is it the farmers market?"

"The farmers' market. I love these markets. Everything is so fresh and the flowers..."

"I think we're going to follow Cezanne for a while," Ruth said. "Why don't we meet for lunch at the cafe Gerard mentioned, Les Deux Garcons? At 12:30? That should be enough time, I would think."

"Sounds good. We'll see you there. Okay with you?"

Russell nodded. "See you." He looked at his pocket map.

The farmers' market filled the square under the clock tower, booths and stands offering fresh food, flowers and produce. Bottles of honey were stacked alongside wheels of cheese. It reminded the Hunters of the market at Lyon, but on a much smaller scale.

"Just smell the air," Elizabeth said. "Flowers, olive oil, mint, so many wonderful smells. Can you imagine my mother here? She would have loved all of this and stopped at every stand. I remember when she would tell my sister and me about how she would go with her parents to the farmers market in her tiny town, a village really, and would get to buy a pastry, a cookie or a cupcake. She described it so vividly we could smell the sweet icing on the cupcake."

"You miss her, don't you?"

"Terribly." Elizabeth's eyes filled. She tried a smile.

Russell placed his arm around her narrow shoulders. "So do I," he said. "Did you ever talk with her about what her dreams were? What she wanted to be?"

"All she ever said was that after she married my father and then became pregnant she knew what she wanted most was to be a good mother. Once, when I was being a bratty teenager, and said something hurtful to her, she said to me, 'I loved you before you were born.'" Tears rolled down her face.

"She was the best," Russell said, wiping at his glistening eyes. "Did she teach you how to listen to a painting?"

Elizabeth paused, wiping her eyes and face with a tissue. She took a deep breath, composing herself. "I suppose she did. Not directly, but I remember how she would hold us on her lap and page through art books, pointing out all the details in the paintings. She would ask us what we thought the children were saying in the picture, or what a big splash of water sounded like. But the first time I can recall 'hearing' a painting was in grade school when we saw 'The Angelus.' I could just hear the bells ringing, the farmers knowing it was time to go home. All the sounds of the fields came to me. My mother gave me the gift of wanting to learn."

"It's a great gift to give someone."

They toured all of the stalls, purchasing a small bottle of honey and some cheese for snacking as they walked. They easily found the Cours Mirabeau and looked for the famous restaurant. The pre-lunch crowd was gathering, the restaurants spreading tablecloths, setting silverware and glasses. Behind them came the sounds of drums, a steady marching beat. They turned at the sound and saw a crowd marching toward them, banners raised on long poles.

"A parade? Is this a holiday?" Russell asked.

"I don't know. Oh wait, I know what it is. This week is election week for the new president. This is a political parade, see, there's a banner for Sarkozy."

"I hope this doesn't turn into a riot with bottle throwing and tear gas. Maybe we should get away from here."

The parade was indeed political, but well controlled, each group of supporters leaving a space between them and the others as they waved their banners, chanted slogans and pounded on drums and blew whistles.

The Hunters kept moving forward, searching for the cafe, as the slow parade passed peacefully. The Weinsteins were at the cafe entrance when they arrived.

"Hi. How do you like the parade?" Mel asked.

"A little scary at first, but it seems peaceful enough. Maybe we should try it in our elections. What's the story for lunch? Are they open?"

"Yes and no. They don't serve the full lunch until 1:00. You can get drinks and snacks, like peanuts or olives now."

"I think I'll need more than that. Is there anything else nearby?"

"I noticed a few cafes on a side street we passed. Maybe we could find a sandwich shop or a pizza."

"Pizza sounds good. Maybe it's time to get our stomachs back on American food," Mel said.

Ruth shook her head.

They walked back the way they had come, looking down the side streets until they found a cafe advertising pizza and sandwiches. The waiter greeted them and seated them at a sidewalk table under a maroon awning where they ordered pizza and drinks.

"I think I'm ready to go home now," Mel said as the pizza arrived. They divided it quickly, passing wedges around the small table. "I've had a great time, but it's time to get back to my own bed and my own chair, you know?"

The pizza was very thin, in the French style, almost a flat bread, with ham and Gruyere cheese.

"Well, at this time tomorrow, we'll be in the air, on our way."

"I can't believe how quickly it's gone. We made the reservations more than a year ago, just after my mother passed on, and now we're on our way back," Elizabeth said. She bit into her pizza slice. "Delicious."

"That's the part of aging that really hurts, when you lose your parents. What did she die from?"

"She just died in her sleep. She had been in a nursing home, being treated for Parkinson's and dementia. It was a very difficult time, watching her decline. She finally refused all food, and slipped away. She was the most wonderful mother. She always wanted to travel and see the great museums and art galleries. We would spend hours looking at art books."

"Did she ever get to travel?"

"No, there was always some reason not to go. It was always going to be 'next year,' but 'next year' never came."

"There are many people like that," Mel said. "Not us. We decided that we're going to do as much as we can as long as we can. After paying for our kids college and weddings and a divorce, what's left is ours."

"Good for you. I think we need to get moving back to the bus," Russell glanced at his watch.

The group finished eating, paid the bill, and started back to the meeting point at the fountain. The bus was waiting as promised, the travelers waiting for the doors to be opened. They sipped from water bottles, some gently fanning away the rising heat with their maps. They had lost most of their initial enthusiasm for sight seeing, and seemed ready to resume their usual life back in their homes. It would be good to sleep late and do nothing for a few days.

The bus doors hissed open, and the boarding began, Gerard stationed at the front door, offering his assistance. "Did you have a nice lunch?" he asked.

"We had a pizza, French style, on a flatbread. It was excellent, with Gruyere and ham," Elizabeth said. "Just delicious."

"Thank you. I prefer it because it is so light, compared to the Italian," Gerard commented. "You have excellent taste, Elizabeth."

The interior of the motorcoach was cool, and the passengers lowered shades to block the bright sunlight as they left Aix behind. The usual chatter and picture sharing was gone, with most of the folks dozing off.

Chapter Twenty Three

"Bonjour," Gerard announced after an hour's travel, waking the dozing group.

"We are now in Draguignan, the location of the Rhone American Cemetery, where we will be making a brief stop. This cemetery commemorates the battle that occurred near here in August of 1944, two months after D Day in Normandy. American and French troops landed from St. Tropez to St. Raphael, while paratroops landed inland. The victorious armies advanced through the Rhone valley all the way north to Lyon and beyond, meeting the Normandy forces east of Dijon. We will gather at the chapel for a brief ceremony. I understand that Mr. Merlino has a relative buried here and he will be laying a wreath on his resting site."

Frank Merlino raised his hand in acknowledgement. He stood in the aisle, taking the microphone for Gerard. "Hi. I will be placing a wreath on the grave of a cousin of mine who was killed when his plane was shot down during the invasion. He was just 19 years old, with a promising future as a professional baseball player. I would like to thank the French government for maintaining this sacred ground for our brave men and women."

The passengers climbed down the steep steps and dispersed, some headed for the restrooms and others to the wide paths of the cemetery, with its straight rows of white crosses and Stars of David on a brilliant green lawn. The grounds were perfectly groomed, not a piece of litter of any kind. The buzz of a lawn mower from the far side of the grounds barely reached the ears of the group.

Russell read out loud from his guidebook. "According to this guide, the cemetery is more than 12 acres, and sets at the foot of a hill covered with cypresses, olive trees, and oleanders. The headstones are arranged in straight lines, divided into four plots, and grouped about an oval pool. At each end of the cemetery is a small garden. On the hillside overlooking the cemetery is the chapel with its wealth of decorative mosaic and large sculptured figures. Between the chapel and the burial area, a bronze relief map recalls military operations in the region. On the retaining wall of the terrace, 294 names of the missing are inscribed. Rosettes mark the names of those since recovered and identified."

They moved toward the chapel, stopping to take pictures along the way, and pausing at the large relief map set on a platform. The bronze map showed the invasion beaches, the units that landed, the 3rd, 45th, and 36th United States divisions, and the push up the Rhone Valley all the way to the linkup in the north of France. A guide explained the sequence of events and how the battle progressed with a long pointer. The travelers recognized the towns they had just visited on their cruise. It was hard to imagine people dying there in the now quiet streets.

The interior of the chapel was cool and filled with sunlight streaming through the stained glass windows. The English speaking guide formed the group into a tight circle. The windows displayed the seal of the United Stares in stained glass.

"I invite you to join in the singing of the national anthem of the United States of America," he said. The men removed their hats, and placed their hands over their hearts, waiting for the song to begin.

"Would someone please begin?" he asked.

"Oh, say can you see..." the song began, with the powerful baritone voice belonging to the man known as "Just Plain Bill." It was obvious that he was indeed a trained singer, as the notes reverberated in the small room, the rest of the travelers joining in. A collective chill passed through the group as an immense sense of pride swelled in the rising voices. They joined hands, tears appearing at the closing notes. They had never felt so proud to be Americans, overwhelmed by an innate sense of patriotism.

Frank moved to the altar to lay the wreath for the young man who had died so long ago. He placed it reverently on the marble, knelt and blessed himself in the Catholic way, and said a short prayer, his wife and the other two women standing behind him.

The ceremony over, the travelers strolled quietly to the waiting bus.

"That was something," Russell said. "I always get choked up when I hear the Star Spangled Banner in a foreign country. I don't know why, but I never feel more American than when I'm somewhere else."

"There is much to be said for patriotism. It is a real emotion, not some political cliche," Mel stated. "We need more of it."

"I was surprised at Bill's voice. He sings beautifully, powerfully. He must have had training," Ruth speculated.

"There he is. Let's ask him," Mel said, approaching Bill and Vicky. "Hey, Bill, you have a great voice. That was just beautiful, leading us like that. Did you ever sing professionally?"

Bill stopped, startled by Mel's forwardness. "Oh, thanks. No, I never had professional training. I sing at our church, and I do musicals with a small theater group in our home town, but nothing really professional. I would have loved it."

"Bill has always had a great voice and he had the lead in all our high school musicals," Vicky explained. "I always told him he could have been a professional singer."

"But my family needed me in the store," Bill said softly.

Vicky rushed to explain, "Bill's dad and uncle owned a hardware store, and Bill is the oldest son, so he entered the business. Singing became a hobby."

"Hey, the store gave us a good life. I did what was right for us. If it hadn't been for that damned Home Depot, we'd still be in business."

Mel nodded. "A lot of small merchants have suffered because of them. It's hard to compete with their prices."

"It wasn't just the lower prices," Bill said. "What pisses me off is that for almost fifty years our store was open six days a week, with Friday a 12 hour day. We gave personal service, we helped people figure out how to build things, how to lay tile, everything, at no charge. We even did free delivery for years. And when money was tight, we carried them on our books. A lot of people died still owing us. But Home Depot shows up, and our 'loyal customers' disappear."

Bill's face was red, his anger displayed. Vicky reached for his hand. "It's okay, Bill. Our kids are raised, the grandkids are beautiful, and we've had a wonderful vacation, haven't we?"

Bill softened, squeezing her hand. "Yeah, you're right, Vicky. You can't have everything, but at least we have a good family. It's been a good life."

"And what about this trip?"

"It's been good, Vicky. I really liked the boat. You were right."

Vicky beamed. She raised up on her toes, slipped her small arm around Bill's neck, and pulled him downward for a cheek kiss.

"Thanks again for the singing, Bill. You were great," Mel said. "I never kiss men." he joked.

Chapter Twenty Four

Nice was the final destination on the tour, a jewel of a city on the Mediterranean Sea, more than 4,000 years old. Through the centuries, Nice, originally founded by the Greeks, kept passing between Italy and France. It sits next to Monaco on the Bay of Angels, a blue crescent of water with a roughly pebbled beach.

The motorcoach slowly moved along the Promenade des Anglais, paralleling the sea and its spectacular view. Gerard kept his conversation to a minimum, knowing that the visit would be brief, with just time for an early dinner, then an early bedtime in anticipation of the return flights. Some of his charges would be rising at 3:00 am. For those opting to stay on for an additional three days, there would be a separate agenda.

Gerard was ready for the tour to be over as much as the passengers were. It had been possibly his best trip ever, with good people, perfect weather, and minimum disruptions. The illness of Agnes was upsetting, but he had done the correct procedure, getting her the best medical care, and had even gotten Shirley safely on her way back to her home. He had checked throughout the day, but there was nothing to report about poor Agnes. She was stable. The business with the British passengers and Brenda was really not his concern, and that matter was closed. Best of all, he had Sophia's contact information in his wallet.

He guided his people into the hotel lobby where they were pre-registered, and saw them receive their keys. He checked into his room and began reviewing his messages before returning to the lobby in two hours to hold the final meeting.

The Hunters checked in and entered their room. Their bags had been delivered.

"If there is one feature of this trip I really appreciate, it's not having to schlep our bags around every day," Russell said. "This is nice. I guess we just need to leave out what we're going to wear on the plane tomorrow morning, and the toilet articles. Are you beat? Need a nap?"

"No. I'd like to take a short walk, if we can, and see the ocean and the Promenade. And we can find a place for dinner with our friends later. We have a few hours, I think," Elizabeth said.

"We have a little more than two, and I would enjoy a cocktail by the sea if you would. Let me freshen up a bit, change shirts, and off we go."

Russell disappeared into the bathroom as Elizabeth consulted the travel guide once again. It had been a smart purchase. They both hated wandering aimlessly and missing interesting places because of ignorance. It was a long way to travel, and they didn't want to waste time when they were in a new land.

"I've found a place for dinner, I think," she said. "There is a square near here, next to the sea, that is popular with students. It has many cafes, ice cream stores, and outdoor entertainment. That usually translates to cheap but good food and interesting people. I'll call the Weinsteins and Sonia and Sally for a time and we can go. Did you talk to Durgan? Is he coming?"

"Yes, I did talk to him and he said he would join us," Russell said. "I need to leave him a message after we find the place for dinner. I also talked with Kevin and Pamela, but they're staying on for 3 extra days here, so they won't be dining early. I enjoyed my morning talks with him. I'll miss them."

"I'll meet you in the lobby. I'll see what the concierge recommends."

Elizabeth consulted with the young attractive woman at the desk about their needs and she agreed the Place Rossetti would be suitable for them. It was a short walk from the hotel, in the old town, clearly marked. She also recommended a specific restaurant famous for seafood.

Elizabeth suggested a 6:30 reservation for seven people. "We'll be in the final meeting, so we'll leave from there."

"Would you like me to make your reservation?" the concierge asked as Russell appeared, freshly scrubbed and dressed in a yellow shirt.

"Why don't you? Thank you so much."

She dialed the restaurant number. Russell turned to Elizabeth, asking "Don't you want to see the place first before making a reservation?"

"That's what we're going to do now. If we don't like it, we can pick something else and cancel this one."

"I see. Very smart."

"Every once in a while…by the way, I like your shirt. Nice color."

Russell looked down at his shirtfront. "Thanks." He smiled.

The street in front of the hotel had light traffic and the Hunters were able to cross over to a small park with wooden arbors covered with newly sprouted wisteria. The pale purple flowers were fragrant with the smell of spring. The park was empty except for a few homeless souls sleeping in the sun. They scurried through an intersection under construction, and entered a large square surrounded with three and four story buildings.

An almost hidden tunnel with wide steps led down to a narrow street which emptied into an open plaza, lined with small cafes and larger restaurants. All offered the very best and freshest seafood in Nice.

"Well, I think we'll be able to find a place for seafood. What's the one she recommended?"

Russell took a piece of paper out of his shirt pocket. "Cafe Cote d'Azur."

"And it's right here. Look."

The cafe was just a few yards to their left, in the last row before the Promenade and the sea. The cafe was in the middle of setting up for the evening trade, but they could see inside as the waiters worked. Like all the cafes on the street, rows of outdoor tables and chairs were arranged in neat ranks. Sky blue umbrellas aided in finding the Cafe Cote d'Azur at a glance. They looked at the posted menu on the white walls. It was almost exclusively seafood, with mussels a prime feature.

"See anything good?" Russell asked.

"I'm thinking of the grilled sardines. Remember when we had grilled sardines in London, in that small restaurant behind Harrods? I forgot the name."

"Yes, I do remember. They were fantastic."

"Okay. This place is fine with me. You?"

"Fine. Feel like walking?"

"Time to see the Mediterranean Sea."

They walked hand in hand under an archway toward the Promenade, crossing over with the traffic signal light to look down on the pebble strewn beach. "I guess you get used to the pebbles," Russell speculated. Just a handful of people were on the beach, blankets spread over hastily cleared spots. The waves were small, breaking quietly along the crescent of impossibly blue water.

"We are looking across to Africa, aren't we?" Elizabeth asked. "I love traveling. Maybe we can do a cruise on the Nile next?"

"Why not? I've always been fascinated by the Egyptian civilization. They seem unworldly, like they came from another solar system."

They stood holding hands, staring at the waves, thinking of the places they had been, the sights they had shared in their years together. Russell's arm went around the small shoulders of Elizabeth, who moved closer. There were times when words weren't necessary.

"How about buying a girl an ice cream?" Elizabeth asked.

"That I can do. And there is an ice cream cart."

While the Hunters were enjoying their ice cream on the Promenade, Gerard was consulting his checklist for departure day. He confirmed with the hotel baggage handlers the room numbers of all those who would be leaving on early morning flights. The guests would be instructed to have their bags packed and outside their rooms at specific times. Vans to transport the travelers to the airport were scheduled, beginning in the early morning hours. He would get little or no sleep this evening. He was used to it; he had done it many times before. Several people had asked for the email addresses of all of the passengers, intending to keep in touch with new-found friends. The hotel office was supposed to have copies made for him to distribute at the final meeting. Finally, he called about Agnes, only to receive the same answer of "no change." He was hoping for better news to give to his soon-to-leave guests. Tonight he would receive envelopes with gratuities for his services. Although the group seemed generous, and he had had few problems, he had no idea what amount of money to expect. Of more concern to him was the evaluation forms each passenger was asked to complete. A serious complaint could endanger, and even end, his career. The agency relied heavily on comments from its customers and would be sending detailed forms to the passengers' homes in the next few weeks. He had no control over those comments. He realized he had offended Mel, the man from Florida, but hoped his curtness had been forgotten, but …he looked at his watch again, called to be certain the meeting room was ready, and selected a jacket to wear. It was time to say goodbye.

The meeting room was on the first level of the hotel, just off the lobby. Hand lettered signs pointed the way. Gerard had discovered that more chairs were needed and was carrying a stack of three through the milling crowd. "In here, please," he called. "Please come in and be seated."

The room filled quickly, the crowd eager to complete the meeting and still have time for a pleasant dinner on this last night. Gerard noticed the now familiar groupings in effect, the Iowans in one cluster, the single women in another, Frank and the Golden Girls, the Hunters, just returned from their walk, and the Weinsteins, now joined by Durgan, with Sonia and Sally. Kevin and Pamela sat at the far wall, smiling at some private joke. Moira and Kate sat separately, not even making eye contact. It was going to be a long flight home for them. Bill and Vicky were near the door, gratefully acknowledging the compliments he was receiving for his earlier singing of the National Anthem. The ceremony had been deeply moving, and totally unexpected.

"Bonjour," Gerard began. "Say it with me."

The travelers laughed and shouted a group "Bonjour!"

They all had remembered their first meeting upon arrival in Paris, when Gerard advised them to always open a conversation in France with a hearty "Bonjour." They had been jet lagged and surly at the time.

"Now you say it. Was I right? You should always listen to Gerard," He waved his finger. "I have a few announcements, and a few handouts, then you can be on your way to dinner or whatever you prefer. First, no change for Agnes. I have an email list of those who chose to be listed, which I will hand out, and I will send an email to all of you when I receive any information about Agnes." He began passing out the lists.

Gerard completed the email list handout and proceeded to outline the checkout procedure, the bags outside the door, the timetable for the van departures, and other administrative details. His final act was to pass out a brief evaluation form for completion, with the reminder that a longer, more detailed form would be mailed by the agency to the traveler's homes later.

"Time to go," Mel said. "I'm hungry."

"Me too. Everybody ready?" Sonia asked. They gathered their purses and papers and moved to the door.

Gerard paused. "Are you leaving?"

"We have dinner reservations. Is there anything else that has to be settled tonight?" Mel asked.

"Not really, but I would appreciate your feedback."

"It will be in the mail. This is for you. Thank you very much for a good job, especially with Agnes and Shirley." Mel handed him an envelope. Russell followed, and the entire audience began to line up with their gratuities for Gerard. He was misty eyed as he shook hands, shared embraces, and said goodbye. His job did have some special benefits.

The small band crossed the street, strolled through the park with the pale wisteria, and admired the buildings in the government square. As they found the steps leading to the row of restaurants, they saw the familiar faces of Frank and the girls. They were having trouble getting down the steps in the dark passageway, Frank patiently offering his strong arm to Peggy.

"Well, hello there. Need a helping hand?" Russell offered.

Frank looked up at the sound of Russell's voice. "Oh, hi. Yeah, I could use some help. Can you help Ann Marie? It's hard to see in here and she has trouble looking down. Bifocals."

The added helpers quickly stepped in and assisted the ladies. They passed into the plaza with its row of cafes, alive now with the early evening crowd, a greeter outside each restaurant inviting customers to dine at their special seafood establishments.

"Thanks, guys," Frank said as the group reassembled. "This has been a hell of a trip." The Golden Girls and the other women were chatting as Frank wiped sweat from his forehead. "One more meal and we are gone."

"Rough one, huh?"

"Harder than I expected. Everything takes so long. You know, the wife and I, we travel a lot. We get up early, we get moving. We eat what's served, we take pictures. Simple. Now we wait and wait. They don't like French food, they don't like the coffee, they're tired of looking at paintings. I tell you, we'll never travel like this again."

"Maybe they should give you an envelope with a gratuity," Mel suggested.

Frank laughed. "One last meal. Then we're gone. What are you up to?"

"We're having a farewell dinner with Sonia and Sally at Elizabeth and Ruth's suggestion," Russell said. "And Durgan, the single guy. We've gotten to know them a bit and they're really a lot of fun. They're the Merry Widows, not the helpless ones. They can handle themselves. So can Durgan."

"Isn't it interesting how some people can just move on and go with things, and others just sit and wait for the world to take care of them?" Frank asked. "We have a nice neighborhood center where we live in Florida, and some people are always there, taking classes, learning things, keeping active, taking trips. I don't mean trips like this with the boat and all, but little trips to museums and gardens and school plays. They get out."

"It's the secret to a happy life when the years march on," Mel said.

"It's time for us to march on," Russell noted, catching Elizabeth's signal. "See you Frank. It was a pleasure meeting you and your ladies. Take care."

"Yeah, same for me. Take care, my friend," Mel added, shaking hands.

"Same to you," Frank said.

Elizabeth led the way, deliberately passing the Cote d' Azur. "Let's walk down to the end of this section. We're early."

Russell realized she was waiting for Frank and the girls to move on. She had no desire to listen to complaints over dinner.

After a short walk to the end of the square, they returned to the cafe where the young woman greeted them warmly, and introduced herself as Michelle, checking their reservation, and offering them their choice of seating, inside or outside the cafe. Since it was a pleasant evening with no wind, they chose an outside table with a view down the entire colorful street. Russell summoned the waitress and ordered three bottles of wine for the table.

"I hope everybody likes white wine. Elizabeth and I would like to treat with some wonderful Chardonnay Delmas from the south of France, a local wine, perfect for seafood. Gerard recommended it."

"That sounds wonderful. I have never enjoyed wine like I have on this trip," Sonia said. "But the last time we did this I went and blabbed my life story. It's someone else's turn tonight."

The waitress placed wine glasses in front of the party and struggled to open the chilled bottle of wine. Her attempt to use the corkscrew had failed, the cork breaking off in the bottle.

"If you will allow me," Russell said, reaching for the wine. The waitress handed him the bottle and the opener, grateful for any assistance. He adjusted the corkscrew, shoved the device further into the remains of the damaged cork, and slowly eased it out of the bottle with a noticeable 'pop.'

"Voila!" he said in triumph. The waitress beamed, her face reddened.

"I am new at this position," she explained as she poured a taste of the wine for Russell's evaluation. He sipped slowly, then swished the wine in his mouth, breathing in to enhance the tasting through the aroma.

Russell nodded, raised his glass. "To new friends, new adventures, and hopefully, many more of each."

"Hear, hear," was the response as glasses clinked.

"Ummm, that is so good," Sonia said.

"It's so fresh tasting. Not sweet or cloying. I think it tastes like apples, but with a kick," Elizabeth guessed, her brow furrowed in concentration.

"I taste lemons. Not a lot, but definitely lemons," Mel said. He held his glass away from his face, staring at the color.

"You're both right," Russell said. "Gerard recommended this wine and said it was loved because of its unusual apple and lemon taste. I had no idea it would be this good."

"Good God, Sonia, listen to us," Sally said, rolling her glass in her hand, staring at the soft yellow wine. "Sitting in a cafe in France, talking about wine and what it tastes like. I used to think all that talk about tasting different things in wine was just nonsense made up by wine snobs. The only thing I ever knew about wine was it was either red, white, or rose, like Mateus, remember that? There's so much to learn, isn't there?"

"Here's something I learned," Mel said. "If you have knowledge about something, like how to enjoy wine, don't hide it. If others think you're a snob, the hell with them. That's a problem they have, avoiding learning because they're the real snobs, proudly ignorant. Learn and enjoy and never apologize for your enjoyment."

Durgan sat quietly, a small smile on his lips, watching the others, enjoying his wine.

The waitress interrupted with menus and some suggestions. Her English was excellent, even her knowledge of American slang. She replenished the basket of rolls and butter. The diners ordered their preferences, accepting offered suggestions from the very knowledgeable waitress.

"Okay, Mel. It's your turn to tell us your story of life," Sonia said, her face flush from the wine."

"They don't want to hear that. It's boring."

"Wait a minute, Mel. It's your turn, so dish. What were your dreams and how did it all work out for you?" Sally prodded.

"What's to say? My father was a fabric cutter who died young. I went to college and studied business, then got into business in sales and later manufacturing, mainly women's clothing specialties. I married Ruth, worked hard, traveled a lot. We had kids, three, two of whom drove us nuts. When I sold the business and retired, we decided to move to Florida where my older brother was, to get out of the Jersey snow. We lived in Morristown, in New Jersey. We like Florida, but it does get very hot in July and August."

"What about your dreams?"

"My dreams? I wanted to have a good job, not one that would kill me, like my father's did. I wanted to make enough money to take care of my wife and kids, live in a nice house in a nice neighborhood. I got all that, plus a bonus I had never thought about. I found Ruth, my perfect mate. We have enjoyed every minute together. That is a dream come true I never dared to wish for."He re3ached for Ruth's hand, squeezed it gently.

Glasses clinked for continued good fortune.

"What about you, Durgan?" Sally asked. What's your life story?"

"Sally," Sonia glared.

"You don't have to talk about it if you don't want to," Russell said quietly.

"No, that's okay," Durgan said. "The truth is I'm not exactly a grieving widower, like everyone seems to think." He reached for his wine as his words spilled out. "I am a widower, and I miss her, but it wasn't a happy marriage like you guys seem to have."

"Were you married long?" Elizabeth asked.

"Not really. About 15 years. It was the second time for both of us. I was with the first wife for three years. Just kids, I was right out of the Navy. It was a big mistake, all sex and rock and roll. I swore I'd never do it again. So, after the divorce, I threw myself into work, got my CPA, started making some decent money, a nice quiet life. Then I met Kit. She was divorced, one son, a nice kid. I was lonely and so was she. We got along."

"So it was more a marriage of convenience?" Ruth asked.

"I guess you could say that. The truth was we were both bored after a few months, knowing it was a mistake. We were oil and water. But you don't get divorced because you're bored, do you?" Durgan said, tilting his glass as he drank.

"Our kids did," Mel said. Ruth was silent.

"Anyway, after a few years, we both knew there was no spark, nothing special. Just two people living together. She spent all her time playing bridge, I watched sports on TV. This cruise was my idea, a last shot at something different that might turn things around. I guess I was a lot like that guy, Prufrock, you told me about, Sally."

"What happened to her, medically, I mean?" Sonia asked.

"Cancer. The deadliest kind. There were no symptoms at first when we booked this trip. Then she started losing weight, having pain. Five months later, she was gone. Don't get me wrong, I do miss her, and I loved her in my way. We didn't have the greatest romance, but she was a good person," Durgan said, sipping his new drink."I think most marriages get like that."

Russell glanced at Elizabeth. She met his eyes, shook her head slightly.

"I'm so sorry."Sonia said.

"What are your plans? I mean when you get back home?"

"I just bought a small condo in Florida, at New Smyrna Beach on the Atlantic. I'm planning on living there part of the year, in the winter, probably fishing every day, morning and evening tides. I need to learn how first. Maybe a little golf, and a lot of reading, something I never seemed to have any time for," Durgan explained. "If it works, I'll maybe move there full time, sell the house in Leominster."

'So, no dating activity?" Sally smiled.

"No, not for me," Durgan smiled broadly. "I've decided to spend what time I have left just doing what I want, on my time and my terms. I'm comfortable with myself."

"If you ever want surf fishing lessons, Rehobeth Beach is always open, right on the water," Sally smiled over the rim of her glass. "I know the right people."

"Do you have mermaids singing there?" Durgan asked."I don't think I've ever heard them singing."

"Well then, maybe it's time you did."

"I'll keep that in mind," Durgan lifted his glass.

The platters of food arrived, steaming and rich with the aromas of spices and herbs. There were steamed mussels, oysters on the half shell, and three kinds of fish with fresh vegetables. Russell and Elizabeth looked at their platters of six grilled sardines, garnished with fresh lemons and aromatic broad leaf parsley. They would be messy to eat, but there were plenty of napkins available, with fingerbowls for the final cleanup. They broke off pieces of crisp bread and feasted on the bounty of the Mediterranean. The wine disappeared as they all ate with a lusty appetite, sharing tastes of each others food, knowing it might be a long time until they had another experience like this magic evening.

When the dinner was finished and the plates cleared away for the dessert serving, Mel turned to Ruth to suggest it was her turn to speak of her wishes and dreams. The effect of the wine lured her into speaking. Mel called the group to attention.

"I was raised in a very strict religious household, Jewish, of course, with rules for everything," Ruth said. "I didn't have many choices to make. I was lucky to get to go to college. I was thinking of becoming a lawyer, not really focused on anything. Then I met Mel. Our mothers set us up. They said we would be perfect together, and they were right. This was in the late fifties, so things were different then. Women didn't work if their husbands had a good job. They stayed home, had kids and became a mom. That's what I did. Being a good wife and mom became my dream. I think I reached it. Now the kids are gone, just Mel and me. Our plan is to see as much of the world as we can, enjoying every day."

"You're so lucky to have each other," Sally said. "My Chester was never much fun, to be honest, but I still miss him, like in the evening when he would sit and talk about his day and the Yankees. He loved baseball. That was okay with me, because I had Sonia to talk to and visit. I understand your feelings now, Durgan. Even if your mate isn't perfect, when they're gone, you still miss them."

The dessert plates were cleared and coffee was offered. Mel called the waitress aside, and excused himself. When he returned to the table, she followed with seven brandy snifters on a silver tray.

"What's this?" Russell grinned as the glasses were distributed. "Brandy?"

"Well, you know, I figured that since we're in France, we should have a French after dinner drink-the brandy of Napoleon. And Elizabeth has to tell her dreams."

Elizabeth reached for her brandy. "I suppose it is my turn. Are you going to propose a toast first, Mel?"

"Yes. How about to all of our dreams, those that came true, and those that came close? "

"To all our dreams," they drank.

"Well, Elizabeth?"

"I'm catching my breath. I'm not used to strong drinks." She placed her brandy on the place mat. "Well, let me see, where should I start?"

"How about a year and a half ago?" Russell said.

"Yes, that's about when we decided to take a cruise. It was just after my mother's funeral. She had had Parkinson's disease, and then developed dementia, which put her in a nursing home." She paused, breathing deeply, gathering her thoughts. "For the last year of her life, she never spoke or opened her eyes. It was the most heartbreaking experience of our lives. My mother loved being a mother. That's all she really wanted. Her grandchildren adored her. She was Nana, in the best Italian sense of the word."

Elizabeth paused and sipped her drink. "Her dream was to travel the world and see the great art treasures in the magnificent museums. That dream did not come true. She became an armchair traveler, pouring over art books while my father found one excuse after another not to travel or spend money. He wasn't a bad person, just intimidated by life and its pitfalls. He never got over the memory of the Depression. He also wasn't adventurous at all. So, in a very special way, this trip is a realization of her dream."

"Tell them about how you listen to paintings," Russell urged.

"Oh, Russell, that's just something I do."

"You listen to the paintings? Now that's interesting. How do you do that?" Ruth asked.

Elizabeth explained, "When my mother would show us art books, she would turn the pages and ask us to tell her what we saw in the picture. It built our vocabulary, and it was fun. We'd make up stories about what we saw, what the people might have said, and what sounds we might have imagined." She reached for her snifter, stopped, and returned it to the table, changing her mind.

She continued, "One day in school, we looked at a painting called The Angelus. It was by Jean Francois Millet, a French painter. When I looked at it, I could hear the church bells in the distance, the bells ringing the Angelus, calling the peasants to prayer. I smelled the freshly plowed dirt, heard the cries of birds heading to their nests. I found myself part of another world of peace and beauty. My dream, for me and my dear mother, was to come to France to see if I could really listen to the paintings. I wanted to go to the scenes and stand where the artist stood and used canvas and brushes and paint to capture that scene for all eternity. Yesterday, in Arles, we stood where Vincent van Gogh stood, and saw what he saw, when he painted *Starry Night over the Rhone*. As I looked at the night sky, I understood his desperate need to capture the beauty around him, and I realized that living life with a passion like he had is in itself an act of beauty. I was able to listen to van Gogh and hear what he was saying."

The group sat quietly, absorbing Elizabeth's words.

Russell broke the silence. "I think we have all learned something about ourselves and our needs during this journey. I know I have. I hope we can all meet again sometime, somewhere."

"Well, if we rent a villa in Italy…"Elizabeth began.

"We'll talk," Russell said, smiling as he raised his brandy glass in a salute.

"Adieu, France."

The End